# DESERT DELUGE

*Author Helen Hamilton writes horror fiction. In her mid-thirties, Helen's focus on her career is starting to pay off with her novels becoming popular. She's on a tight deadline but distracted by the need to pack up her childhood home after the death of her father fifteen months ago.*

Helen travels from Brisbane to the outback and is reunited with her first lover. Challenging circumstances threaten to derail their future as they battle the troubles from the past.

Kelly Wells is the Officer in Charge at a remote police station. Her abilities are admired, and she has the respect of her team. Why then, is life so complicated?

*This story is set in a fictionalised version of the remote South Australian opal-mining town of Andamooka, during the real major storm events caused by Cyclone Kelvin during the Summer of 2018.*

I0593173

This edition published in 2022 by Centred in Choice
"Sharing Australian voices, stories, strategies and skills with
the world."
First published by Centred in Choice
ABN 17 601 690 975

National Library of Australia cataloguing-in-publication data:

Author: Heather Anne Gordon

Title: *Desert Deluge*

ISBN 978-0-6451250-3-0

# DESERT DELUGE

## HEATHER ANNE GORDON

# DESERT DELUGE

# PROLOGUE

# ABC WEATHER NEWS, KIMBERLEY REGION

## CABLE BEACH - BROOME, WESTERN AUSTRALIA

### 6:15 am Sunday, 11 February 2018

Ryleigh Stone adjusted the collar of her Country Road linen shirt to straighten the microphone. The soft pink linen was organically and ethically sourced: most likely, nobody would ever ask, but she was ready for the question should it arise.

Striking chestnut eyes framed by long black lashes aimlessly tracked the dunes of Cable Beach. The sun had risen a half-hour earlier in a dazzling display of rosy gold and mauve, tinting the sand and water a glorious pink. The beach wasn't deserted, but at this hour the few visitors were quiet and thoughtful, basking in the sound and beauty of early-morning nature.

It was quiet, serene, and all rather lovely, really.

It was also uncomfortably warm, with humidity over 90 percent. Ryleigh sighed, trying not to think about whether the glue on her eyelash extensions was rated for extreme conditions.

*I know **I'm** not rated for this weather*, she thought, grumpily. She could feel her makeup sticking tiny strands of hair to her face - hair which had already begun frizzing in the tropical heat despite being straightened only an hour ago.

*What on earth possessed me to move to Broome?* she asked herself, not for the first time.

When the same question was inevitably posed in one form or another by colleagues or fans, she had a ready list of go-to answers selected for her audience: for some, she waxed lyrical over the artistic communities; for others, the lure of ancient culture and history. And if in doubt, it was always safe to praise the gloriously dramatic landscapes.

The only answer never to cross her lips was the truth: that at her lowest moment, Ryleigh had been handed not only an escape route but a huge opportunity to launch her career. Decidedly on the rebound, looking to be literally anywhere else, she had jumped at the opportunity when the national broadcaster served up salvation in the form of an on-camera role in the Kimberley region.

*Stupid, so stupid. Falling for a uniform.* Ryleigh admonished herself, gazing grimly outwards to the ocean. *Could you have possibly been any more of a cliché?*

The uniform in question was the Senior Sergeant at Roxby Downs Police Station in South Australia, Kelly Wells: clever, reliable, and possessed of a wickedly sharp-witted humour all the more engaging for its elusive appearances. Add in a muscular body, fascinating grey-green eyes, those thick black lashes…

Ryleigh's sigh spoke volumes of regret and

recrimination. She'd had been charmed enough to believe, for a while, that she had been the one to snare Kelly's heart.

*And the cliches pile up,* she thought, ruefully.

Kelly had so much going for her, but 'commitment-phobic' did not even begin to describe the woman. In retrospect, it was clear Kelly had one foot outside the relationship all the way along. The failure of her relationship with Kelly was infuriating and heartbreaking in equal measure – but, Ryleigh reflected, straightening her shoulders, it had also got her here.

She wasn't going to waste the opportunity to turn those dusty desert lemons into *spectacularly* sparkling lemonade.

"You're live in…" her camera operator warned, counting down with her fingers, "…three, two, one."

Ryleigh brought a twinkle to her eyes and turned her brightest, most engaging smile to the camera as she relayed the weather report with the turquoise waters of Cable Beach in the background.

**"The Bureau of Meteorology has identified a weak tropical low over the Northern Territory's Tiwi Islands. It is anticipated that the low will move across the ocean, gathering strength before moving south-westwards over land.**

**"The prospect of this low building into a tropical cyclone is high. If so, this will be the third such event this season, after heavy rains from Tropical Cyclone Hilda in late December, followed by flooding and damage from Tropical Cyclone Joyce in January.**

**"Stay tuned to ABC radio for updates and emergency warnings.**

"This is Ryleigh Stone in Broome. Back to you in the studio, Gabrielle."

*And why stop at lemonade? Ryleigh thought, turning her face to the sun.*

*I'm going to make champagne.*

# PART ONE

# CHAPTER ONE

## ABSALOM LANE, ANDAMOOKA, SOUTH AUSTRALIA

**6:30 am Sunday, 18 February 2018**

Helen stopped at the entry to the living room. The hazy smell of dust filled her nose - the pervading aroma of Andamooka overwhelming everything else. If there were dead mice or rats, they had decomposed long ago, their bodies a desiccated sacrifice to the desert.

It had been fifteen months since she'd visited her childhood home.

Fifteen months since her father's funeral.

The simple room, its couch and armchairs in their faded slipcovers, family photographs covering every level surface, seemed to have settled into the loss. When she had last been here, it had felt as though any second might bring with it her father's joyful laugh, his heavy tread... but no longer. A sense of emptiness seemed to have descended along with the dust.

Helen reached out a steadying hand against the

couch, sucking in a tremulous breath. With her father gone, she was completely alone in the world.

The image of her sister flashed across her mind.

No.

Maxine had turned her back on her family years ago, after what had happened.

The darkest day of their lives.

\*   \*   \*

Helen's father had forever insisted on referring to her mother's murder as that terrible day. It was easier that way, he'd said. What he'd meant was that if they didn't mention murder, they didn't have to talk about the trial or the fact the accused was Maxine. Daughter of the victim.

There wasn't even another suspect. As hard as she and her father had fought to find some way – any way – to verify her sister's insistence that she was innocent, the evidence and an eyewitness left no option for other interpretations. The jury was unanimous.

The Supreme Court Justice had been coolly dispassionate in handing down a life sentence to the nineteen-year-old. Businesslike as he declared that no parole would be considered until the minimum term of twenty years was served.

As a child the experience had unnerved Helen in ways she couldn't explain; as an adult she found herself wondering at the life experience of a man who could so calmly commit someone to serve a sentence spanning longer than their entire life to date.

Their last vision of Maxine was of her bowed back in the Port Augusta courtroom, flanked by uniformed police. Her sister never raised her face to her family, even as the verdict was read out. Worse, she had adamantly refused to communicate with them in any way since the day the trial ended. Year after year, their letters had been returned unopened.

Helen had taken the hint and stopped bothering.

Eventually, so had her father.

So many times, Helen had considered going to see her sister in prison - but after so many rejections, she'd recognised the futility of the effort. Even so, she couldn't help but keep Maxine in her thoughts over the years, hoping she was safe.

That had ended the day Maxine hadn't bothered coming to their father's funeral.

Helen had made the necessary calls and confirmed her sister would be permitted to attend on compassionate grounds. Andamooka was less than a day's drive from the Women's Prison in Adelaide.

But Maxine hadn't come; hadn't reached out in any manner. Not even a sympathy card.

In that moment, Helen physically felt the last thread of her relationship with her sister snap, stretched beyond all redemption. On the day of the funeral, she'd buried her father along with any childish hopes for reconciliation with her sister.

A few months later, just before Christmas, Helen received notice of an application for parole. Since Maxine's first act as a new prisoner had been to prohibit her family from receiving any information about her during her imprisonment, the parole application provided Helen with the first information she'd received about her sister's life since incarceration.

In a legal twist that she found darkly ironic, her

status as *daughter of the victim* had finally allowed her the insight into Maxine's life she'd been forbidden from receiving as *sister to the killer*.

The Parole Officer reported that Maxine had been an exemplary prisoner and positive role model for new prisoners throughout her term. She had even completed a Bachelor of Communications and Media through distance education.

Helen's feelings about her sister's accomplishments were complicated, as all things inevitably seemed to be when Maxine was involved. Genuine happiness and pride in the purpose Maxine had found in her life, sadness for the past, and a strange new sense of loss that this stranger was even further from being the sister she remembered.

As a child her sister had been athletic and energetic, excelling in team sports and even playing cricket at the state level in her final year of high school. Never strolling anywhere: always striding briskly, chin forward, as though whatever plans she had would vanish if she didn't race towards them. She'd hated the confines of the classroom and spent her lessons watching the clock slice away the seconds as her feet tapped the floor in countdown to the next activity.

Helen tried to visualise her sister poring over research behind a desk. Tried, in vain, to reconcile *Maxine Hamilton, Communications Specialist* with beloved big sister *Maxie...*

Who, in two decades, had not once put pen to paper to write to Helen or their father.

*It's Maxine who let me bury Dad alone. Maxine who sent back all the letters unopened,* her heart had whispered. *It has to be Maxine... because Maxie could never be so cruel.*

For Helen, Maxie died that Christmas.

She didn't recognise Maxine, who had risen in her place.

Putting aside her personal hurt, Helen fully supported her sister's application. With the Parole Board's approval, Maxine secured a release from prison, albeit under strict conditions: she would have to advise Community Corrections where she was living and where she was working, no drink, no drugs, no 'questionable' social contacts, and she would have to report to a Parole Officer for the rest of her life.

Helen was, of course, completely unsurprised when her sister failed to get in touch after her release.

*I've learned to get by without you just fine, **Maxine**.*

\* \* \*

Helen had arrived in Andamooka late the previous night after a long drive from the Adelaide Airport. She had wearily gone through the required motions: switched on the electricity at the meter, checked the water level in the rainwater tank, and turned on the electric pump for flushing the toilet and showering. Finally, she had wiped out the refrigerator, switched it on and made sure the dodgy door was firmly closed. When she'd eventually slunk into her childhood bed, exhausted, dark dreams and shallow sleep had chased her until the morning.

Her last visit home had been for her father's funeral.

There had been no reason to come, until now.

Sinking into the couch, she rested her head against the padded cushions and thought gratefully of Mr and Mrs Sharpe, the closest neighbours.

*Ray and Lorraine*, she reminded herself.

The Sharpe's had been good friends of her parents since she was a child. She had been invited to call them by their first names around five or six years ago, but it still hadn't quite stuck.

Before heading back to Brisbane after the funeral, Helen had asked if the couple would mind looking-in on the property from time to time. It had warmed her heart when Mr Sharpe had confided that they had already planned to do a weekly check on the way to church to make sure the house remained safe from trespassers.

Helen knew the house was not even close to being 'on the way' and that they were being kind by downplaying the inconvenience, so she had eventually persuaded them to accept a small payment in exchange for the service. But even though the agreement was only to check on the house once a week, she knew Mr Sharpe – Ray, she caught herself again – quietly incorporated it into his daily walks more often than not.

A few weeks after returning to Brisbane, she'd come to the belated realisation that keeping her spare key at the property was a security risk. Lorraine had told her she'd see what they could do, and then Ray had called back a few days later to let her know he'd installed mechanical keypad locks on the house and shed. He wouldn't even let her pay him for his time, only the cost of the locks.

Between the improved security and Ray's ongoing vigilance on his walks, Helen had been able to sleep at night without fearing the worst for her childhood home. It had allowed her the time and distance she'd so desperately needed.

She'd been caught completely off-guard when she'd heard from the insurance company on Friday, advising they would not renew the homeowner's policy due to its extended time untenanted. She had sixty days to remedy the situation, or there would be changes to how she insured the property.

That phone call had changed everything.

Suddenly, she realised how very long she'd left the house abandoned. It was one thing to prevent trespass, but entirely another to provide the level of care and maintenance it required. Left vacant, she knew the house – her father's legacy - would fall into disrepair.

She couldn't let that happen.

The idea of renting it out had been swiftly discarded: the complex responsibilities of a long-distance landlord made that option intolerable. At the same time, she couldn't imagine ever wanting to live in the home again, wrapped in the shadows of her family's absence.

Selling seemed the least-worst choice from a range of unsatisfying options.

Before she could even put the house on the market, though, there was a lot of work to be done. Going through a lifetime of what her parents had accumulated would not be an easy task, nor a pleasant one.

Their father's Will had - entirely uncharacteristically, she thought - left Helen 'the sole inheritor of all my chattels, goods, and assets'. The wording, presumably drafted by the lawyer, was jarringly at odds with her father's manner of speaking.

With her eyes closed, she could imagine Robert Hamilton standing in the yard: feet planted solidly on red dirt, faded blue polo straining across his broad chest. Arms spread wide in an expansive gesture taking in the house, the distant opal claim, and - knowing her dad - the world at large. In her mind the archaic, formal wording became, *"It's all yours, kiddo. Do whatever makes you happy,"* delivered in that familiar rumbling bass with his huge grin.

She blinked back tears along with a smile.

*I'll do what I can, Dad.*

Her first priority was the family home: an eccentric house on an odd-shaped block. Loosely bordered by low grey scrub and red dirt, the house had been built room-by-room by her father's hand, with each add-on distinctive in style and reflective of the materials available at the time. The family joke was that the house was "more *ramshackle* than *chateau*", a description which still brought a small smile to her face even in her current mood. She supposed she'd have to find a more meaningful description for the real estate agent, but right at this moment she couldn't find the emotional space to take it on.

Far easier to be pragmatic about the working machinery inherited with her father's estate: practical and functional, with no sentimentality attached to any of it. The '82 HiLux diesel 4WD ute, ostensibly white beneath layers of dried clay, rust, and silica dust, remained where her father had parked it slightly askew in the shade of the carport. Up the road, about ten kilometres away, she knew there would be opal mining equipment at his claim – *my claim, now* - out at White Dam.

When she'd first been told of her inheritance, Helen had thought she understood her father's rationale for leaving everything to her, but she hadn't agreed with it. Once the property sold (if it ever did – properties could sit for a long time in Andamooka waiting for a buyer), she was determined to put half the proceeds into an account for Maxine, who could take it or leave it as she saw fit.

Now, surrounded by her father's space, Helen realised he would have anticipated her reaction. He'd seemed to know her better than herself, sometimes. She felt a tug at her heart as she recognised that putting everything in her name had been a gesture of trust in Helen, not a weapon wielded against Maxine.

*He knew I'd look after her.*

Taking a deep breath, she thrust herself off the couch. Tried to steel herself to the task of picking through the chattels of her parents' lives, left behind like emotional landmines. Full of memories, but achingly empty of the people remembered.

*How can I do it?* she thought, looking around. *Where do I even start?*

A sob rose in her throat, a stifled whimper.

*How can I let them go?*

A deep breath, and a decision.

*OK. Simple plan: start with the things that definitely aren't for keeping.*

She knew she was putting off the emotionally gruelling work of sorting through keepsakes and personal items, but rationalised that the key part of 'productive procrastination' was *productive*. Any step forward was a step in the right direction.

The plan seemed reasonably uncomplicated until she had stepped through each room methodically opening wardrobes, cupboards, and drawers to get a sense of the job ahead of her. How had she never noticed the enormous amount of stuff her father had kept? 'Uncomplicated' did not in any way describe the tasks ahead.

Like an iceberg, for every one-tenth of inventory out in the open, nine-tenths lurked in boxes and cabinetry.

Overwhelmed by the scope of the project, she needed to withdraw and rethink her approach. Instinctively, Helen retreated to the kitchen. It was where she and her parents had always gravitated, for some reason, whenever there was a serious matter for discussion or if she needed advice.

*Maybe it's because bad news always goes down better with a gingersnap biscuit?*

Pity there weren't any biscuits handy. She'd have to add them to the shopping list. And maybe some other comfort foods while she was at it.

*New plan: caffeine.*

She hauled her old coffee maker down from the cupboard. Her father had enjoyed instant coffee, and Helen's 'coffee snobbery' had been an ongoing joke between them. Strangely, it seemed to make the kitchen emptier now, as though the echo of jokes that would never be spoken had carved a hole out of the familiar space.

The brew process finished as she glumly opened and closed the pantry cupboards. After so long, all the canned and dried food stores would be out of date or damaged by the intense summer heat. Unfortunately,

Andamooka's town services did not include rubbish collection; instead, a vast trench in the ground served as the town rubbish dump. Without a sturdy vehicle, navigating the rough roads was out of the question. She chewed on her lip, silently cursing her own stupidity.

*There's no way I'm getting out to the dump with that poxy little rental car.*

Andamooka's lack of services had never bothered her before, but she realised she'd started taking urban life for granted. Life in the city didn't require checking the water tank levels; didn't require an electric pump to get water inside; didn't require careful management of food and perishable items. Didn't require a sturdy 4WD just to dispose of the rubbish.

*I was so concerned with the weekly rental rates on the car, I didn't even think about what I needed beyond getting here.*

Helen's frugality was another joke she shared with her father, and it crossed her mind that he'd be laughing at her self-inflicted predicament right now.

\* \* \*

Her father had taken a very different approach to money, seeing it as something to be spent when it was available: Robert Hamilton's largesse whenever he'd win a parcel of opal from his claim was legendary.

As a family they'd gone on several overseas holidays - sometimes for months at a time. Helen had always suspected this was why they'd never been allowed to have pets. According to their father, it was because cats and dogs were devastating to the local wildlife, but she was quite sure the actual reason was so that he could bundle the family into the truck and go exploring the world on a whim.

It would be hard to argue that the trade-off wasn't worth it.

One year, he'd splurged on a brand-new Winnebago, and for three glorious months they'd driven through the centre of Australia to Darwin before following the west coast back to South Australia – and then, when the money had run out, so had the holiday.

The girls had reluctantly returned to Andamooka's tiny school. Helen remembered how claustrophobic it had felt after revelling in the vast spaces and kaleidoscopic beauty of the outback for months on end.

Their dad had returned to his opal mining; their mum, Ruth, to cutting and polishing opals, raising their family, working on craft projects and volunteering with the Country Women's Association.

As a man motivated by experiences rather than possessions, only once had her father considered their living accommodation worthy of investment: back in 1985, when the Woomera hut they'd been living in blew over in a dust storm. A toddler at the time, Helen was far too young to remember the event, but she'd heard the story from her parents more than once.

She'd always loved the way her mother had told the story, like the princess in her own personal fairy tale: how Robert Hamilton had knelt before her, just like the day he'd asked her to marry him, and faithfully promised *'his Ruthie'* that he would build her the home she deserved – a solid house, built from stone, with ventilation shafts for summer cooling.

He'd kept that promise, painstakingly hauling huge rocks from the creek to create their family home. Some floors were stone, while the others were concrete, mixed one bag at a time – the bags of cement purchased in Port Augusta long before the road from Andamooka had ever been sealed, while Roxby Downs township was still in the planning stage.

The details of the process were long lost to Helen's childhood memory, but hazy fragments remained of days spent happily playing in the dry creek bed with her sister as their father hefted rocks by hand into the tray of his ute.

Her father, Robert Hamilton, had been a big man with a big heart.

Helen remembered her dad's pride in his wife, recalled his playful protests that Ruth was 'far too good' to be with a bloke like him, and he didn't know what he'd done to deserve his luck. Once, after a few beers, he'd chuckled she was 'too damn good for this damn world', Helen recalled.

She'd often thought of that horrifically prescient phrase after *that terrible day*, and always hoped her father hadn't remembered saying it.

There was nothing that could have induced her to ask.

# CHAPTER TWO

**7:15 am Sunday, 18 February 2018**

Fearing that this train of thought may lead her down a dark hole, Helen wrenched her thoughts back to the immediate problem: disposing of perished supplies.

She contemplated using her dad's ute. Would it even start after all the time it had been sitting under the carport? She had to hope so: beyond her immediate concerns, she also knew that sooner or later she'd have to check on the mining equipment at her father's opal claim at White Dam. The road out that way was notorious for destroying small vehicles, and her rental car wouldn't stand a chance.

She gazed out over the sink, through the window, and inhaled the fragrant aroma from her cup as she cast a thoughtful eye to the ute before looking further afield. Her eyes narrowed: the sky had the look of a dust storm approaching. Helen leaned further over the sink, peering up to see if the blue hen on the weathervane could provide any more information.

Helen could remember her sister asking once, *"Why is the chookie in the sky so blue?"* Her father had laughed and thrown Maxie in the air and said that if the chookie was blue and the sky was blue there was nothing to worry about.

Today the chookie was blue against a dull pinkish-beige sky. Definitely dust today. From the northwest, according to the blue chookie.

As a child, she'd often wondered how it knew.

A faint memory tickled her thoughts - had she heard something on national radio as she was driving last night? The hours on the road had started to blur together after a while, the long stretches hypnotically repetitive ... but thinking back, she thought she recalled something about a cyclone up Broome way.

*That's right. What was it called...Kevin?* With a mental snap of her fingers, the answer came to her. *Kelvin!*

It had always amused her writer's brain that devastating storms were so innocuously named. It would be one thing, she felt, to be made homeless by Cyclone Bonebreaker or Hurricane Destructo. A person could understand that. Respect it, even. But Neville? Bruce? *Edna,* for goodness' sake? Being worked over by a cyclone that sounded like it had merely wandered out aimlessly from the geriatric ward in search of a warm cup of tea just seemed to add insult to injury.

She tapped the fingers of one hand thoughtfully on the outside of the cup as she considered the likelihood of *Kelvin* traipsing all the way down to Andamooka. The Summer rains did tend to come out of Broome's cyclones, but there had already been fairly high rainfall in December and January. She didn't see it happening again this late in the season. It seemed more likely that February would provide its usual bounty: heat, dust, wind.

*On that note, it might be a good idea to check outdoors before it gets too bad out there*, she thought, nabbing her phone from the lounge room where she'd left it. *I can take some photos for the real estate agent while I'm at it.*

Helen took a moment to survey the surrounding area through the lounge room window, gaze roaming out into the distance, trying to imagine how a prospective buyer would view the house and the town she grew up in.

The township of Andamooka had grown haphazardly up along the creek with its original opal diggings, sprawling lazily over a landscape of rosy-orange dirt, grey shrubs, yellow grasses. There were more than twenty opal fields with open cuts, shafts, bore holes, and tunnels.

The 'big bust' of the mid-noughties had seen property prices in Andamooka drastically plummet after mass redundancies at the Olympic Dam mine. Entire families had abandoned the area in search of employment, turning the previously thriving town desolate - seemingly overnight in Helen's memory, though she knew the reality was a more like an erosion: slow, inevitable, and utterly relentless.

Izzy Bullock, the real estate agent, had gently explained to Helen that if her father had sold before the bust, he'd have been able to ask around $220,000 for the property. Now it was worth perhaps a tenth of that.

It was a moot point to Helen - she knew her father

would never have left Andamooka. His spirit was bred for the outback; he could never be content anywhere else. Much as he enjoyed his visits to the coast and towns, the desert always called him home. Though her father had been completely supportive of her move to Sydney, Helen imagined she could feel the weight of previous generations of Hamiltons judging the ease with which she had left home and heritage behind.

Eyeing the view beyond the window, Helen admitted to herself that only those who were born to the desert would appreciate Andamooka's beauty. City dwellers would see only the rusty corrugated iron and the dust.

The house would not sell quickly.

For a hundred practical reasons, she knew she should feel burdened by that knowledge, but in a quiet corner of her heart it gave her hope that the eventual buyer would look beyond the surface and grow to love the property as her family had.

But first she needed to get it on the market.

With the dust in the sky this day, the ambient light had a pinkish quality.

*Not a good day to photograph the exterior of the house, she thought. I'll stick to photographing the shed along with any interesting items out there, and then try some exterior shots tomorrow morning – and maybe at dusk if we get a gorgeous sunset.*

Stepping back into the kitchen, she grabbed her cup and drained the last mouthful of coffee as she gazed into the distance beyond the property line. Off to the side, she could just see the top of the State Emergency Centre. Just out of view on the other side of the hill, she knew, would be Roman Szubanski's little house.

It gave her an idea.

Roman lived in Alaska for nine months of the year, only visiting Andamooka during Winter to mine his opal claim at White Dam. She knew Roman; he'd been friends with her dad, and she found him easy to get along with. It crossed her mind that it might be worth waiting for his visit to see if he would want to buy the opal mining machinery.

Weighing the pros and cons, she had to acknowledge that while it would be a salve to her conscience to know that the equipment went to someone she knew would respect and care for it, the main 'con', unfortunately, was a big one. Waiting for Roman to fly in would mean having the equipment sitting unused until mid-year at best. It was a long time to spend in limbo, without any guarantee that Roman would even want it.

*And I've already let it sit there too long.*

Turning from the window, she leaned back against the counter, fingers tapping on the countertop as she sought more practical avenues to dispose of the equipment.

It would be best to ask at the bottle shop, she decided. It was the one place people reliably congregated twice a day: at the end of night shift to buy the day's supplies, and then in the afternoons to buy slabs of beer, bottles of wine and spirits for the evening's drinking session. All the local news flowed into and out of the bottle shop, and there was every chance that the gossip grapevine would prove the fastest way to find a buyer for the machinery. She could ask to put up a notice in their window, too.

Her eyes roamed the kitchen ceiling – *needs de-cobwebbing* - as she took mental inventory of the equipment to be disposed. There would be a 50-tonne dump truck, an 8-tonne excavator - *reconditioned engine on that one,* she recalled - a D53A dozer, and a noodling machine at the site. Probably some other sundry bits and bobs.

*Actually,* she acknowledged grimly, *that lot together is probably worth more than the house.* The proposition of the unwanted machinery competing for value against her family home made Helen feel slightly queasy, and her lip curled in distaste.

*Maybe I'll just give it all away,* she thought, conflicted by the idea. On the one hand, it wasn't just her inheritance she'd be giving away – half that value would rightly be allocated to her sister.

*On the other hand, Maxie would agree with me,* she thought, defiantly.

She couldn't care less what Maxine might think.

The irony that the thriftiness which so amused her father was also the reason she could afford to be irrational in this decision did not escape her notice. Helen had always preferred to plan her finances and make sure she had a buffer. The highs and lows of opal mining had made her acutely aware of the ease with which money could come and go.

She wrinkled her nose and aimed a wry half-smile at the sky.

*Laugh it up, Dad,* she thought, imagining him chuckling at her predicament.

\* \* \*

When Helen's love of writing had propelled her from Andamooka to the University of Sydney, she'd secretly feared that she'd built the idea up too much in her head. Coming from a remote outback town, she didn't know if she'd ever be able to find a place for herself in the city or in the university culture.

Worse, she knew that she didn't really have any benchmark for her own academic capability – being the highest achiever among her peers didn't fill her with confidence when there were so few people her own age in the area.

Despite her fears, the university experience had turned out to be everything she'd hoped for, both academically and in terms of extra-curricular opportunities. Whenever her part-time work and full-time study schedules allowed a breather, she'd attended readings – both poetry and prose – and every other literary or cultural event the university offered. It had been a magical time of growth for her, both personally and in her writing expertise.

The stars had continued to align in her favour after graduation, when the work she'd done throughout her study paid off with a permanent job offer at the end of her degree. Jumping on the opportunity, Helen had thrown herself into the publishing world for over ten years – starting first as an editorial assistant, then working her way into the position of Executive Assistant to the Director of Publishing.

It had been a calculated trade-off – the hours and responsibilities of her new role allowed less time for creative writing, but every cent of the wage increase was funnelled directly into her savings plan in the hope that one day she'd be able to make writing her full-time career.

When her first adult horror novel was picked up by niche publishing house *The Screaming Scribe*, she'd crossed her fingers and hoped for the best. Two years later it had become a bestseller, and the release date for book two had been adjusted to take advantage of the buzz. Contract offers for books three and four had allowed her to quit her job and focus on writing full-time.

Of course, giving up that financial stability had required sacrifices. In particular, moving from her townhouse in suburban Sydney to the little one-bedroom apartment in Brisbane had been a difficult decision - but doing so had allowed her to retain the east coast lifestyle she'd grown to love, and the rent at her new apartment was barely a fraction of what she'd been paying. It also didn't hurt that Helen's discretionary spending was limited to the occasional meal delivery when she was deep in the creative process: she wasn't a party goer, her shoes were sensible, jewellery non-existent, and her expenses minimal. Moving was a financial risk, but a calculated one.

When book three had come out last August and raced up the list, she knew she'd made the right decision: Helen Hamilton had officially 'arrived' as an author.

Looking back, she was profoundly grateful she'd been able to share the success of her first two books with her father. He'd understood that the travel requirements to promote her book didn't allow for visits to Andamooka.

Instead, he'd come to her in Sydney and Brisbane:

a proud dad, just happy spending time with his 'little girl'. He'd been genuinely enthusiastic about seeing the things she thought were wonderful about her city, and as a born explorer, he'd been happy to wander on his own when she was unavoidably detained by meetings.

On one such random wander, he'd even found a new favourite coffee shop for her. It had hurt, for a while, visiting the café after his death, but at the same time it had served as a reminder of the good times they'd shared.

After the funeral, life had moved on without concern for her feelings. She'd gone from mechanically plodding one foot in front of another to a chaotic storm of activity. The escalation had felt completely outside of her control, and the past three months had been a non-stop blur of one book tour and publicity event after the other.

Then came the news she'd received en route to Andamooka: the possibility of a movie option with a small independent company. The idea filled her with excitement and terror in roughly equal quantities.

It was amazing. It was incredible.

It was utterly, *incomprehensibly* **overwhelming**.

\* \* \*

Helen's eyes lit upon, and then deliberately slid over, the laptop bag resting on the kitchen table. Her publisher was pushing her hard, desperate to receive the completed manuscript. In the whirlwind of the past few months, she'd struggled to carve out precious minutes to work on her fourth novel. She'd even attempted to turn the long drive to Andamooka into productive time by thinking through her current storyline, but so far it was stubbornly refusing to come together.

*Because of course that's just what I need, to round out this not-at-all stressful occasion. Writer's block.*

Helen had brought the computer along with the hope that she would get at least a little work done during the stressful weeks ahead of her. It had seemed like a brilliant idea at the time, but now she could see that she'd set herself up between a rock and a hard place: any moment not working on the novel felt like a broken promise, while every moment not spent on the family home would be a betrayal.

She huffed a noise that was half-frustration, half-snort of wry amusement. She would never complain about the strain of her workload - what writer wouldn't jump at the opportunities she'd received, particularly so early in their career? But it was all so uncertain. Even as an established author, she didn't feel secure or flush with funds.

*Or with friends.*

The notion flashed across her mind before she stamped it down, irritated.

*Save that drama for your characters*, she thought, with an internally directed glare. It had been entirely her own choice to limit her social circle, and she wouldn't allow her inner dramatic streak to delude her into pretending otherwise.

The simple fact was that the time and energy channelled into bringing her dreams to fruition hadn't left space for cultivating new friendships. Acquaintances who might otherwise have become friends had slowly drifted away, their efforts towards a stronger connection rebuffed one too many times.

The social engagements she did engage in were strictly on a superficial, sporadic, and – above all – low maintenance basis, mostly with other authors or people in the trade. In moving from Sydney to Brisbane she'd left behind her social circle without regret, and she knew that if circumstances ever required her to move internationally, she could abandon the Brisbane circle just as painlessly.

But a small part of her quietly grieved the paths that had taken her so far from the very few people she had loved. Her connections were few, but they ran deep.

Dad.

Maxie.

*Kelly.*

Helen pointedly held up the image of Kelly to her inner thoughts as indisputable evidence that thinking about friends as a quantity was unutterably foolish.

What truly mattered was the *quality* of friendship, and what she had with Kelly Wells was incomparable to any other relationship in her life.

\* \* \*

Helen couldn't remember a time when Kelly wasn't by her side – at least emotionally, if not physically. They'd grown up together, played together, been in the same class at their regional area school. Everything in her life until she graduated high school and drove away without looking back had included Kelly – even her first kiss.

Thinking back to that last year of high school, they'd spent every possible moment together, hoarding time and memories as though they were a resource to be rationed out later, when life inevitably pulled them apart.

They'd lost their virginity together that last year. Camped out in their swags along Opal Creek towards Lake Torrens, with the Milky Way illuminating the sky above, it had been tender and loving and startlingly pleasurable.

Afterwards, they were still best friends, with no false modesty or shame to ruin the moment for them. They had always been everything to each other, and it felt entirely natural that their first time would be together.

They had never tried to redefine the relationship. If Helen were completely honest with herself, she couldn't deny there had been sparks ... but what did they know about sparks between women in Andamooka? Male conversations in derogatory tones about 'lezzos' overheard at the pub. Boys making crude gestures and offensive comments about same sex couples.

To Helen, the most important thing was that Kelly was still her best friend; would always be her best friend. Even if their life plans led them far apart on divergent paths.

They'd both had plans past graduation: Kelly had talked about joining the Navy after high school, and Helen was off to Sydney to become a famous author.

In the end, Helen's career had gone pretty much as planned. Kelly's had not.

After fleeing an abusive husband when Kelly

was little, Kelly's mum Margaret had struggled before finding refuge in Andamooka and building a comfortable life for them both. Then, just as Kelly was ready to leave home, Margaret was diagnosed with an autoimmune disease.

The Country Women's Association had been strongly protective of Margaret when Kelly was young, and in the process, Margaret had forged lifelong friendships. The CWA assured Kelly that Margaret would always have the support of their members.

Kelly knew they were sincere, but she couldn't bring herself to turn her back on her mum. Instead, she decisively aborted her plans to join the Navy, abandoned dreams of travelling interstate and overseas, and enrolled with the South Australian police force, secure in the knowledge that she could be anywhere in the State and still get back to Andamooka within a day or so.

Even from the outset, Kelly had seemed completely at ease with that momentous decision, and Helen knew she was unlikely to have second-guessed her choices or wasted time frivolously pondering the path not taken.

Kelly had always been relentlessly pragmatic.

Helen knew that Kelly's work kept her extraordinarily busy: the Far North Local Service Area covered seventy percent of South Australia, and Kelly and her team were often called to jobs without notice, sometimes without appropriate equipment. Remote area policing was no place for fragile spirits. Those who succeeded in the job had been forged by necessity into adaptive and resilient lateral thinkers who could 'make do' in challenging situations, often without support.

It wasn't surprising, then, that Kelly had flourished in the environment, and - from what Helen had gathered - genuinely loved her job.

Kelly was a Senior Sergeant now, the Officer in Charge at Roxby Downs Police Station, based only twenty minutes from Andamooka.

\* \* \*

Thinking back to her father's funeral, Helen was struck again by how incredibly lucky she was to have Kelly in her life. Kelly had been her strength when Helen had no strength of her own.

At the time, Helen hadn't been in a mental state to fully appreciate how much Kelly's help had meant, or even think about how difficult it must have been for her to take time off at minimal notice. That understanding had come later, after the fog of grief had lifted.

What had initially been a blur of despair had slowly given way to clarity, and she'd realised with ever-increasing gratitude and warmth how Kelly had been at her side all throughout the process, gently supporting her to make the decisions that had to be made. She'd even slept on the old couch each night, knowing that the quiet dark would be when Helen would feel most alone.

*Oh, my god*, Helen realised with a start. *She slept on the couch! I didn't even offer her dad's bed...or Maxine's.*

As she groaned in retrospective self-reproach, a second revelation hit her. Her eyes widened and her hand came up reflexively as though to ward off the realisation: she hadn't talked to her best friend since their farewells after the funeral.

Worse, she hadn't even called to say she was coming to Andamooka!

*What was I thinking?!*

A swell of shame washed over her as she acknowledged the truth: she hadn't been thinking; not even a little bit. She'd been reacting. Every day since the funeral. If she wasn't escaping reality in her writing, she was drifting along through life, refusing to return fully to the world that had hurt her.

*And that's exactly how you end up in stupid situations like dragging a flimsy rental car out to the harshest environment possible... or turning up in town without letting your best friend know,* she thought sourly. Decisively straightening her shoulders, she took a deep breath and hissed it out between her teeth.

*Well, it's time to pull on the big girl panties, Helen. Time to rejoin the land of the living.*

# CHAPTER THREE

## ABSALOM LANE, ANDAMOOKA, SOUTH AUSTRALIA

**8:00 am Sunday, 18 February 2018**

The idea of calling her best friend was exponentially more appealing than dealing with the unknown potential of the shed, but Helen knew she'd already procrastinated too long on the task.

*Complete this job first. Call Kelly as a reward after.*

Pulling a white barista-style apron - included as a bonus with her last coffee order - over her t-shirt and cotton shorts, she stepped determinedly outside to survey the contents of the shed.

The wind and the heat had picked up, and Helen jolted as a piece of random grit flicked off the edge of her eye. As a child, she had easily tolerated the heat and dust.

*When did I lose the knack for living in the outback?*

She nearly turned around and went back inside. The ventilation shafts her father had drilled deep underground cooled the air, drawing it below the earth before hand-dug tunnels brought it up again through floor vents in each of the rooms. The underground temperature was a constant twenty-three degrees Celsius, making the house bearable during hot weather – so long as the wind was blowing to create the downdraft for the ventilation system.

The downside, of course, was the dust that travelled with it, and she made a mental note to remember to check the vent covers inside the house. She knew from experience that if the wind was high and they weren't fitted properly, the wind would literally scream through the small openings. The unearthly howling could raise goosebumps on even the most stoic person.

Helen entered the combination for the keypad on the shed door, with another quick grateful thought towards Mr Sharpe for fitting it for her.

*Definitely a better deterrent to thieves or trespassers than a padlock or key entry*, she thought.

The interior of the shed was as she'd expected: full of items to be sorted, only some of which had any obvious purpose. There was a discouraging number of cardboard boxes and dusty glass and plastic containers piled high that might contain sentimental treasures, or even a hoarded parcel of opal, but more likely contained off-cut lengths of wire, random screws and nails, and other things that 'might come in handy someday'.

Her dad's tools were mostly hung neatly above the rough workbench. Those might be able to be sold. The piles of paint swatches nearly as old as she was? Not likely.

A small grin tugged at her face despite her mood.

*Ahh, yes, the paint swatches.* That was from the time that her father had decided there was no money in opal, and he would become a house painter. He did get a few paid jobs, but it was clear his heart wasn't in it. The opal called to him.

She opened her camera app and took a selection of photos.

Should she have a clearing sale? It felt grubby, but there was nothing here she needed, and she hated the idea of consigning anything to rubbish that could be used by someone else.

Maybe a 'clearing giving-away' instead.

*Come one, come all. Just don't make me put a dollar value on my father's life.*

Her sandals left scuff marks on the dusty cement floor as she squeezed around the items piled high on every surface. Having successfully navigated the maze of memories back to the open door, her hands abruptly white-knuckled on the doorframe as the ambient light, the smell of warm dust, and her shadowy grief conspired to conjure the memory of *that terrible day*, bringing every nuance into horrible clarity.

Her father's deep moan of devastation.

Her sister's hysterical cries.

Her mother's body lying on the dusty ground.

And the blood. The smell and the sight of it everywhere. Pooling on the pavers and soaking the hungry earth, life leached from multiple stab wounds.

Panting, Helen shut her eyes and sunk to her knees, forcing down the memories and rising panic until the swirling dread receded to a more liveable level, memories shoved down into their boxes for the time being. Tentatively, she reopened her eyes, breathing deeply and willing her heart rate to slow back to normal.

Unwilling to tread back over the ground that held that tainted vision, Helen staggered to her feet and walked stiffly towards the town cemetery. Both of her parents were buried there, along with her paternal grandparents. She'd never known her maternal grandparents; they had died before she was old enough to form memories. Her mother did have one sister, who had lived –was presumably still living - in Italy, but the sisters had never been close.

Helen's family had travelled to see her aunt once, during one of those boom times when the Chinese opal buyers had come with their small planes to the dirt airstrip and paid generously for the beautiful stones. Her aunt had shown minimal interest in her nieces; even less in travelling to Australia.

Aside from a condolence card sent with a couple of childhood photos after Helen's mum had died, they'd not heard from her aunt in the years since.

The wind buffeted her towards the cemetery. It wasn't particularly far, but the breeze had picked up even more of the sharp, gritty dust, and she wished she'd thought to bring wrap-around sunglasses for protection.

A hand-built stone fence surrounded the cemetery. The wide arch curved broadly over the main gate, ANDAMOOKA CEMETERY wrought plainly in rusting metal.

Like the town itself, the cemetery spoke of simplistic functionality and isolation. No cramped graves here: the residents of this gated community had an abundance of space, blanketed by pinkish dirt beneath an endless sky.

She settled herself on the simple stone bench her father had added after her mother's death and reflected on their lives following *that terrible day*.

In that one unthinkable moment, Robert had lost his wife and one of his daughters. He felt it was his duty to stay strong; provide reassurance to Helen and find exoneration for Maxine. He had, he believed, too much responsibility to allow him the luxury of living his loss. Instead, he would walk here and sit for long minutes each evening, sharing his thoughts, plans and fears with his beloved wife. Only in those quiet moments could he unburden himself, grieve without judgment.

At the same time, Helen had felt as if she had stepped into the twilight zone: everything was muted, grey. Words without meaning, no solid ground on which to walk. It was the kind of thing that happened someplace else, to *someone* else. But it had happened to them. To her and her father. To their world.

Dad talked around it; Maxie wouldn't talk at all.

It had taken a long time for life to start to feel normal again.

Helen's eyes rested on the headstone her father had chosen and dedicated to his wife.

*Ruth Hamilton*
*1959 – 1998*
*Loving mother of Maxine and Helen*
*Beloved wife of Robert*

Helen hadn't yet organised for the stone to be engraved with her father's details; another task she hadn't had the emotional strength to contemplate.

Looking down, she noticed that the rectangular plot had been neatly edged with slates from the creek, cemented-in to prevent erosion and disturbance by burrowing wildlife.

*The funeral director must have organised that,* she thought, and added a mental reminder to go by his house and thank him for arranging it on her behalf.

From her seat on the bench, Helen looked over to the distinctive gravesite of one of Andamooka's most-beloved residents. As unconventional as the woman herself, her grave supported the framework of a tree over a metre tall, fashioned from twisted wire threaded through two massive rocks for stability.

Crafted by an admirer with love, the tribute was as complex as the inscription was simple.

*Nóra Esterházy*
*1932 - 1984*

Helen remembered the stories her mum had told the girls about the life of the remarkable woman she'd known.

Nóra had been born in Budapest, Hungary. She wasn't yet a teen when her parents were taken to the concentration camps; her father first, and her mother only a month or two later. Nóra and her sister, Krÿstÿna, had stayed for a while with their grandparents and other relatives, before their grandmother pushed the sisters out to seek a better life.

Nóra never spoke of what happened to her and Krÿstÿna after that. The story always skipped ahead to the day she arrived in Australia on a Red Cross boat in 1957 from Hungary via France.

She could never bring herself to talk about how

she'd lost her sister along the way.

Helen remembered the way her mother had marvelled at Nóra's character and resilience, holding her up as an example to her girls about what true strength really looked like.

Arriving alone in a country that didn't speak her language and held no family or friends, Nóra was determined to start her new life free from oppression and persecution.

Hitchhiking overland from Melbourne, allowing the winds of fate to lead her through towns and settlements, she'd eventually landed in Andamooka and the freedom it offered. Her life had taught her a justified fear of government authorities - but out here the government had minimal interest in, and effectively no oversight of, its citizens.

This was somewhere she could build a life.

From that point onwards, Nóra had lived entirely on her own terms. She built her own house, noodled for opal to pay the bills. She named her mining claim *Krÿstÿna*, and her home became *Sissi's* in tribute to her sister.

Notoriously independent, she quickly made it clear that she neither wanted nor needed a permanent man in her life: instead, she'd had 'friends with benefits' long before the phrase existed, refusing to be cowed into submission by the societal standards of the time.

Nóra asked nothing from anyone and was never in anyone's debt.

*It's not surprising that Andamooka loved her all the more for it*, Helen thought, flashing a fond smile towards Nóra's grave. *This town was built by feisty underdogs; we know our own.*

Nóra never bore children, but she had generously provided practical assistance to the town's young mothers and been cherished by them in return. Helen recalled her mum saying that Nóra had been a true friend and support both during and after her difficult pregnancy with Maxine, and had helped her with the baking, cleaning, and laundry.

Nóra hadn't been afraid to take Helen's dad to task either, telling him exactly how he should help his wife - something her mum had recounted with laughter as she described how remorsefully attentive he'd been after Nóra had given him his wake-up call.

The town had been rippled by grief when Nóra died in 1984. In the final act of respect and admiration available, her gravesite had been crafted with love to become a monument true to the woman herself: complex, multi-faceted, and proudly unique.

*Rather than being crushed by her life*, Helen mused, *Nóra became unbreakable. She saw the worst that people are capable of, and it only made her more determined to help those who needed it.*

She wondered whether her sister's time in prison had forged her similarly. According to the Parole Officer, Maxine had spent over fourteen years on the purpose of improving rehabilitation outcomes for women prisoners.

Maxine's focus had first been towards developing and implementing a range of self-improvement programs, and these had ultimately led to limited freedoms for prisoners to attend university, deliver public speaking engagements, or even run their own radio programs.

At much the same time, she had lobbied for female

sanitary products to be classified as items of 'essential dignity', successfully arguing that these were not luxury items but basic hygiene necessities.

More recently, in the last few years of her incarceration, she had created a support group for women preparing to reintegrate with society after prison, with the aim of increasing personal resilience and creating job opportunities through community networking groups.

While it was still a little early to truly gauge the efficacy of the support group in reducing recidivism, the Parole Officer had noted that - combined with the self-improvement and educational programs previously implemented - early results did seem quite promising.

As a young teen, Helen had sat through every hour of her sister's trial. She had never believed her sister was a killer - or perhaps *'believed'* wasn't the right word; there was a disconnect between the clear evidence in front of her, and what her heart told her. Though her father had never said as much, she was certain he had felt that same dissonance.

There was a part of Helen that still clung unwaveringly to the faith of her teenage years. That part desperately wanted to believe the picture the Parole Officer had painted: that Maxine had not only endured the harsh environment but had heroically improved the lives of others along the way. The idea filled her with a glow of warmth and loving pride.

But try as she might, she just couldn't quite buy into the story as it was presented. As an author, Helen was innately aware of timelines from a narrative point of view - and it was impossible to ignore that the timelines in Maxine's story *just so happened* to conveniently align with the times that she personally had the most benefit to gain from each program.

*Just because she cut you off, it doesn't make her a bad person,* she thought crossly, reminding herself not to be uncharitable. *Maxine has done a lot of good, regardless of her motivations.*

Rising from the bench, she began the trek back along Miner's Way towards the house.

Spinning dust-devils whipped at her apron, throwing grit in her face. The rough gravel road pierced the soles of her flimsy sandals, and sharp-edged detritus flew on the swirling wind to slice at Helen's feet. Her nostalgic mood made it feel personal, as though the Outback was snarling a reprimand at its wayward daughter for abandoning it for so long.

# CHAPTER FOUR

**9.20am Sunday, 18 February 2018**

Back at the house, Helen brushed down her clothes and tossed aside the offending footwear. She had to smirk at the folly of wearing the white apron – now dusky pink and brown-streaked - to the cemetery, as she poured herself a glass of water from the fridge.

Wiping her face with a cloth dampened from the sink, she looked at it thoughtfully before repeating the action with the chilled water.

*Much better.*

Helen checked her phone.

*Would now be a good time to give Kelly a call?*

Perhaps she could head into Roxby Downs, and they could have lunch together.

Helen thought back to her last visit. Fifteen months ago, Kelly hadn't had a partner. It struck her anew how very long it had been since she'd spoken with her best friend: fifteen months was a *huge* gap.

Since her last visit, Australian federal law had legalised same-sex marriage. She had no doubts that Kelly would have rung her to announce an engagement, but for any relationship short of that status? Probably not. Kelly had always been cautious, and the pressure of a community-facing role would have only strengthened that trait, Helen thought.

While the lead-in to the plebiscite had amplified the voices of an ugly but vocal minority, it had also encouraged same-sex couples to make their voices heard. Helen wondered whether the Roxby Downs community had grown more accepting as a result of the frank discussions taking place across the country. She feared it would take time and persistence to break through the entrenched attitudes in regional towns.

As for herself, Helen had never been in any serious relationships. She had been focused strictly on her plans: get through university; get a job in the publishing industry; write a book. When pressed, she'd always said there hadn't been time or energy for anything else, but for the first time, she wondered – was lack of time the real issue, or had she just been drifting along in a personal fog?

Thinking about it honestly, she knew that when she truly wanted something, she made it happen. Whatever her other failings, lack of ambition wasn't one of them - so, if the part of her life that included intimate relationships was on permanent pause, it was because she'd allowed it to happen.

She sipped the cold water thoughtfully. Had she ignored those needs to avoid having to deal with *that terrible day*? In truth, had she or her father ever really dealt with the ramifications of that loss and the shocking violence that preceded it? Had it just been easier to immerse herself in her studies and then her work?

Now, here she was - suddenly mid-thirties, and alone, and uncertain about so many things.

"Less thinking! More doing!"

Helen spoke the self-reprimand aloud, giving herself a mental shake, and following up with a gentle hand-slap in punctuation to the thought for good measure.

*Being in this house has me obsessing about the past.*

Helen picked up her notepad and focused on what she should be doing: taking inventory and making a list of the items she wanted to keep, and those she felt compelled to send to her sister. She restrained her emotions and determined to be ruthlessly practical in her selections.

She went first to her father's bedroom and began sifting through decades of her parents' lives. The faint scent of mothballs swirled in the wardrobe. The clothes were all in good condition, and most could be donated, aside from her father's work clothes. Those were fit only for the rubbish dump.

There wasn't any jewellery, other than a few inexpensive pieces belonging to her mother. Somewhere, Helen knew, there would be an opal necklace that she intended to keep; an heirloom piece handed down through her father's family.

She made a note of the item on her list but didn't see it in the jewellery box.

A makeup table and mirror sat at the end of the double bed. Her father had left the area essentially untouched: the perfume his wife had worn, her few cosmetics, all remained where Ruth Hamilton had left them … everything, Helen thought, except the lipstick her mother had loved. One of her friends had originally picked it up for her on a whim, amused by the name - 'Ruthless Red' – but her mother had loved the shade and made it her signature colour. Helen thought she recalled seeing it when she was picking out her father's clothes for his funeral.

*Now, where have you gotten to, little lipstick?*

With a pensive hum, Helen opened the shallow centre drawer, but found only a hairbrush and handheld mirror, both covered in fine dust. She gently lifted the curtains to check behind, careful not to raise too much dust – no lipstick – then got down on hands and knees to peek beneath the bed.

She couldn't restrain a short, self-pitying groan.

*More boxes. Of course,* she thought, rolling her eyes with a sigh. She made a mental note to check under the rest of the beds and – realising another area she'd initially overlooked - on top of the wardrobes.

*OK, no more diversions, distractions, or treasure hunts. Get on with it, and the lipstick will turn up when it turns up.*

Helen knew enough basic psychology to be aware that the mind tended to fill in what it expected to see, particularly during a time of extreme stress. She probably hadn't even seen the lipstick or necklace last time she was here.

At least she could be certain of one thing: the opal necklace would be somewhere safe, and the lipstick couldn't have gone too far. Her father wouldn't have parted with either of them.

*So, stick to the job in front of you, tidy up the clutter, and eventually you'll find everything.*

Unfortunately, it was easier to give herself a pep talk than it was to implement it.

Helen could be extraordinarily single-focused when there was an intellectual puzzle or a research path that grabbed her fancy, but housework and cleaning had always been a challenge. Her own home was entirely minimalist purely so she wouldn't have to invest more than a handful of minutes tidying. Dealing with a large volume of sorting, reorganising, and cleaning would be a challenge at the best of times; doing it when every step in the exercise came with the risk of emotional damage was that much harder.

*Focus,* she reminded herself.

There was a lot to be done.

# CHAPTER FIVE

FOUR NATIONS ROAD, ANDAMOOKA, SOUTH AUSTRALIA

**9.35am Sunday, 18 February 2018**

Standing in the middle of a homicide scene was the last thing Senior Sergeant Kelly Wells wanted to be doing on a Sunday morning – any morning, for that matter. Yet here she was.

Kelly surveyed the back yard where Lorraine Sharpe lay prone on the dusty ground not a dozen steps from her back door. Dark crimson blood, from what appeared to be multiple stab wounds, stained the victim's dress. Strangely, it didn't appear to have run down the sides to pool in the dust beside her. Maybe there was more beneath the body, but Kelly would have to wait until the doctor arrived to check it out.

She shook her head with a barely audible growl of frustration.

*Who in the hell would do this to a woman nearly seventy years old?*

Lorraine had lived in Andamooka her whole life. She baked for the church fundraisers. She taught Sunday School.

*This doesn't make any sense.*

Detectives Deer and Heath were two and a half hours away, recalled from duty in Port Augusta where two separate demonstrations – one for, and one against - were underway in relation to a proposed nuclear waste dump.

The northern site where the Princes, Stuart and Eyre Highways converged was causing delays on the bridge crossing Spencer Gulf, where anti-nuclear protestors lined the roads. The southern site, at the turn off from the Augusta Highway to the Flinders Ranges Way, was just as problematic, with pro-nuclear demonstrators threatening to rally and further disrupt travel. A heavy police presence had been brought in to ensure the safety of road users and demonstrators at both sites, with officers travelling from Adelaide, Whyalla, and Port Pirie.

The township of Andamooka was too small to warrant a permanent police presence - instead, a small fibro-cement building served as temporary office space on an as-needed basis. Unfortunately, the building wasn't sized for a full response team, so the Roxby Downs unit had secured the crime scene and were all working on location.

Kelly cast an eye to the sky. The weather conditions were noticeably deteriorating, putting serious strain on their timeframe to collect physical evidence. With the majority of regional police tied up at the demonstrations, Kelly's team were carrying out evidence collection under the direction of Major

Crime via radio from Adelaide.

Her two Senior Constables were working the body: Harry Flugelman collecting evidence, while Geralt 'Gerry' Chadowski photographed the scene. Nearby, Constable Sheila Roberts was documenting the evidence with her usual meticulous attention to detail.

Working nearer the fence line were Constables Morgan Fowler and Bronwyn King, both called in from their days off. High-visibility vests over their khaki police uniforms made it easy to pick out where the officers were working their grid search in the hot wind. Morgan was the youngest member of the team and keen to prove herself; Bronwyn, by contrast, was solidly procedural, having come from a background in highway patrol.

Rounding out the team on site were the newest members, Constables Ashley Zone and Jett Bullock, both of them mature-age graduates – Ashley coming via the fitness industry, and Jett from Social Services. The pair were a surprisingly good fit with the local community: Ashley's background as a personal trainer had led her to set up a range of youth group activities that were proving popular, while Jett's skills made him the natural lead in diminishing tense situations and helping victims of crime.

Kelly looked at her phone, checking the time. She had been advised that a doctor was currently en route to certify that death had occurred. If her judgment was correct, she should be seeing them within the next fifteen minutes.

The dispatcher hadn't advised which of the two local doctors would be attending, and she quietly hoped it wasn't going to be Garry Guthrie. The man was competent, no doubt, but had an irritating tendency to forget where his religious beliefs ended, and her personal rights began.

*Really not in the mood for his passive-aggressive bullshit on top of everything else today*, she thought. She could feel her shoulders tighten in expectation, and deliberately stretched to release the tension as she mentally reviewed the current evidence.

So far, the investigative team had found no reason to suspect that anything had been taken from inside the house. Not even the cash in Mrs Sharpe's handbag was missing.

The murder appeared to be senseless and unprovoked.

Kelly glanced over at the body, calculating the damage. An interrupted burglary would usually be the most likely scenario, but experience told her that a startled intruder tended to strike and run. It wasn't possible to be sure until the doctor arrived and moved the body, but her bet was that there was a lot more damage than would be expected from someone trying to flee the scene.

Her mind turned to the only witness.

Ray Sharpe, Lorraine's husband, stated that he'd arrived home at seven thirty that morning from what he'd referred to initially as a *business trip*, although further questioning revealed an appointment with a medical specialist in Adelaide.

Kelly understood, though found it eternally frustrating, that male witnesses – and it *was* almost invariably men - were reluctant to divulge medical information to investigative officers because they feared the 'town grapevine' would immediately spread news of their illness.

She knew the obfuscation was instinctive, not premeditated, but it grated at her. Allowing pride to lead a witness into falsifying any element of their Statement could not only bring their entire testimony into question but could significantly misdirect an investigation by blurring critical timelines, distances, or associations. And in cases like this, every minute wasted in getting to the truth was time gifted to the killer to escape…or kill again.

With a mental sigh for the follies of men, she continued her review of Ray Sharpe's statement.

He'd driven all night to get home, arriving at 7:30am.

When he'd unlocked the front door and come inside, he'd noted how quiet it was. The television was usually on from first thing every morning, so he assumed Lorraine must be sleeping in – she didn't tend to sleep easily when he was away and was sometimes up until two or three in the morning, leaving her groggy the next day.

He'd quietly put down his bags, heading in to make a cup of tea to surprise his wife in bed. As he entered the kitchen, he immediately noticed the back door standing open. Realising she must be outside hanging up washing, he went out to greet her.

As he approached the threshold, he saw his wife sprawled on the ground outside.

*It all fits*, Kelly thought, looking down at the victim, *but it's not much to go on.*

Rigor mortis had begun its slow, inevitable trek through her body. The coroner would make the decision, but Kelly was guessing Lorraine Sharpe had died a few hours before her husband arrived home.

Since the victim had been alone the night before, and had a history of insomnia under those circumstances, it would be difficult – she hated to admit, maybe impossible - to determine *when* her attacker had arrived, or *why* she had apparently let them willingly inside.

The front door had been locked when Ray Sharpe had arrived home; he was certain he'd used his key to enter. No windows were broken or open. Logic dictated that if it were an intruder, and not a guest, they must have entered through the back door - yet there were no signs of forced entry.

Had someone knocked, and Mrs Sharpe stirred from sleep thinking it was her husband?

Had grogginess prevented her from considering that her husband wouldn't have had to knock?

Perhaps she'd assumed he'd forgotten or lost his key?

Kelly turned to Constable Roberts, "I'm going to talk to Mr Sharpe again. Can you me know when the doctor arrives?"

"Will do," Sheila nodded, briefly making eye contact over her clipboard.

Kelly made her way into the house through the kitchen to the living room, then down the short hallway to the guest bedroom where the victim's husband was temporarily located.

The team had needed to ensure that Mr Sharpe remained away from the official activities, but it was too hot to ask him to wait in the car. Kelly did not want him in the main bedroom: she wanted the crime scene technicians from Port Augusta to examine the bed Mr and Mrs Sharpe had shared for more than forty years, and she wanted to be subtle about it.

While this end of the transportable house had not yet been examined, there was nothing on first viewing to indicate the killer had entered either of the two spare bedrooms. Ushering the man into the guest bedroom facing away from the back yard had seemed the best way to keep him insulated from proceedings and the terrible scene outside.

Ray Sharpe had been slumped forward in the armchair between the two single beds, head in hands, fingers curled into his short grey hair, but he looked up as Kelly paused in the doorway. He had strikingly cornflower-blue eyes, under incongruously black bushy eyebrows at odds with his hair, which had been grey as long as Kelly had known him.

Today, those eyes were bloodshot, red-rimmed, his face sombre.

"There are people I need to call," he said, voice wavering. "Arrangements need to be made."

Ray and Lorraine Sharpe didn't have any children, but Kelly knew that both were active in the church community and had many friends around the local area.

"I understand," Kelly said softly. "We'll finish up here as soon as we can."

She sank down on the edge of the bed to his right, bringing herself to the same level as the man in front of her.

"I know we've asked you a lot of questions today, but there are a few more," she added gently. "I'm sorry if it seems like we're treading over the same ground, but it's critically important that we get a complete picture."

Sharpe reached up to scratch blearily over the morning fuzz of shaving regrowth, hand shaking ever so slightly. "Sure, sure. Whatever you need."

"About what time do you and your wife usually go to bed at night and get up in the mornings?"

Kelly needed to determine whether the scenario where the intruder had awakened Mrs Sharpe was the most feasible, or whether it was more likely she had already been up.

Had she come into the living room, discovered the intruder, and ran out the back door?

Or had she answered the door thinking it was her husband?

The latter seemed the most logical since there was no sign of forced entry. There was no indication the locks on either the flyscreen door or the solid wooden door had been tampered with whatsoever, and a woman nervous at being alone in the house would certainly have ensured they were locked in the first instance.

What *didn't* fit was her manner of dress: she wasn't wearing a nightgown or pyjamas.

Neither did the bed show any sign of use, being neatly made.

Whatever Lorraine Sharpe had been doing, she had either risen early, or not gone to bed at all before trouble appeared at her home.

"Since we retired," Ray Sharpe began, with a shuddering sigh, "we've been staying up to watch the late news. Then we have a glass of milk with a splash of brandy and talk about the next day's plans, the weather."

His shoulders moved up and down as if he didn't really know what else to say.

"A few nights ago, we were talking about what we might do for our birthdays this year." Anguish pooled in his eyes. "I don't know what in the world I am going to do now."

"Eleven-thirty? Midnight?" Kelly asked gently, redirecting him back to the question.

Sharpe nodded. "That's about right. She's always found it difficult to sleep when I'm away; says the house is too quiet. She probably fell asleep in front of the television, for the noise."

Or she was awake when her killer arrived.

"Do you both have mobile phones?"

Kelly opted not to use the past tense: the man was aware his wife was dead, no need to point out the obvious.

"She's always refused to bother with one. Always preferred the house phone."

The home's landline was in the kitchen, with an extension in the bedroom.

If some unidentifiable sound had awakened her, why not stay in the bedroom to call for help? The phone was right there.

Or if the intruder had come in the back door, why run outside?

Whatever her intent, Lorraine hadn't been fast enough to escape her killer.

Sharpe reached out a hand and put it on Kelly's arm, his eyes intent and expression serious.

"I told the officer earlier that I called Lorraine around half-past eight, but I think ... I think I might have been wrong. I think it might have been more like nine. Can you please let them know? It might be important. Can you ask them to check the outgoing calls on my phone? It's out there somewhere… probably the table?"

Kelly nodded, making a note. "I'll do that, and make sure the record is corrected, thank you, Mr Sharpe." She patted his hand reassuringly, and he removed it, settling back into the chair.

With a deep breath, he continued.

"I let Lorraine know that I'd checked into the motel at Port Pirie. She's always worried I'll fall asleep on the drive home if I don't take a break. I napped for a few hours, but couldn't get settled… I knew that storm was coming in. If it flooded, I'd get stuck outside of town for who knows how long. Around three in the morning I figured I'd be better off pushing through to home and sleeping in my own bed, so I packed up and drove straight through."

Tears formed in the corners of his eyes, and he roughly knuckled them aside. His voice was husky as he muttered, "I wish to God I hadn't gone at all."

"Mrs Sharpe sounded fine when you spoke by phone?" Kelly asked the old man.

He nodded. "We just talked about the doctor's visit, and the shopping I'd done on the way out of town." He sucked in a breath on that thought, scrubbing at his face. "I've just remembered. The shopping is still in the truck."

"Would you like me to get one of the officers to bring it inside for you?"

Ray Sharpe closed his eyes and considered the question for a moment.

"No, it's okay. I didn't get anything that needs refrigerating on this trip, and I need to keep the bags separate; a few are for the church group. I'll have to," his voice caught, "...have to go and see the pastor anyway. He'll be busy with church this morning."

He lowered his head into his hands. "I can't believe this. I can't..."

"When I first arrived," Kelly began, "one of the things I asked you to do is to mull over the idea of who might have wanted to hurt you or Mrs Sharpe."

The old man lifted his head, his gaze an open wound.

"But that's just the thing, Kelly. *No one.* We don't have a thing in this world worth killing for. There's a few thousand in the bank for emergency money, but we don't keep any here at the house. We haven't offended anyone or made anyone angry. We don't have any enemies." His eyes were pools of pained confusion. "It just doesn't make *sense.*"

The answer, while unenlightening, tracked with what Kelly had expected.

Growing up in the area, she was aware of the Sharpes in a general way. They were friends of Robert Hamilton and she'd seen them at Helen's house regularly over the years, interacted on a passing social level. She knew they had a reputation locally for their good works in the church community, and that they were considered reliable and steady.

They certainly weren't the type to attract trouble.

Nor did their lifestyle invite greed or resentment. The simple prefabricated house had been transported across the sand dunes from Woomera during the early 1980's: like so many others, it had a generic steel frame with aluminium cladding and was small and modest, filled with furniture focused more on functionality than style. Nothing evident that could bait a thief.

And yet, Lorraine Sharpe was dead.

*Murdered. And for what?*

"If you think of anything at all, however unimportant it may seem," Kelly said, "let me know. For now, we'll operate under the assumption this was a stranger passing through looking to steal money or something easily converted to cash."

Except … one hundred and fifty dollars in cash remained in the victim's purse. Her credit card was still there. There were no computers or expensive electronics, aside from the laptop Ray Sharpe had taken with him on his trip. The old television was not valuable enough to bother stealing. No jewellery or other goods that were readily marketable. Quite a few of the older generation still dealt in opal, but Sharpe had assured Kelly there was none stashed on the property and that his wife's jewellery had only sentimental value.

Her instincts screamed at her that this killing wasn't the action of a thief or a crime of opportunity.

*It has to be personal.*

A knife was missing from the block on the counter, and – pending forensic confirmation – it seemed the most likely murder weapon. So far, the knife hadn't turned up in her team's search of the house and property. The murderer had likely taken it with them.

Kelly found the choice of weapon both intriguing and perplexing: a kitchen knife was a weapon of opportunity. The killer didn't appear to have brought one to the scene – of if they had, they hadn't used it, and had taken it away with them.

Had they arrived with positive intentions before something went terribly wrong?

Kelly knew that the public generally underestimated how much actual determination or excessive adrenaline was required to create more than one stab wound – even if the first one had been made in anger. From what Kelly could tell, Lorraine Sharpe had *at least* four stab wounds in the back, and no other visible indications of injury.

It spoke to a crime of significant passion: hatred, fury, devastation … *betrayal*?

None of her thoughts showed on her face as she waited for Ray Sharpe's response.

Sharpe exhaled deeply. "If it's okay, I'll just stay in here until you people are done. I can't see… can't be there for what has to be done."

"Is there anyone I can call to pick you up? You might be better off out of the house until we're through here."

His head shake was an emphatic rejection.

"I need to stay. I need to be here when they take her away. This is our home. I can't… just, no. No, Kelly. I'll wait."

Kelly put a hand on the man's shoulder and gave it a squeeze. "Let me know if I can get you anything at all."

Kelly moved back into the living room and found Constable Bullock.

"Jett, can you please keep an eye on Mr Sharpe?" she said quietly, "I don't want him to do anything irrational."

"Of course, Kelly," he replied in equally hushed tones, "I'll be sure to check in on him".

Kelly pushed down her remorse that Ray Sharpe was going to have to endure more of the grim investigation taking place in his yard. It would have been better for the poor man to go to a friend's place and stay for the day – or maybe a couple of days, considering the storm coming.

Kelly exited the house, grimacing at the sky. Judging by the inky clouds gathering above the dust, the storm was headed straight for them. She'd hoped they'd get lucky: often, rain seemed to circle around Andamooka - the old timers talked about the town being in a 'rain shadow'. Where Roxby Downs and Woomera would get soaked, Andamooka would often get just a few sprinkles.

*Not this time*, she thought.

Ex-tropical cyclone Kelvin had already drenched the Kimberley and Pilbara regions of Western Australia, then gone on to drown the AＯangu Pitjantjatjara Yankunytjatjara lands of Central Australia yesterday. Now, it seemed, Kelvin had turned his eye to far north South Australia, seemingly infinite in his capacity for destructive rain.

Kelly located Morgan, who had been doing a grid search of the yard in the rapidly rising wind. "Anything?"

Morgan shook her head. "Nothing yet. No tracks of any kind." Morgan gestured to the hard-packed gravel driveway that led from Four Nations Road. "I walked the length of the drive just in case whoever came last night had gone off the gravel. No luck. Didn't find any footprints anywhere around the house, either – but this bloody wind is moving every grain of sand."

"Good work. But make sure everything gets a second look by a fresh set of eyes, please, Morgan. I don't want anything missed."

"Sure thing. Can you hold here a tick so that nobody disturbs the area? I'll go grab Harry."

At Kelly's nod, Morgan headed around the house to find the Senior Constable, leaving Kelly alone with her thoughts again.

It certainly hadn't escaped Kelly's notice that the manner of death was eerily reminiscent of Ruth Hamilton's some twenty years ago. Ruth Hamilton, too, had been stabbed in the back, her body face-down on the ground in her own backyard.

Uneasiness slid through Kelly. She hated the idea that when Helen heard this news, she would be forced to relive that nightmare all over again.

The doctor's car arrived at the same time as the Clinic's ambulance, and Kelly felt a weight shift from her shoulders knowing the body would be moved soon. She had begun to fear that the storm would hit before the doctor's arrival, which would have brought a whole new level of difficulty to an already challenging situation.

The combination of remote location and low population meant that some agency functions were allocated differently in the outback: in this case, the Clinic ambulance would transfer the body back to the Roxby Downs Hospital morgue, before a different car transported the body to the Forensic Science unit nearly seven hours away in Adelaide. Normally, the body would be moved by air, but with the storm it simply wasn't a sensible option.

The two specialist remote area nurses with the Clinic Ambulance readied the equipment to cover and lift Lorraine Sharpe into a body bag. Kelly didn't recognise either of them, which was unusual.

*Joy and Kal must be on leave*, she thought.

Doctor Rosemary McGregor climbed out of her car, much to Kelly's relief. She suddenly realised she'd been gritting her teeth in expectation of Dr Guthrie, and deliberately unclenched her jaw in a smile of greeting.

Tall, slim, and capable, Rosemary exuded an aura of self-assurance and competence, though her no-nonsense attitude won her fans and detractors in equal measure. She'd developed a reputation in town for not suffering fools - something she in common with Kelly. The two had quickly developed a mutual respect and, as time had gone by, something akin to friendship.

The doctor's chin-length black hair was cut into a practical bob that the immediate frenzy of wind threw into her eyes: Kelly heard her huff in exasperation as she tucked a wayward piece behind the arm of her red-framed glasses, only for it to blow out again seconds later as she nodded to Kelly in greeting.

"Really nice weather you've put on for me," Rosemary observed drily, pulling on her latex gloves.

Kelly smirked in response. "You know you love a challenge".

The rattle of the gurney being pulled from the ambulance drew their attention.

"That storm is picking up steam," Rosemary said. "I've got a feeling we're going to be in for it tonight.

I was watching Ryleigh's latest weather report from Broome - looks like they've avoided any loss of life, but Kelvin's inflicted some serious damage."

As an ex-Roxby resident, the glamorous weather reporter was on first-name terms with both of them.

*Well, maybe not me anymore*, Kelly thought with an inward wince. To say their relationship hadn't ended on a positive note would be much like suggesting the docking of the *Hindenburg* had encountered some minor technical issues.

Rosemary inclined her head towards the house. "So. Got ourselves a murder, hmm?"

"Afraid so. Lorraine Sharpe."

Rosemary frowned thoughtfully, trying to place the name. "Not one of my patients. Is she churchy? Most of them go to Garry Guthrie." At Kelly's brief nod, the doctor continued, "Is the husband here?"

Kelly nodded. "He found her. Got home this morning. The back door was wide open, and his wife was outside on the ground."

The doctor made a sympathetic noise. "The poor bastard," she said with a shake of her head. "He must be shattered." She reached out to Kelly and clapped her on the shoulder. "Well, let's get on with it. See if we can't bring some clarity to this shit show."

Kelly grinned at Rosemary and made an expansive 'after you' gesture. It never ceased to amuse her how much the elegant doctor's speech patterns changed depending on whether she was with patients or peers. Her patients would have sworn butter couldn't melt in her mouth.

With a quick wave to Harry and Morgan, who were reviewing the search grid, the pair walked around to the back of the house together.

Gerry and Sheila had just finished up their work around the body. Releasing the scene to Kelly, they moved on to the main living areas of the house.

The gurney wheels crunched over the gravel as Rosemary crouched down and began her examination of the victim.

As the doctor carried out her tasks, Kelly stepped back, reviewing the scene from a different perspective. She ignored the body on the ground and visually examined the back verandah. Nothing stood out: a simple small table and two chairs unsoftened by cushions; some small machinery parts abandoned on the porch. There were no scuff marks in the dust around the abandoned items that would indicate the murderer had taken an interest.

The walkway from the back door to the path was clean and generally free of dust besides that whipped along by the increasingly angry winds. Kelly concluded that the path was likely swept by Lorraine Sharpe every day: while simple and unpretentious, the tidiness of her home spoke to her houseproud nature.

Kelly looked to the mat on the ground in front of the door, then traced the path to where the body lay. Other than the dead woman, there was nothing whatsoever to suggest foul play.

If anything, it was *too* clean.

That was the rub that chafed at Kelly. The entire scene felt wrong; staged. Intended to send a message.

*What was the message?*

Considering that nothing had gone missing – at least nothing that Ray Sharpe had noticed beyond the potential murder weapon – this had to be personal. If that was the case, the real question was: who had a grudge against Lorraine Sharpe?

*And why didn't her husband know about it?*

The couple spent most of their time together. Kelly had seen them around town, shopping in Roxby Downs. Always together: at church, at community functions, at the café. As far as Kelly knew, they were only apart when her husband had his Adelaide appointments, or if he had a water delivery to do - and that was rarely, these days. He'd become the backup driver since his retirement.

Whatever had happened here after Ray Sharpe spoke to his wife by phone, there *would* be a motive.

And probably a secret or two.

"Kelly?"

Kelly moved towards Rosemary and crouched down next to her. "You find something?"

"Maybe." She pointed to the victim's throat, visible now that the body had been moved onto its back. "See that fine red line there?"

"I do." Kelly squinted thoughtfully. "It's too shallow to be a ligature mark, wouldn't you say?"

"Definitely not a ligature. I'm thinking something more like a thin chain. Perhaps a crucifix? Her killer may have yanked it off her."

Maybe there was something missing after all?

Kelly leaned in. "I reckon you're right. Mr Sharpe didn't mention her having a favourite necklace, but I'll ask him about the possibility." Kelly frowned, looking closer. "Is she wearing *make-up*?"

Despite the lividity caused by lying face down for all these hours, the victim's lips were ruby red, her cheeks painted.

Strange, for a woman with no plans other than to go to bed.

Stranger still, Kelly couldn't recall ever having seen Mrs Sharpe wearing such a vivid shade. She had always been a sparrow of a woman: understated makeup, simple clean nails. A woman of brown, taupe and beige, never red or bright colours.

Even the dress she had died in was a muted mustard-gold, not a shade to attract attention.

"Certainly seems out of character, and especially odd in the circumstances," Rosemary commented, voicing Kelly's own thoughts.

Kelly tilted her head as she looked at the victim's face.

*Lipstick, blusher, eyeliner... but no mascara, eyeshadow, or brow pencil.*

Had she been interrupted while getting made-up?

Kelly beckoned Morgan and asked her to send Gerry to take more photographs.

"What really bothers me, though" Rosemary said, her brow furrowed, "is the lack of blood. It doesn't seem like nearly enough for her manner of death."

"I noticed." Kelly shrugged. "I thought there'd be more of it under her. What's your estimate on TOD?"

"Unfortunately, the best I can say is that she died somewhere between midnight and four o'clock this morning. It's a difficult call considering her body has been outside and the sun is warming up. And the wind isn't helping."

In response to Kelly's enquiring look, Rosemary clarified, "No flies to use as a guide. The local species, *lucilia cuprina*, disappears when the wind picks up. Their wind speed threshold is only about 30 kilometres per hour."

"Ah, I see. That's a pity." Kelly paused, looking from the body to Dr McGregor. "If you find anything else, Rosie, can you call me ASAP?"

"You'll know as soon as I know," Rosemary assured her. "She'll be off to Adelaide for the full forensic analysis. By road, I imagine; can't see them flying in this weather."

"Definitely by road," Kelly agreed, "there are flight warnings are already in place. There's an SES warning for the Far North Local Service Area. We're going to be on our own up to twelve hours – it's going to be too dangerous for emergency responders. National Radio has started issuing warnings for the northeast and northwest Pastoral areas."

There was a short pause where Rosemary and Kelly looked deadpan at each other before breaking into open grins, mutually acknowledging the exchange of their respective expertise as both slightly pretentious and a little competitive.

It hadn't been strictly necessary, but it lightened their mood.

"Admit it," Rosemary said, nudging Kelly, "you were secretly impressed with the bit about the flies."

Kelly chuckled in agreement, the pair hunching their backs in camaraderie against the wind as they turned towards the house.

"Kelly, wait up a second," Jett called out as he intercepted the pair, adding "Hi, Doctor McGregor" with a professionally courteous smile.

Interpreting that she was not required for this conversation, Rosemary excused herself with a polite nod to both of them and continued on her way.

Jett waited until the doctor was a few steps away before speaking.

"Kelly, I was just thinking... do you want me to take a ride over to the Hamilton place on Absalom Lane and see if she heard anything? Out this way, sound carries pretty well in the dark."

Jett was correct. The road was sparsely populated, and sound would carry, particularly at night. Then Kelly frowned. "The Hamilton place is unoccupied," she reminded Jett. Helen hadn't been home since her father died.

Jett's face froze for a moment as he pondered his next words, clearly caught off guard.

"I uh...I think she arrived yesterday? My wife spoke to her on the phone about the house."

A familiar tension rippled through Kelly. "You're talking about Helen Hamilton?"

Jett nodded. "I thought you knew. She's taking a few weeks to get the house ready to go on the market." He offered a meek smile in an attempt to diffuse the tension. "You know Izzy's a real estate agent. They know *everybody's* business."

"Helen's selling the place?"

Again, Jett nodded. "As far as I know, as soon as she clears the place out, it's going on the market. I guess with her dad gone and her living in Brisbane, it's no use to her anymore? And Izzy said the insurance people have been giving Helen a hard time about the house being left vacant. It looks like her dad left everything to her... I reckon he must have disowned the sister."

"That certainly fits," Kelly agreed, a little stiffly.

She hadn't known that part either, but she'd assumed as much.

*How could Helen come here and not tell me?!*

They'd been friends since they'd been kids. Best friends. Helen always called her when she was in town. They'd have lunch or coffee.

A sudden thought had adrenaline firing in her veins, chasing out her hurt feelings: houses were a good distance apart in this area, but if Lorraine Sharpe's killer were desperate enough, they may have sought another house to hit when they didn't find what they were looking for.

*If Helen's home, she could be in danger!*

"I'll take a ride over to the Hamilton place," Kelly said, projecting calm professionalism. "Make sure everything's okay over there."

Jett, having noticed the hastily-hidden flash of panic, hastened to reassure her, "Helen should be okay; Izzy spoke to her just this morning before we got the call to come here. She rang to tell me I needed to pick up the kids after school. Mentioned speaking to Helen."

"That's good to know, but it won't hurt to follow up." Kelly was grateful for the news but needed to see for herself. "Like you said, sound carries at night. Maybe she heard something and didn't realise it was important."

Jett gave her a nod and they both stepped aside as the gurney carrying Lorraine Sharpe's body rattled past. Ray Sharpe's ashen face appeared at the front door with Ashley. He descended the few steps on shaky legs and shuffled behind the body of his wife as she left their home for the last time. Kelly decided it would be kinder to allow the grieving man some time alone for the moment; she could ask him about the necklace later today.

She strode to the police vehicle and climbed in. The realisation that she hadn't heard from Helen in months – no, a *year* plus a couple of months – had her berating herself. She shouldn't have allowed this much time to go by without sending Helen a text message or calling. Helen was alone, and probably felt Kelly had abandoned her.

Helen had taken her father's death hard. Her grandparents had lived well into their eighties, and she'd expected her dad – strong as an ox and half as broad - to do the same. Kelly had done all she'd could to help Helen with her father's arrangements and anything else Helen needed before and after the funeral; still, she should have followed up.

Kelly turned the vehicle round and drove along the gravel driveway towards Four Nations Road. She had idolised Helen for as long as she could remember. Their relationship couldn't even be defined by calling it a mere friendship. They'd flitted along the boundary edge of something more, and even when they'd parted ways after high school, Kelly had always felt sure that Helen would be there as a friend no matter where their lives took them.

Had that somehow changed since her father's death?

*I should have done more to remain in contact.*

Helen had thrown herself into her latest book release; Kelly had recognised her need to keep busy, keep focused, and had made the decision to hold off on contacting Helen until she was ready to grieve.

Now, she was wondering if she'd done the right thing.

*Did I leave it too long? Did she think I abandoned her?*

Kelly had kept up with Helen's travels and the accolades for her books through the publisher's social media pages. Kelly felt so proud to know her, and knew Helen deserved the success. But on the heels of the thought came another: *has all the media attention changed things between us?*

Helen was rushing towards stardom and Kelly was steady in her job: advancing up the ranks, relocating to different regions of South Australia to get a range of experiences. Solid, dependable, reliable Kelly, the natural balance to Helen's creativity and big dreams.

*Solid, dependable,* boring *Kelly,* she thought, sadly.

Even if Kelly were able to carve out a space in Helen's days while she was here, would this be the last time they'd see each other? Once she'd sold the family home, Helen would have no reason to come back to Andamooka.

It felt as if straps had suddenly tightened around Kelly's chest, forcing the breath from her lungs.

Helen had been gone for seventeen years, ever since she'd left for Sydney and University. But she'd never been *gone*-gone - she'd always come back to visit; Kelly had known she would. Helen would always come back to see her dad.

No matter where their respective lives took them, Kelly hadn't expected that to change.

*There's nothing tying her to Andamooka anymore.*

Kelly rolled to a stop at the end of the driveway that led to the Hamilton place. She stared at the house where she had played as a kid. It was nothing flash to look at: hand-built by Robert Hamilton with huge rocks from the creek, joined with cement and some oddly stark fibro cement additions. The forty-four-gallon drums protecting the ventilation shafts stood like sentinels along the creek line. It looked almost deserted now, aside from the old Toyota HiLux and what she assumed was Helen's car parked under the shelter of the carport.

Her mind shifted seamlessly into investigative mode as she looked at the unfamiliar vehicle. The number plates indicated the little hatchback was registered in Victoria, which meant it was probably a rental – most of the rental companies registered their vehicles there for cheaper rates. No branding to indicate the rental company, though.

Eyes moving past the car to the house, Kelly's thoughts travelled back to her history with Helen. Warm memories of days spent roaming the sand dunes and the mullock heaps as kids. Afternoons stretched out on the floor of her room as they listened to music when they should have been doing homework. They'd even sneaked some beer from Robert Hamilton's stash in the fridge in the laundry once - they'd gone camping out towards Lake Torrens and drank the beers and laughed like fools, then chucked their guts up.

Helen Hamilton had always been an important part of Kelly's life, no matter how far apart they had been geographically. Even though Kelly had been working in regional South Australia in postings at Port Augusta, Port Pirie, Gawler, and across the outback, while Helen was firmly city-based, moving only from Sydney to Brisbane.

*Andamooka's always been our shared history. Our place.*

Her stomach fell further. Maybe Helen had met someone. Maybe she was getting married and deliberately cutting old ties for a new and better life.

Kelly glanced at the ominous sky. With the murder on the adjacent hill and this storm coming in, this was about the worst time Helen could have come home.

But here she was, and Kelly wanted – needed – to see her.

She opened the door of the vehicle and climbed out. She removed her high-visibility vest and carefully hooked it over the head rest. Her gut was tied in a thousand knots, and she suddenly felt completely out of place.

Damn it. Everything about this day was wrong.

# CHAPTER SIX

## ABSALOM LANE, ANDAMOOKA, SOUTH AUSTRALIA

**10.30am Sunday, 18 February 2018**

Feeling unready to tackle her parents' room, Helen decided her bedroom would be the simplest place to start. She'd already picked through her childhood belongings over the years and taken what she'd wanted after moving to Sydney and then Brisbane.

It hadn't taken her long to get distracted, even so. Sitting in the middle of the floor, she turned to the next page in the journal she'd kept in her senior year of high school. She'd started a new journal every year from age ten, and by the time she was fourteen it was an established tradition.

She decided the journals had to be kept; most other things would be donated.

Even at nine years old, Helen had wanted to be a writer. She'd listed all sorts of story ideas in her journals since that time. Flipping through the pages, she'd had to laugh at the silly thoughts and childish ideas she'd shared with her journal. She'd been utterly certain she would grow up and become hugely important: she would travel the world and send brilliant postcards back to her family. By the time Helen reached the final journal, her plot ideas had matured, the rambling run-on sentences giving way to the seeds of a budding writer: jotted-down combinations of words and images that she'd thought evocative, ideas for characters and names, and thoughtful reflections on her day.

Helen smiled as she read the passage following her first kiss with Kelly. They had been so young. Full of dreams, racing towards their futures like a tsunami.

A blush crept across her face and her heart rate picked up as she read the jumble of words she'd scrawled after their night together. She remembered how giddy and nervous they'd been; how Kelly's hands had shaken as she'd touched her.

But it was Kelly's eyes that Helen would never forget. Between kisses and licking and sucking, Kelly had stared at her with deep intensity as her fingers had probed and explored and brought her to a throbbing climax in their shared swag under the glorious night sky.

It had been a long time ago. Kids grew up. Dreams changed. Relationships changed.

*People* changed.

Helen closed the journal on a jumble of emotions. Pushing to her feet, she placed the journals at the foot of her bed. She cleared her throat and swiped her hands on her cotton shorts.

"Okay," she said aloud as she gazed around the room. The journals, she would keep; the rest of the room held only artefacts of a life she'd unreservedly left behind.

Steeling herself, she moved on to the bedroom which had once been her sister's.

Technically it still was, she supposed.

Since *that terrible day*, Maxine's door was always closed. Helen tentatively opened the door, unable to shake the feeling that she was being disobedient and disrespectful in stepping through the threshold. Inside everything was as it had been the day Maxie had been taken away; the room frozen in time for twenty years.

*Actually, it's not as dusty as I expected*, Helen mused. *Dad must have vacuumed and dusted from time to time.*

It made sense when she thought about it. She knew he'd never really given up on Maxine.

Helen stood in the middle of the room and gazed around the space, momentarily taken aback by how impersonal the room looked, before recalling why. After finishing High School, Maxine had moved to a boarding college in Adelaide to attend University, studying to be a Physical Education teacher. She'd only lasted a semester before being abruptly expelled for using drugs … although she had sworn she was innocent of that charge, too.

She'd been back only a few weeks when their lives changed.

Helen wondered what had happened to most of her sister's personal effects after the expulsion. It didn't look like she'd brought many home with her.

*Probably sold them in Adelaide for Totally Not Drugs*, Helen thought snarkily, before dismissing the thought as uncharitable.

How was she supposed to decide what her sister might want, and what to donate? She couldn't possibly imagine what – if anything – in the room would hold sentimental value for Maxine.

*Probably none of it, all things considered...but I'll hate myself if I throw out something important by mistake.*

The best idea, she decided, would be to box up everything other than the furniture, and ship the boxes to her sister. Of course, she didn't know where Maxine was staying, which was more than a minor flaw in that plan. Perhaps she could rent a storage unit for the boxes until she could track down Maxine.

A sudden thought brought a smile to her face - Kelly would probably know how she could go about getting an address. She made a mental note to ask her.

*I might celebrate that decision with a well-deserved cuppa*, she concluded, wiping the sweat from her forehead.

It had been a while since she'd experienced an Andamooka Summer.

Her father had generally visited her every Christmas, happy to trade the mid-Summer bake for the comparatively pleasant weather in Sydney. He'd always enjoyed seeing new places. He'd been relentlessly enthusiastic about any touristy experiences, her favourite coffee shops (although he laughed at her every time) and the scenic drives she'd taken him on.

Later, when she'd moved to Brisbane, the weather along the river had been a complete change for him from Andamooka's dry outback heat, and he'd struggled at times with the oppressive tropical humidity. But he'd never complained, just grinned and told her to take things a bit slower with her old man; that he wasn't built to breathe water like a fish.

Tears blurred her vision. He'd been a good man and a fantastic father.

*God, I miss him.*

For the first time in years, she desperately wished her sister were here.

\* \* \*

On *that terrible day* when the police arrived and attempted to restrain Maxine, something had snapped inside her. In that moment, her sister had turned completely feral, kicking out and screaming wordlessly as the police dragged her away from their home, gone over some edge that no one else could see.

Her father had pushed for the courts to see this as a mitigating factor, but the jury had viewed things differently. Despite the expulsion from college, there had been no drugs in her system, no history of mental health issues. The court was satisfied beyond a reasonable doubt that Maxine was guilty of murder, not manslaughter. The judge had condemned her to a life sentence, despite the pleading of her family and no history of previous violence.

In desperation, their father had even hired a retired cop friend-of-a-friend to conduct a private investigation. Ultimately, what he found only confirmed what local law enforcement discovered – there was no evidence that anyone else had been at the scene other than Maxine and the witness, Lorraine Sharpe, who arrived merely by chance.

Even so, Helen had never truly accepted the idea that Maxine had murdered their mother. Whatever other problems she'd had, Maxine had loved their mother too: Helen was certain of it. She simply couldn't imagine any situation in which her sister would commit such a terrible act.

But Maxine's refusal to keep contact was a different matter. Though her father never spoke of it, she had watched what it did to him.

*   *   *

Shaking off the painful memories, Helen moved towards the living room. Once she'd made her final selections, the packing would begin.

Izzy Bullock, the real estate agent, had delivered boxes for Helen to use for her personal collections and the donation items. The rest would be inventoried and prepared for sale by Izzy.

Helen was relieved not to have to be involved in the process; she didn't even want to be in town when the sale was held. It was one thing to box things away, and another to stand by as other people debated the value of her family's worth as they picked through the accumulations of a lifetime like seagulls fighting over chips.

In the kitchen, Helen put her coffee machine through its steps again. She cradled the warm mug and wondered what kind of madwoman she was to be drinking coffee in the heat.

The smart move, she acknowledged, would be to have a glass of water, turn on the radio, and tune into the national station to keep abreast of the approaching storm. She wasn't going to do any of that – particularly the last bit.

Frankly, she had been enjoying the silence.

There was never total silence in Sydney. The sounds of the city proved an endless stream: the wail of sirens; the blaring of horns from impatient drivers; the moan and screech of buses; motorbikes weaving through traffic; the constant flow and disjointed conversations of pedestrians; and the ferries on the harbour. An incessant hum of life.

The relocation to Brisbane had brought with it a quieter life along the river that soothed her mind and helped her writing flow. But Brisbane couldn't match Andamooka for silence.

The slam of a car door closing echoed through the front of the house, and Helen almost dropped her mug. She recalled vividly the rarity of unexpected visitors while she was growing up. No one travelled all the way to Andamooka unless they confirmed you were going to be home - and even the locals checked first, because opal mining did not keep to a timetable in her dad's head.

Helen glanced at the clock on the stove. Izzy wasn't supposed to come until Monday. Placing her mug on the counter, she moved in the direction of the bump, bump of a round of knocking. Rather than go straight to the door, she stopped by the louvre window and peeked out beyond the shade cloth screen.

*Kelly!*

That instant rush of joy; it always happened when they caught up after time apart. Helen had come back to visit her father at least once a year, and she always spent time with Kelly. Each time like the one before, always that instant jolt of joy.

Less normal was the way her heart bounced into a frantic rhythm as her face flushed with the memories of what she'd read in her journals only minutes ago.

Struggling to compose herself, Helen unlocked and opened the door.

"Helen!" Kelly's full lips spread into a wide grin. "I didn't know you were coming home!"

Without hesitation, Kelly reached around Helen and hugged her tight. The heat radiating off her khaki uniform soaked through Helen's thin t-shirt. Helen melted in Kelly's embrace, Kelly's unique fragrance filling her nose though the dusty air.

Helen had feared their bond might have faded after so long apart. Obviously, that wasn't the case at all.

"I'm so sorry, my mind's been all over the place. I should have called when I arrived in town." Helen drew back with a wide smile. "Come on, get in out of the wind and dust."

Kelly stepped inside, lifting her head, scenting the smell of fresh coffee. "Oh, good, I've come at the right time!" she exclaimed, rubbing her hands through her short dark hair to shake out the mad restyling carried out by wind and dust over the past few hours.

"You timed it well - I've only just poured a cup."

Helen wrapped her arms across her chest to restrain the impulse to hug her friend again, but couldn't restrain the huge grin on her face.

She noticed Kelly had grown even more tan under the outback skies, and the contrast with her smoky green eyes was startlingly hypnotic. She opened her mouth to comment on it, before the unfamiliar and discomforting feelings from earlier made her turn and focus on the coffee instead, unwilling to voice the compliment in case it was …misinterpreted? Correctly interpreted?

Helen didn't know which one was more accurate.

Back when they were in school, and Kelly had insisted that she was joining the Navy after graduation, Helen had her doubts. Kelly's love of the outback had run bone-deep even as a child, and Helen had never been able to imagine Kelly on a ship, endless miles from the desert.

To her mind, Kelly was built of slate and granite, dust-pinked skies, the green and brown of eucalypts. A crystal opal sparkling with hidden depths.

There was nothing of the ocean in Kelly.

Her first view of her friend since the funeral had confirmed for her that Kelly was where she belonged. Like the Sturt Desert Peas that Helen adored, Kelly had come into her full bloom in the desert.

For her part, Kelly tried her best not to stare too closely at Helen. Her hair had grown long over the past five or six years, and now fell thick, treacle-dark and shiny in a hastily-made, lopsided braid down her back. The cotton shorts showed off shapely legs with curving thighs.

This was Helen in her element: straightforward, unpolished, authentic.

"You always make great coffee," Kelly complimented Helen as their eyes met. Anything to distract her from the rounded breasts in the light green t-shirt.

Helen moved across the room and leaned against the counter near the sink, ensuring a safe distance since her every nerve ending still jangled at seeing

Kelly. "How've you been?"

"Good. Busy." Kelly held up her hands in a weighing gesture. "You know how it is: tourists lost in the desert, brawls down at the pub, family violence, intervention orders, road crash rescues...road crash deaths. And, of course, the drugs sucking in more and more young people. Same old, same old. How about you?"

"Yeah, good – but busy," Helen echoed Kelly's answer. "I've spent the better half of the past year on the road doing signings and speaking engagements." She sighed, staring at the floor morosely. "Everything but writing. Now I have a deadline breathing down my neck and no idea how, or even if, I can meet it."

"Everyone's really proud of you, Helen. You made the big time."

Helen smiled wanly, seeing the honest praise in Kelly's eyes.

"I was lucky. Lots of writers far better than me don't get the right breaks. It's a feast or famine business."

"You beat the odds." Kelly savoured more of the coffee. "I always knew you would."

From most people, this would have been a platitude - but not from Kelly. Kelly was the one person she'd dared to use as a sounding board on her story ideas, trusting her to provide fair and balanced criticism and suggestions. Knowing how important Helen's writing was to her, Kelly had always given her honesty she could rely on.

When Kelly had told Helen that she was going to be famous one day, she'd meant it with every fibre of her being.

"How's your mum doing?" It suddenly struck

Helen that she no longer had any family for anyone to ask about. The jolt of realisation felt strangely unreal. Maybe she was just unsettled by the unexpected emotions at seeing Kelly. Or reading those journals.

"Really well, actually! She still has regular visits to Adelaide to her rheumatologist. Do you know, she sacked *four* before she found one she liked? But she's doing heaps better now. The clinic nurses give her the Biologic injections each fortnight." Kelly grinned mischievously as she added, "I think Dr Guthrie might be just a little bit afraid of her."

Helen laughed. "More power to her. She's amazing." *Like you.* Helen barely bit back the words.

Okay, no more reading in the journals for her.

"Oh, she's *something* all right," Kelly agreed, with a half-grin. "I tell you what, though, she's come ahead leaps and bounds with the new meds. She's back to bossing everyone around at the CWA Op Shop and doing her quilting in the evenings."

Kelly raised her cup to take a sip before interrupting herself excitedly, "Oh! And she was totally chuffed when she suddenly got a lot of interest in her work after *Arty Andamooka* promoted it on social media - now she reckons she's going to start a shop online so that when she's too old to boss everyone around, she'll have something to fill her time."

Kelly's mother, Margaret, was wonderfully skilled, and Helen couldn't help the huge grin that spread over her face.

"That's fantastic! She's so talented, it did seem a shame that only the local community ever got to see her work. I've got one of her quilts on my sofa at the apartment and I just love it." She laughed, "Even had a delivery guy compliment me on it once!"

Kelly smirked over her coffee cup at Helen, who was clearly oblivious to the likely reason for the compliment. *Honestly have no idea when someone's flirting with you, do you?*

Helen went on, blithely "I'm not at all surprised she's still running things, though. Your mum is an amazing organiser, and tough as nails."

It was an accurate assessment, and Kelly nodded in agreement. Margaret had struggled to get away from her husband Brian's coercive control before fleeing to the desert town to make a life for her daughter and herself in Andamooka. The CWA had taken her under its wing, and time and experience had brought out the confident, competent woman hiding in the terrorised shell. Margaret had never forgotten their help and had been strongly active in the CWA and community improvement programs ever since.

Kelly paused for an appreciative sip of coffee.

"She actually moved in with me at Roxby a few months back, but still drives out here most days. You know Mum; this is where her heart is."

Kelly sat her empty mug aside, sitting upright in the chair and affecting a magisterial pose as she stated, in the tones of one delivering a formal verdict: "She loves your books, by the way. In fact, she calls you *'amazingly talented'*." She grinned at the look of delight on her friend's face.

Helen couldn't hold back the smile. "Oh, Kels, that's so sweet of her - I know horror isn't her genre. Please thank her so much for me, it means a lot to me that she's read them."

"Are you kidding me? *Read them?* She has them on

pre-order!" Kelly laughed.

Standing up and taking her cup to the sink, Kelly looked over her shoulder at Helen. "You know, we need to tee up some real time together while you're here. Last time it was much too hard to think of anything except your father. But it feels like *forever* since we caught up."

Kelly was right, and the truth was, Helen wasn't sure when she would next be getting back this way. Catching up would be a good thing.

"Definitely," she agreed. "It's been *way* too long."

With agreement reached, Kelly's attention flicked back out to the angry weather building outside the window. "You know the edge of that storm will likely hit us hard later today."

"I do, and I'm prepared, honestly. I have food and plenty of water in case the power goes off and the electric pump can't work. Unfortunately, I think Dad's generator is out at White Dam, but I have bottled gas for the barbeque and to heat water for coffee."

Helen paused, before adding in mock earnestness, "More importantly, I've ordered enough wine through *Elsbeth's Little Shop of Everything* to stay happy throughout the entire event."

Kelly laughed. "Sounds like you're all good."

"Hmm....mostly? Once I get all the things packed up around here, I might actually be able to relax."

"Well, that settles it." Kelly gave a nod. "As soon as this storm passes and I'm rostered off, I'll come and help. I'll even bring pizza from Roxby - and *you*, clearly, can provide the wine."

Growing up, they'd loved pizza. If they were together, there was pizza involved. The memory had

Helen smiling.

"I will gladly take any help I can get, and pizza would be great. I knew sorting the house was going to be a difficult task, but I'm not sure I've ordered enough wine for two people to do the job. I can always get a top-up at the bottle shop if it comes to it, though."

Kelly waved off the concern.

"We'll be fine. There's always coffee!"

Helen couldn't help laughing as she agreed, "Yes, there is *definitely* always coffee."

"You heard anything from Maxine?"

Helen shook her head. "Maybe one day, but not so far."

"It's too bad. I always looked up to Maxine. I never understood what went wrong."

"None of us understood. I hoped in time we would become family again, but I guess she can't forgive us for being unable to keep her from being convicted of mum's murder."

Helen wondered, as she had hundreds of times, *if Maxine didn't murder mum... who did?* And was this unknown person still running around free?

Kelly tensed her shoulders. "Um, on that note...I have some bad news," she said with a grimace.

Tension slid through Helen. "What's going on?" A trickle of uneasiness slid through her veins. She barely supressed a shiver, and couldn't help the quake of shock that shuddered through her as Kelly gently explained, "Lorraine Sharpe was murdered last night."

Quiet words for such a thunderous event. Helen had lived in Sydney for more than a decade. There were murders on a too-regular basis because of the sheer number of people jammed into the area. Brisbane, too, had its share as a busy city.

But this was *Andamooka*. Population approximately three hundred. It was nearly unthinkable.

The reality that it was her neighbour, a woman she had known her entire life, made the news even more stunning.

"Oh, Kels, no! I was just thinking about them both this morning! What happened?" Aside from Kelly and her mum, Ray and Lorraine Sharpe had been the closest thing to extended family that Helen and Maxine had. "Is Mr Sharpe all right?"

"We are trying to piece it all together," Kelly said, worry etching itself across her face. "Mr Sharpe is fine; he'd gone to Adelaide for a specialist appointment. He arrived home early this morning and found her."

Helen's hand went to her mouth. Her stomach flipped and her chest tightened with disbelief. "How awful. I can't believe it."

"I'm so sorry to have to pass on this news. I know you and your family were close with them both." A small, sad smile tugged at one corner of Kelly's mouth. "Do you remember how hard she worked to fix the dress you wore to the Year 12 Formal? You were absolutely gutted because you'd ordered it, waited forever for it to arrive and then it didn't fit."

Helen smiled sadly. She had forgotten all about that dress.

It had been a stress-filled time as she tried to shift her image from shorts, t-shirts, and sandshoes, and she'd ordered a glamorous dress to celebrate the end of school and the start of her new life. She'd been utterly devastated - in the soul-searing way only a teenage girl can be - when the dress turned out *far* too big in the chest, drawing attention in the worst way possible.

'Aunty' Lorraine had come to the rescue, unpicking and resewing until the dress wasn't entirely embarrassing - and although Helen had been paranoid on the day, it looked perfect in the photos.

"She was a lifesaver on more occasions than I can recall."

Lorraine Sharpe and Helen's mum had been close friends. The Sharpes often came over for shared barbeque meals – and always brought baked treats along, which made them The Best Neighbours Possible from the girls' perspective. They had no children of their own, and Helen supposed that she and Maxie were their surrogates.

When her mother died, Lorraine had cooked and cleaned and done laundry for weeks, keeping the family going when they needed it most. Helen and her father would have been lost without the couple. The community had been supportive in spirit, but it had been the Sharpes who had stepped up, taken over the cleaning, and let people know about a catering roster.

"I should go over there." Helen said, wanting to help, as the Sharpes had helped them so many times.

"We're still going through the crime scene," Kelly explained gently. "It'll be a while before we release the property."

Kelly ploughed the fingers of one hand through her short dark hair.

"When one of the constables mentioned that you

were here, it really scared me, Helen. The Sharpe's house isn't all that far. I feared the killer might have come here after…" she drew in a weary breath, "… after he left their house."

"Do you have a timeframe for when it happened?" Helen hadn't arrived until very late the previous night.

"The doctor estimated time of death from sometime after midnight, up until maybe four in the morning, but it's difficult to say considering her body was outside."

Helen's breath trapped in her throat. "I rocked up about a quarter-past eleven last night."

The idea that someone may have been next door murdering poor Mrs Sharpe while Helen was pottering around at that same time twisted inside her.

"Did you encounter any other vehicles after you turned off the Olympic Dam Highway?"

Helen shook her head. "No, I'm sure there wasn't anyone else on the road. It was pitch black out, so I'd definitely have noticed any headlights." She thought for a moment. "I don't remember any lights on in town when I came along Opal Creek Boulevard or Christmas Hill Road, either. Just the few streetlights near the Bottle shop, and that light over the State Emergency Service sign."

"Did you call and let the Sharpes know you were coming?"

Another shake of her head. "I didn't. It was kind of spur of the moment. I'd hit a wall in my work and thought maybe the change of scenery would…" she shrugged, looking for the words. "I don't know… shake things loose?"

"You drove all the way from Brisbane?"

"I'm not a masochist, Kels!" Helen looked aghast at the very thought. "No, I caught a flight to Adelaide, hired what was, *in retrospect*, a totally inappropriate little car, and drove up here."

Helen gave a winsomely apologetic smile as she added, "I didn't want to ring from the airport lounge: there's always so much other noise interfering, it's impossible to hear yourself think, let along carry on a conversation. Plus I didn't want to be worrying anyone if I decided to stay the night in Port Augusta, and then didn't arrive at a prearranged time."

Kelly couldn't help teasing her friend, "Nice try, Hamilton, but I've *already* forgiven you for not calling me, so the puppy-dog eyes routine was totally wasted." Her face became serious again, as she added, "Were you in and out of the house for a bit when you first arrived? Maybe unloading your bags?"

Helen bit her lip in thought before confirming, "I think…yes, I definitely was. Yes. I came in and turned on the electricity at the meter, but then I had to go back out and turn on the water pump and bring in my suitcase". She thought for a second. "Oh! And I had to go out again to get my laptop. It was probably about, um, maybe half an hour or so before I remembered it was still in the car, so …maybe around midnight? I'm not 100% sure, sorry Kels."

It was evident to Kelly that Helen was genuinely dismayed at being unable to provide any actionable information. "It's fine, honestly," she reassured her friend. "You didn't hear anything in the distance? Maybe a shout or the sound of a car door closing?"

Helen concentrated hard on those few minutes

of going in and out when she first arrived. "No. Nothing. It's a different kind of quiet compared to the nights back home. It was so soundless, I honestly think I would have been startled by any noise, but I can't be completely certain, sorry."

Kelly stared at a her a moment longer and Helen realised she had just called Brisbane home. It was, she supposed: but even so, a part of her would always consider Andamooka home.

"Have you looked around outside since you arrived?"

"A little. I checked the shed… oh and walked to the cemetery. Do you really think the killer came through here after what he did?"

"Just trying to cover all the bases."

"What…what actually happened?" Helen wasn't sure she wanted to know the details but at the same time, she needed an answer.

*You're a horror writer*, she reminded herself, *you automatically go to the darkest place. It's probably not what you're thinking.*

"She was stabbed. In the back. Repeatedly."

Helen's entire body stiffened, and her face turned stony.

*Then again, maybe it's worse.*

So that's why Kelly was here. This wasn't just about proximity.

As if Kelly had read her mind, she asked, "You're certain you haven't seen or spoken to Maxine?"

*And there it is.*

After all these years, and no matter that Kelly had known Maxine, her sister was suddenly a person of interest in another murder.

"I haven't seen or spoken to her." Helen hadn't intended for her tone to sound so frosty, but the question triggered a defensive instinct she couldn't control.

"I'm not accusing Maxine of anything, Helen. These questions are standard procedure."

*You used to believe in Maxine like I did. Maybe I don't know you as well as I thought.*

"So, exactly *why* would Maxine kill Mrs Sharpe after all this time?" Helen's arms had crossed over her chest in a classically defensive pose. She hadn't intended to let Kelly see how this line of questioning irritated her, but there it was.

"Maxine spent a lot of years in prison primarily based on Mrs Sharpe's testimony. Now she's out and no longer required to have day to day supervision."

"And what… you think that having lived out twenty years behind bars, she desperately wants to return for another round?" Anger sparked deep inside Helen. "Interesting theory."

Without waiting for Kelly to respond, Helen turned and walked to the front door. Kelly following morosely.

"Well, thanks Kelly, but much as I appreciate you checking in, I really must get back to work." Helen smiled stiffly as she held the door open.

"I'll check on you later today," Kelly offered. "I'll bring that pizza and help with the packing."

"I'm fine. Really." Her tone thawed momentarily as she added, "Please tell Mr Sharpe I'm thinking of him, and that he has my sympathy."

Kelly nodded. "All right. You know my number if you need anything."

Helen watched Kelly go and promised herself she would not need anything.

*Some things about this bloody place never change,* she thought bitterly.

The newspapers and the community had been all too ready to condemn Maxine for her mother's murder, slavering salaciously over the tragic scandal like some tasty morsel. A loving mother was dead – murdered – and the masses had wanted someone to blame.

She just hadn't expected to see that same mentality echoed in Kelly.

Hesitation slowed her next thought, but Helen couldn't ignore the undeniable truth in Kelly's words. It *was* Mrs Sharpe's testimony that sealed Maxine's fate: if her sister wanted to hurt anyone for what had happened to her, that poor woman would have been the Number One target.

Helen closed the door and held her forehead there.

*No,* she told herself. Her sister wouldn't come back here.

*Maxine wouldn't kill anyone.*

But what if she was wrong?

# CHAPTER SEVEN

ABSALOM LANE, ANDAMOOKA, SOUTH AUSTRALIA

**11.30am Sunday, 18 February 2018**

Helen stalked around the lounge room.

With the benefit of a bit of time to think, she could acknowledge to herself that she shouldn't have allowed Kelly's suggestion to get under her skin. Kelly had been right to ask the question: she was just being a good cop. Maxine was a *logical* suspect, given the circumstances.

But her sister was not a killer. Helen had never believed her to be capable of murder and she wasn't going to start now. Whether Maxine ever spoke to her again was irrelevant.

Helen closed her eyes and took a deep breath, willing herself, for the thousandth time, to try and remember anything that might have been important evidence.

\* \* \*

There had been blood all around her mother's body. The butcher's knife her mother had been using for the lamb roast had been rammed over and over into her back. Maxine was covered in her mother's blood.

Maxine insisted that she'd pulled the knife from her mother's back and tossed it on the ground in an attempt to help her. She'd turned her mother over and attempted CPR.

Helen, arriving home, had fallen to her knees in pure shock. Had been unable to do anything but stare at the scene before her.

She'd been trudging back along Miner's Way from her *secret place* – not that Sissi's derelict house was technically a secret, but she'd always pretended it was – when she'd heard Maxine's scream. The sound had touched her on a primal level; she was running before she knew what she was doing.

Only moments after she arrived, her father returned from his claim at White Dam. Hearing the commotion, he leapt from his vehicle, racing around the house.

Falling to his knees, he snatched his wife from his daughter's arms.

Both father and daughter had been screaming.

Mrs Sharpe had been sitting on the steps of the back porch, weeping, and covered in blood from trying to help as well. She had already called the police.

*   *   *

Lorraine Sharpe had testified that she had been home baking and had run out of ginger, so she'd stopped over to borrow some from Ruth. As she neared the property, she heard Maxine shouting and had followed the noise to the rear of the house, just in time to see Maxine chase her mother from the kitchen and stab her repeatedly.

Stunned by the scene unfolding in front of her, she had frozen in place until Maxine abruptly dropped the knife and just stared, transfixed by what she had done. This triggered Mrs Sharpe into motion, and she rushed forward to help her friend.

She'd said that Maxine remained locked in position for perhaps half a minute, until she suddenly jolted forward, screaming for her to get away - at which point Mrs Sharpe had raced into the house to call emergency services.

When she returned, Maxine was screaming and crying over her mother's body, seemingly trying to revive her... but it was clearly too late.

Mrs Sharpe had collapsed, her legs going weak as reality caught up with her.

\* \* \*

Mrs Sharpe's testimony was heartfelt and compelling. Maxine's fingerprints were the only ones on the knife. There was no evidence of any alternative intruder.

And yet Helen could never quite make it fit. The scream that had flung her into motion on that dusty road hadn't been one of fury, or even remorse.

It had been purest anguish, a soul-deep devastation.

There had to be another explanation. Someone else had to have been in the house. Lorraine Sharpe, by her own testimony, didn't enter the house until several minutes after the murder had been committed. There was more than enough time for an unseen assailant to leave by the front door.

She simply couldn't accept that Lorraine Sharp had seen what she thought she saw.

In researching for her stories, Helen had come across countless examples of people in adrenaline-charged scenarios misremembering what they'd seen or mistaking one person for another. It had only made her more certain that there had to have been a third, unidentified, person in the house.

But now the woman who had cemented Maxine's fate was dead, murdered in the same manner as their mother. Had she died still confident in her story, or had the years allowed suppressed recollections to come to the surface? And, if so, had she discussed them with anyone?

Helen blinked back the burn of tears. After all these years, her mother's murder was still all questions with no satisfactory answers.

She needed room to walk and think.

Stalking out the back door, Helen shivered despite the blast of hot dust-filled air. Her gaze went immediately to the sky. The storm wasn't going to give them a pass. It was coming. Soon.

Bracing herself against the heat and wind, Helen staggered up the hill towards Miners Way, feet instinctively tracing the path to her 'secret place' where she'd played as a child: the decrepit old house assembled from river rocks, reclaimed corrugated iron and local timber built into the hillside by Nóra Esterházy. Nóra had named it "Sissi's" in tribute to her beloved sister, lost in wartime.

With little effort made to contact relatives after Nóra's death, Sissi's had become Helen's private sanctuary as a child. She'd painstakingly carted all sorts of things up the long path to the dilapidated house, placing them in the small loft: a child's table with a couple of little chairs; her favourite set of pink plastic dishes; curtains and sheets from her mother's project stash.

Some locals considered the house to be haunted, but having grown up with stories of Nóra, her child's logic told her that if Nóra's ghost *did* haunt the home, they'd probably get along famously. For all the years she visited, she'd never seen Nóra's ghost, nor felt her presence, but that didn't stop Helen from talking to her like a friend while she daydreamed and created her fanciful stories in the quiet isolation of the loft.

Helen's sandals chafed against her skin as she walked unsteadily uphill over the rough ground. The dust swirled and spun in the oven-hot air.

Unable to shake the belief that her mother's death was partly her fault for being so far away when she was needed, Helen hadn't revisited her secret place since *that terrible day*. Even so, the narrow track winding up the hill was permanently etched in her memory.

When she reached the decaying building, she studied the door for a moment before daring to open it, eyes searching beyond the threshold for any sign of human passage. Surely if someone had been lurking, they would have stepped in the pile of dirt formed by the dust that swirled near the back door.

Taking a breath, Helen opened the door and entered the desolate front room. Old beer bottles had been cast aside in an untidy pile in one corner; in the opposite corner lay a few metal camping plates and a broken aluminium folding chair.

*That's new*, Helen thought, before catching herself and correcting, *well, different, anyway*.

From the dust and dirt that covered them, it looked to have been some time since Sissi's had been used as some teenage secret drinking spot.

*Probably frightened off by the ghost stories*, she thought.

She knew from experience how the wind could howl up here; anyone predisposed to imagine an angry shade prowling the space would have bolted the first time they heard the unearthly scream of wind through the corroded metal. It crossed her mind to wonder if that's how the chair got broken, and she smirked at the thought.

In the dry, desert environment not much had changed. Helen padded quietly through another door and along a short corridor. The room on the end, on the left-hand side, held her *secret place*: a small loft built into the triangular space, with a rickety ladder for access.

Deliberately slowing her breathing, Helen reached for the ladder and started to climb. The wooden steps creaked - one wobbled, shifting a little, and she stilled, waited to see if it would hold her weight. Two more cautious steps upward and she was able to peer back into her own past.

The child-sized table and chairs her father had made for her were still there, seemingly unchanged. Helen's eyes misted over with bittersweet tears. That little set held such good memories: working together with dad, handing him the woodworking tools while he constructed the furniture. Then painting it with mum – she couldn't remember if they did the mint green basecoat together, but she clearly remembered her mum showing her how to stencil the pink and yellow flowers, the two of them giggling together as they worked.

She couldn't help the smile that warmed her face as she remembered the aftermath: her mother had just a little bit of paint on her hands, but Helen had somehow managed to get it all over herself, including – somehow – on her bare feet.

She remembered her mum laughing, "See, this is why I made you wear daddy's work shirt!"

Her dad, sitting in the lounge in front of the television, had looked through to where they'd set up their workspace over strewn newspapers in the kitchen and declared he'd be the prettiest miner out on the fields in that shirt.

*I miss you both so much.*

Pulling herself fully into the room, she immediately noticed the sleeping bag and pillow in the corner.

The *adult-sized* sleeping bag and pillow.

Helen's heart started pounding.

Now she noticed the empty plastic water bottles beside the sleeping bag, and packaging from potato chips and chocolates on the roughhewn wood floor. She picked up one of the potato chip bags and checked the expiration date.

Her chest tightened.

Someone had been here recently.

Helen sifted through the items in the space, checking beneath and inside the sleeping bag and under the bare pillow. There was nothing to indicate the identity of the mystery resident.

She closed her eyes and forced away the little voice in her head.

*It's* not Maxine. *She's not a killer.*

A crack rent the air and Helen instinctively froze where she stood. Fear seared through her veins.

The sound of metal clanging in the wind dominated, but there was a secondary sound – the sound of the ladder being dragged away.

*There's someone down there.*

Helen reached into her pocket, found it empty. She'd left her mobile phone at the house.

Helen wasn't sure how long she remained petrified in the shadowy corner, cowering alongside the wobbly table and chairs she'd played with as a child. Long enough to be soaked in sweat and dehydrated.

Finally, the silence had gone on long enough that she worked up the nerve to peek through the sun-bleached curtains. Outside, Helen saw nothing but the darkening landscape. It was probably about midday, maybe past noon, but already the gathering storm clouds were blocking the sunlight, turning the day to early dusk.

Whoever or whatever had been out there, they were gone now. Helen peered over the edge of the loft.

The ladder she'd used to get up to the loft lay on the ground.

*Damn.*

The fact that it was simply grounded rather than moved against another wall made her pause, though. Maybe she'd misheard; let her fears run away from her when she saw the sleeping arrangements. The ladder had certainly been jostled a bit on her way up... perhaps it'd simply slid down under its own weight - or even been bumped out of the way by some random wildlife seeking shelter from the incoming storm.

*You don't really believe that.*

The distance to the ground was about two and a half metres. She swallowed. Whatever she did, she had to do it soon. The temperature in the loft was really heating up.

She eyeballed the drop appraisingly: it *might* be possible to jump down and get away unscathed, but it seemed likely she'd at least end up with a sprain. The real risk, though, was if she broke a foot or a leg – or worse, both. She would die out here of dehydration before anyone found her.

Especially since she'd basically sent Kelly packing.

*I shouldn't have overreacted.... Kelly was only doing her job.*

"Okay, enough handwringing. How can I make this happen?" Helen murmured thoughtfully, scanning the room. There had to be way down that didn't come with the risk of slow death by desert.

Moving from one side of the loft to the other, Helen peered down through the small openings in the floor where the boards didn't quite fit together.

*Maybe I could throw the pillow down and aim for it.*

Evaluating the odds, she figured it'd be just as likely to explode under the sudden pressure. Either that or slip out from under her and pitch her into a wall.

*OK, clearly that's a non-starter.*

Calculatingly, she looked at the fabrics in the room and considered their tensile strength against her weight.

*Cutting it close, for sure - but maybe? They're probably still good enough.*

So…if she could pull up a couple of floorboards, she might be able to clamber down using the old curtains or the sleeping bag as a rope.

*I could still fall, but maybe not so far or as fast.*

Casting her eye around the room, she came up empty on any better alternatives.

*Well, as far as bad plans go, it's certainly not the worst I've ever had.*

Now that she had something like a plan in mind, Helen went to work methodically. Shoving the sleeping bag aside, she started at the corner nearest the opening first. The gap between the floorboards varied considerably; wide in some areas and marrow in others, the space having only ever been intended for use as storage, not a living area.

Stripping the curtain fabric from the wall, she tore a section off and wrapped her hand in it.

*Too thick*, she thought with a quiet *tch* of disappointment, tossing it aside. *I'll have to have to take my chances with the splinters.*

Cautiously, Helen wriggled her fingers through the wide part of a gap and started to pull with all her might. Creaking and groaning echoed in the air, but the board didn't give.

Determinedly, Helen kept going, from gap to gap along the line, until she found a board slightly looser than the others. After a half a minute of rest, she started to pull again; this time she was rewarded as the board came free from the supports beneath it.

*That gap between the joists is probably a smidge over half a metre*, she thought, eying it. She could get through without catching or scraping herself too badly.

*Well, hurrah. Now all I have to do is pull up a couple more boards, drop through the opening, swing my feet around until they hit against the wall below, and abseil down using the sleeping bag and the curtains as a rope. What could* possibly *go wrong?* she thought, rolling her eyes.

Was she really going to do this?

"Well, it's not like I have any better options," she answered her own unspoken question with a growl, steeling herself for action.

The next few boards came up gratifyingly easily – but to her chagrin, hitching the sleeping bag and curtains together wasn't quite so easily achieved. The curtains were weakened by the sun and shredded readily, while the sleeping bag was bulky even when unzipped.

After positioning it diagonally across the support beam, tied on with the curtain, Helen eyed it doubtfully. *I just hope you hold together long enough not to kill me.*

Lowering her body through the opening and hanging on with her arms splayed out over the hole in the floor also proved more difficult than expected. She struggled to hold her weight while swinging her legs in in the slight left angle she needed.

Her elbows slipped, and she clawed at the floor of the loft and the sleeping bag to find purchase. Heart thundering, she managed to get her fingers into the sleeping bag to stop her fall.

For a moment she could only hang there and try to breathe.

Again, she swung her legs; her feet hit the wall and

sprung back. Cursing, she swung her feet once more: this time the base of her sandal flattened against the wall below the loft and she steadied herself.

She took a moment to relax her trembling arms.

*Come on, you've nearly got it. Don't mess it up now.*

Finally, she dared to slip her right arm through the opening in the floor and step down the wall, holding on to the sleeping bag. With a little grunting - and a lot of swearing - she managed to lower her body one tiny increment at a time. There was one alarming moment when she heard the sleeping bag tear, but it held, even as her body froze in fright.

It wasn't until her feet hit the floor that she realised she'd been gritting her teeth the whole way.

*Ow,* she thought, rubbing her jaw. *Still, that went ... much better than expected. Don't think I'll put my hand up for abseiling or rock climbing anytime soon though.*

Staggering to a standing position, she managed to take a deep breath and look around.

*At least I know the house is clear. If there was someone here, they had plenty of time to ambush me while I was getting down.*

Her legs trembled as she started to walk to the corridor, staggering to the only exit door. She tentatively opened it and looked outside. Still nothing. Just the sound of the wind. No sign of life – animal or otherwise.

Now she ran – staggering from dehydration and muscle cramps from the unfamiliar exercise, but she didn't slow down until she reached the back door of her own place, propelling herself through and into the kitchen.

And then she stopped dead as sudden realisation

hit her.

She'd left the house unlocked. With a murderer on the loose.

*You. Absolute. Idiot.* She cursed her own stupidity. *You've been back in town all of five minutes and suddenly you've forgotten how to lock a bloody door?!*

What if whoever removed the step ladder was here? The image of Mrs Sharpe being stabbed roared through her brain. Her heart, already pounding from the run, felt like it was in overdrive.

She needed her mobile.

She needed to call Kelly.

…She really, *really* needed water.

Still, that would have to wait. If anyone was inside the house, they'd have heard her barging in; it was too late to do anything about that. But that didn't mean she should telegraph her exact position to them by turning on a tap.

Doing all within her power not to make a sound, she eased across the kitchen.

Her mobile was on the kitchen counter. Every second pounded in her brain as she made her way over to it, step by cautious step. Only once the device was clutched firmly in hand did she glance around for a weapon.

She felt a brief moment of nausea as her eyes lit upon the knife block.

*At least they're all accounted for.*

Reaching further along, she carefully lifted a long-tined barbeque fork from the utensil jar with her right hand as she moved towards the doorway to the living room. She held her breath as she eased across the room and into the short foyer. Instinct urged her to run and forget the possibility of an intruder. Get in her tiny rental car and drive away.

*Do you not read your own books? Get out NOW!*

She ignored the warning voice in her head and fumbled with the doorknob. She knew she was running on pure adrenaline and wasn't being entirely rational - but the thought of an intruder in her family space pushed her towards fight, not flight... for the moment at least.

*This is MY house. MY home. Nobody is going to make me scared of it.* **Nobody.** *I'll find them and then I'll...*

*You'll what?* Prong *them into submission?*

"One thing at a time," she muttered under her breath.

Step. Pause. Step. Pause.

Moving quietly through the living room, she checked behind the couch.

*...OK, kitchen and living room are clear.*

She'd been brought up in this house. Her father had built it. She knew every inch of it.

The problem was, the house had been built onto as Robert Hamilton had time and money: whenever another room had been added on, the external doors stayed in place as the house grew outwards. She still had to clear the bedrooms, laundry, toilet, bathroom, and her mother's craft room – and that meant *seven* external doors: heavy, wooden barriers all serving to deaden any giveaway sounds of movement. Worse: the house being built on a slope, there were steps up to some rooms, with no way to approach without being right in the firing-line.

*One thing at a time*, she reminded herself

First: her parent's bedroom. Squaring her shoulders,

she slipped inside, putting her back to the wall. *Oh, smashing, you look just like you're on CSI. That'll come in handy when you need to play a corpse later.*

*Focus!* she reminded herself.

Clear. A quick look under the bed confirmed the conclusion.

Next up: Maxine's room.

Clear.

A swift search of the other rooms revealed the same result. There was no one in the house.

"Okay. Okay."

Deep breath.

*Okay.*

She lowered the barbeque fork, feeling suddenly boneless, and shuffled back to the kitchen. She reached out to put the fork back in the utensil holder, before deciding to hang on to it for a bit.

The front door was locked; she hurried to lock the back door. She had considered locking it when she came inside, but it was in the back of her head that it might be her only means of escape if she encountered someone in the house.

Finally free to take a desperately needed drink, Helen gulped thirstily from the jug on the bench. The water hit her stomach with a glug - a distinct reminder to slow down. Wrenching the linen cupboard open, she lifted out a small towel, wet it under the tap, and wiped the worst of the dust from her face. That done, she rinsed the rag again under the cold tap before draping it over her head in an attempt to cool off.

Feeling slightly better, she looked at her phone, uncertain where to begin. There were calls she needed to make, but where to start?

Kelly, certainly, was on that list... but not first, she decided. No longer in imminent danger, other concerns had shifted to the forefront of her thoughts.

She skimmed through her contacts list and selected Melanie, the legal assistant at Gaia Law, the firm that had defended Maxine. Melanie was retired now, but during the trial she and Helen had become close and remained in touch off and on over the years.

"Hi Melanie, it's Helen Hamilton. I'm sorry to bother you on a Sunday, but I'm back in Andamooka to sell my father's house and I have a problem. I know it sounds weird, but I'm really hoping you might be able to help me out."

Melanie's warm voice was overlaid with concern.

"Andamooka? With all that wild weather going about, are you sure it's a good time to be out in the middle of nowhere?"

"It's definitely kicking up out there, but I'm good for now." Helen replied, with far more confidence than she felt.

"So how can I help?" the older woman asked.

Helen explained about the murder next door, and how terribly the circumstances mirrored her mother's, before moving on to her impulsive walk and what happened at the derelict house.

Hearing herself tell the story now it sounded distinctly over-dramatic to her own ears.

*Plot summary: a ladder fell over at a derelict house, and when I got home my house was exactly as I'd left it. I don't think it's destined for the best-seller lists.*

Cutting her story short, Helen continued, "Look, it's probably nothing, and I've just let myself get rattled ... but I am wondering if there is any way you can confirm my sister's location? I'd just feel better if I could be sure she's where she's supposed to be."

She opted not to mention that the Senior Sergeant in charge – Kelly – had already noted the similarity to her mother's case and was almost certainly trying to track down Maxine herself.

"I'll do what I can. It might take a little while, but I'll call you back as soon I have any news," Melanie assured her.

"Thanks so much. I'll breathe easier once I can be confident this has nothing to do with Maxine."

Important issues covered, they moved on to less troublesome topics, and Helen slowly calmed as the older woman's comforting manner worked its magic on her frazzled nerves. When the call was finished, Helen placed the phone on the counter and decided it was time to put the barbeque fork away.

*Still, there is a murderer out there somewhere. Maybe it would be wise to at least put it somewhere a bit closer?*

Looking around for a useful location, Helen decided to place it on the countertop near the dining room door rather than back in the utensil container. The door between the kitchen and dining rooms was always left open, facing inwards to the kitchen: in that position, the barbeque fork was fairly inconspicuous. There was no reason for anyone to move the door.

*What if someone wonders why there's a fork sitting randomly on the counter?*

Particularly one specific 'someone'. Keen-eyed Kelly would definitely note the oddity of a lone barbeque fork. With that thought in mind, Helen added a metal whisk and the potato peeler alongside the barbeque fork on the counter.

*Oh, yes, that's so much less conspicuous. Nothing to see here!*

Helen dithered another second or two before, with a soft chuff of laughter at her own silliness, she returned the other utensils to their drawer, left the fork where it was, and stepped away from the counter.

"I really need to stop overthinking. Or maybe cut back on the caffeine," she sighed, immediately putting on a fresh pot of coffee. Re-dampening the rag, she put it across the back of her neck, hoping to combat the heatstroke she'd likely acquired from her time trapped in the house without water. She dug around in the drawers until she uncovered a box of paracetamol. Swallowing two with another large glass of water, she leaned back on the counter while the coffee brewed and found her thoughts drifting back to a long-forgotten memory of another day of heat and terror.

\* \* \*

She was about nine or ten years' old, exploring through the mullock heaps. The afternoon was growing late, she realised, and turned to head back home before realising she was lost. Feeling confident about her ability to navigate her way home, she'd clambered to the top of the heap, peering around for a recognisable landmark, but all directions looked equally unfamiliar in their familiarity - endless rolling mountains of white, or dark red or orange, drowning beneath a heat haze that shimmered them into frightening, pulsating shapes.

The shadows had lengthened while she'd searched

for a landmark, and the light had shifted towards dusk. Panic had set in. Her parents weren't home; they'd gone to Woomera for the day.

It was the first time she remembered ever feeling completely and utterly helpless.

She'd known what happened to those who got lost in the desert without water; remembered overhearing a greying old-timer growling about a lost tourist, *"Least they coulda done was stay put instead of wandering off like a bloody idiot. Didn't find the body for days."*

The words hadn't been meant for her ears, but they'd drilled into her mind with an intensity that had never faded.

Whimpering, she'd hunkered down where she was, aware of the ever-present danger of the opal fields - open drill holes. There were two warnings every child learned from the time they could walk – NEVER walk backwards, and NEVER walk the fields in the dark.

She had cried for her parents.

She'd been so tired, and so very, very thirsty.

Maxie had found her as the last light was fading to dark. She'd carried Helen all the way home, given her cool drinks, wrapped her head in wet cloths and shoved cold wet cloths under her armpits. Maxie had gently stroked her hair until their parents came home.

Maxie had pulled Helen out of a swimming hole once too.

A cyclone from Broome, much like Kelvin bearing down on them now, had dumped oceans of water, filling every small dip and the open mining areas to the brim. Once the roads cleared, it was exciting playing in the muddy water and there was enough to jump and swim in, even though they were warned against it. The heat and humidity after the storm meant that safety warnings were disregarded.

*That's the kind of person my sister is. That's Maxie.*

\* \* \*

Determination hardened in Helen's belly. Someone else must have been in the house the day their mother died. Someone Mrs Sharpe hadn't seen or hadn't recognised, making her subconscious fill in the missing gaps.

Helen poured herself a fresh coffee and sipped thoughtfully, returning to the problems at hand. *Someone* had been staying in Sissi's derelict house. A place close enough to access the Sharpe's home. She had an obligation to inform the police in the event that what she'd found had anything at all to do with the Sharpe case.

*Time to call Kelly.*

# CHAPTER EIGHT

ROXBY DOWNS POLICE STATION, ROXBY DOWNS, SOUTH AUSTRALIA

**1.15pm Sunday, 18 February 2018**

Kelly shrugged out of her high-vis vest and slung it over the rack in the corner of her office. Her Akubra hat followed, and she ruffled her sweaty, dusty hair.

It felt like she'd done nothing but spin her wheels all morning. Despite her team's best efforts, they hadn't found a single piece of evidence in the Sharpe home to point them towards the murderer. Fingerprints were still being run through the system, but there were no matches so far. The murder weapon was nowhere to be found - and ghoulish though it was, Kelly found herself hoping the killer had kept it as a trophy, because at least that way there was a chance it'd be recovered.

*More likely they've dropped it down an old mine shaft somewhere. We might never find it.*

Kelly flopped behind her desk, tilting her head back with a grimace. Helen had been just over the next hill from the Sharpe's home. She could have been robbed.

*Or worse.*

Following her abrupt ejection from Helen's place, Kelly had put in a call to Shannon Evans, the police prosecutor she worked with most often. Shannon had promised to look into Maxine's whereabouts and get back to Kelly. If Helen's sister was where she was supposed to be, they had nothing to worry about.

Kelly rubbed her eyes and took a deep breath. She hadn't meant to be so clumsy when she'd brought up the subject of Maxine to Helen... but even so, the question had needed to be asked.

*A woman is dead. I owe it to her to get to the truth, regardless of what that truth might be ... or who I upset in the process.*

She leaned back in her chair and tapped her desk pad with a biro thoughtfully. Like Helen and her father, Kelly had never believed Maxine guilty of her mother's murder: the idea was ludicrous to anyone who knew her. Maxine had been many things – *boisterous, energetic, and opinionated come to mind* – but she had never been prone to violent fits of anger.

*And yet, here we are.*

After 20 years, Andamooka had become the scene of another murder.

In the same style.

And the victim was the eyewitness who had put Maxine in prison.

Kelly groaned. Of all the stupid things, why did Maxine have to choose now to drop off the radar and neglect her probation check-in?

*If Shannon can't definitively place Maxine somewhere else at the time of the murder...*

Kelly shook her head in frustration. She'd pulled up the file on the Hamilton homicide case and gone through the reports. It wasn't her first time reviewing the case: she'd quietly retrieved the case files and reviewed the evidence shortly after being assigned to Roxby Downs station.

As before, she found no missteps in the investigation. No shortcuts taken, no unjustified leaps of logic. The evidence had been limited - but what was there, was damning. Maxine's fingerprints were all over the knife. There was no sign any intruder had been in the house.

Even then, the jury may have acquitted the nineteen-year-old if not for the compelling witness testimony.

*And now that witness is dead.*

On one level she remained convinced that Maxine was innocent, but she couldn't – and wouldn't - let that override her police training.

*The team needs a leader they can trust, and a victim needs justice. Separate the feelings from the facts. Keep them separated. Explore every avenue without prejudice.*

Kelly closed her eyes and forced herself to take a deep breath in and let it out slowly, head in her hands. Purposefully examining and detangling her emotions: grief and injustice over a life cut short; outraged honour and protectiveness because it happened in her region ... and then there was the whole tumbling mess that Helen's unexpected arrival had provoked.

*When we're apart, living such different lives, I start to think maybe I should try and move on. Keep the friendship; try and forget the love I feel for you. Then you pop back into my life and it's like you never left... and I'm reminded why nobody else can measure up to you.*

"Kelly?" The voice from the doorway was hesitant.

Kelly looked up at the station's administrative assistant who had poked her head in the office. *Don't let it be more bad news.*

"Come on in, Chazz," she said, forcing a smile.

Chazz beamed in response and stepped inside. "I was just about to phone the Acacia Café with a lunch order. Would you like me to add yours to the list?"

A genuine smile replaced the one on Kelly's face, as she replied, "What would I do without you?"

Her tone was mildly jesting, but the sentiment was sincere.

Charlotte MacDonell - "Chazz" to her friends - had been hired as a records management and human resource support shortly prior to Kelly winning the position of Officer in Charge. Recognising in each other the kind of kindred spirit for whom the words *"that's just how it's always been done"* were interpreted as a challenge, they had swiftly became a formidable pair.

Kelly had learned that interesting things happened when Chazz was given leeway to work her occasionally ruthless efficiencies into the station's processes. Even if it was a bit like working in a kicked beehive whenever Chazz took aim at one long-standing tradition or another, it had to be acknowledged that the place *did* seem to work much better these days.

"Baguettes for our visitors would be good. Get a variety, please. Oh, and can you make sure one is cheese and tomato?" Kelly reached for her wallet.

"Can do! I'll phone it in and be back in fifteen."

Watching Chazz's energetic bounce out of the office,

Kelly considered how grateful she was that things had worked out despite her having to tell Chazz she wasn't interested in a personal relationship.

Even if Kelly hadn't been intrinsically wary of starting a workplace relationship – particularly one with an inherent power imbalance – the simple fact was that Chazz wasn't the type for a casual fling, and Kelly wasn't capable of anything greater.

Fortunately, Chazz was nothing if not pragmatic: as she'd later explained to Kelly, her mindset was "*It might have been great, but given how bossy we both are, it could have been an absolute nightmare, too. At the end of the day, I'm happy having you as a friend and we probably dodged a bullet on the romance side.*"

In typical Chazz style, she'd accepted Kelly's choice without taking it personally, and seamlessly shifted without any apparent regret to a relationship that *did* work - friendship. A fact for which Kelly was eternally grateful, because - cliché as it sounded - it really *wasn't* Chazz that was the problem.

If last name hadn't been enough of a hint, Chazz's Scottish ancestry was evident in her freckled, creamy skin – she never stepped outside unless gleaming with SPF50 - and shoulder-length auburn curls that defied all attempts at styling. Between the riotous hair, wide smile, and laughing blue eyes, Chazz was attractive in an approachable way, and kind-hearted and funny to boot. Kelly had simply lost her own heart long ago… and, so far, she hadn't been able to get past the idea that the one woman she longed to be with would never return her feelings.

The thought had her mind going back to her meeting this morning with Helen. She'd looked good:

no surprise there, she always did. But weariness had showed on her face, the purple shadows under her eyes clear evidence of months spent burning the candle at both ends.

Years ago, Robert Hamilton had told Kelly that he hoped that one day the two of them would stop pretending they didn't belong together. Kelly wondered if he had ever said this to his daughter.

*Probably not,* she conceded. *He would have waited for her to ask his opinion... or more likely, tell him her decision.*

Helen Hamilton had seemingly known what she wanted out of life since she was just a kid. She'd planned her escape from Andamooka before she was old enough to drive. She'd always said it wasn't because she didn't love the place, it was because she had big plans.

Kelly, for her part, had sketched-in some ideas for the future, but never felt that kind of calling toward any particular path. When her planned Naval career fell though following her mother's diagnosis, Kelly had adapted easily: she hadn't been dedicated to sailing the seas, she just hadn't wanted to stay in Andamooka with Helen gone. It had been easier to pretend that she, too, had 'big plans' than to risk examining her feelings about Helen heading off to Sydney without her.

After all, they'd never been anything other than friends.

Close friends.

*Best* friends.

And they had shared intimate firsts that went well beyond friendship.

But Helen had never wanted more than *"best friends,"* and Kelly couldn't imagine a world in which they didn't have at least that together. Still, Kelly could admit to herself – if not to Helen - that she had been in love with her best friend since she was sixteen years old, and the feelings hadn't faded with time or distance.

*I'm going to have to find a way to apologise for how I went about things earlier. I was right to ask about Maxine, but I spoke like a cop, not a friend.*

Kelly's gaze fell on the television hanging on the wall of the reception area. It was kept on the weather station most of the time, more for the comforting background noise than anything else. Not so comforting now: Cyclone Kelvin was heading right for them, and the flooding would likely be devastating.

On her drive back to the station, Kelly had noted the crowded parking lot at the supermarket. People were stocking up - panic buying, most of them. Helen had said she had everything she needed, and Kelly hoped she was right, because by now it was probably too late to rectify the situation.

Within Roxby Downs itself, and right out to the Olympic Dam Mine, it wasn't too difficult to drive around even after a massive rain event. Even most of the way to Andamooka, where low-lying stretches became filled with water and covered the sealed road, a person could usually get by with a four-wheel drive vehicle if they were careful and cautious.

But the Andamooka township itself was a very different story.

Andamooka had only one sealed road: Opal Creek Boulevard. Built into an ancient erosion gully, this was the main road into and out of town.

Chazz had once opined to Kelly that even entitling Opal Creek Boulevard a 'main road' was flirting with being grandiose – and 'boulevard', she'd stated candidly, took a spectacular level of self-delusion to pull off.

*"It literally means a street lined by trees,"* she'd grumped. *"I'm not sure what the word for a street lined with mullock heaps is, but I really think they should have looked into it."*

Kelly had laughed, never having thought about it before, but having to concede the point.

Opal Creek Boulevard was a long stretch of flat road bounded by a lot of red dirt. The road received a brief highlight as it passed through the town proper - bottle shop, small grocery store with fuel pumps, local town management office, community hall, post office and pub - before listlessly fading off into fundamentally identical desert on the exit from town.

The road was dry and barren most of the time, but after heavy rain, it would became completely impassable. To make matters worse, the remaining roads would turn to sticky clay, becoming treacherous even to heavy 4WD vehicles.

Maybe she would call Helen after the meeting with the team.

Right now, though, the case was a priority, and Kelly needed her whole concentration fixed on working with the homicide team to find the person or persons responsible for attacking an elderly woman at her own home.

*Home is one place a person should always feel safe.*

Kelly was, in many ways, a cynic - but she believed

implicitly that a person's home should be their refuge, and it galled her that this was so often not the reality.

Kelly gathered her notes from this morning and walked out of her office, dropping a $50 note on Chazz's desk to cover the lunches as she headed to the conference room. The already long day was about to get longer.

Detectives Liney Deer and Bec Heath waited in the conference room, reports and photos spread across the table. Chazz had set up glasses with a jug of chilled water; Bec and Liney had already grabbed a glass and Kelly quickly did the same, appreciating the cool refreshment.

"I assume the body hasn't made it to Adelaide yet?" she asked, more to start the conversation than from any expectation of a positive response.

"Hmm. I haven't had any updates," Liney said, looking up from the report she was reviewing, "but last I heard it'll arrive at Forensic Sciences around 5pm-ish. Allowing time for the preliminary examination, I think we'll probably hear something in a couple of days? Maybe tomorrow afternoon if we're really lucky." Glancing out the window at the angry sky, Liney added, "It's a good thing you got the body on the road to Adelaide when you did. The latest weather update reckons there'll be high winds and flooding all the way from north of Pernatty Lagoon right through to Marla."

Bec nodded sombrely. "I don't envy your team working outside in that stormfront. They must have been cursing every minute. They did well, though."

Kelly took the compliment with a small smile and a nod. "Major Crime will be taking the lead now, of course, with CIB support," she said, ceding jurisdiction before adding, "though having said that, there's no telling how long their team will be delayed. There's zero chance they're catching a flight from Adelaide, what with the local airport closed for this weather."

Liney pinched the bridge of her nose, sighing, "Of *course* they're delayed. That's *just* what this case needed: more complications."

"It's not ideal," Kelly agreed dryly, "but par for the course at the moment. We're short staffed everywhere. That anti-nuclear demonstration at Port Augusta isn't helping either. It's blocking the highways east and west of the town."

Bec chuckled. "We drove past an inflatable radioactive waste barrel and lime green three-headed kangaroo as we left. All I could think is that it could get *really* interesting if those balloons catch any of this wind. Someone might end up flying out to sea on a 20-foot kangaroo." She grinned into the distance, clearly taken with the mental image.

Liney narrowed her eyes at her junior officer and returned to the topic with a tone of mild rebuke. "We've had officers working with local Adnyamathanha and Barngarla people, as well as members of the Flinders Local Action Group and Don't Dump on SA. They've been very cooperative, and everything's been peaceful so far. They're just handing out information packs to vehicles." She tapped her fingers on the table, adding "Of course, you just *know* that sooner or later some bright spark will start agitating. We've pulled in support from right through to Port Pirie, Whyalla, and even Adelaide though, so hopefully we have enough visible presence that it'll make any disruptive elements think twice before getting stupid."

There was a pause as each officer considered the situation from their own experience and perspective.

"Ray Sharpe must have driven through the demonstration zone last night." Bec said, changing the subject.

"That reminds me ... where is Ray now? Is he staying with a friend?" asked Kelly.

"After we finished securing the crime scene, we left a scene guard. Ray argued about staying at the house and cleaning up after we finished. He didn't want anyone else to do it." Bec winced a little in sympathy.

Liney noted, dryly, "We firmly disagreed with him about that. Unfortunately, he refused to stay with friends. Said he'd just be a burden and 'bad company' right now. Eventually we relocated him to one of the holiday rental shacks on Treloar Road."

"He was *very* insistent that he'd be alright on his own." Bec's tone betrayed her doubts that the decision was the best one in the circumstances, but Kelly understood. Given that the man's wife of nearly fifty years had been murdered, it wasn't surprising his decision wasn't entirely rational.

"Unfortunately, you can't force people to do what's best for them. The best you can do is try to minimise the fallout," she said, as much to remind herself as Bec.

"It's early days yet, so we have an officer with him," Liney said reassuringly, correctly reading the direction of Kelly's thoughts.

Bec's tone was subdued. "I just wish he'd gone to a friend's house, or even to his pastor. He shouldn't be with strangers right now."

Kelly pictured Ray Sharpe's eventual return to his family home alone. "Did you tell him about the professional cleaning crew that travels from Port Augusta?"

Bec nodded in the affirmative, glad they could at least spare the old man some pain - whatever people thought in the moment about wanting to clean up the scene themselves, the reality was always deeply confronting.

*Although in this case, there isn't even much to clean up.*

Kelly felt a pang of sadness at the thought that a woman's life could be erased with little more to show for it but some fingerprinting mess at the end. The storm itself would probably see to most of the blood outside: dried flakes flung wide on the fast-travelling dust, the rest turned to liquid by the pouring rains and swallowed by the thirsty soil.

"How's it looking in respect of any evidence from the outer perimeter of the scene?" Kelly's tone was brisk and professional, providing no evidence of her inner musings.

"No vehicle tracks, and no footprints. We got nothing," Bec stated baldly. "We've put out a bulletin on radio and social media, asking for anyone who may have seen or heard something, but haven't heard anything yet." Her tone wasn't optimistic. "In the meantime, we've checked the list of friends Ray Sharpe provided. Unfortunately, it seems that no one spoke to his wife yesterday or last night."

Kelly glanced at Liney to see if she had anything to add.

"My team are running the details through the

databases, but so far we haven't turned up anything of note - other than the obvious similarities between Lorraine Sharpe's murder and Ruth Hamilton's all those years ago."

"Yes ... about that. I put a call in to Shannon Evans. She's getting me a location on Maxine Hamilton."

Both Liney and Bec nodded.

"Did you confirm Sharpe's alibi?" Kelly had known the man since she was a kid, and she hated to treat him as a person of interest, but it was standard operating procedure. He was the husband of the victim, so he had to be ruled out.

"I did," Bec confirmed. "I was able to verify he attended his medical appointment in Adelaide on Saturday. After that, it gets a bit harder. He says here" - she tapped her notes with a biro - "that he settled in at a motel before changing his mind and heading out ahead of the storm somewhere around a quarter-past three to three-thirty in the morning. I was able to verify that the check-in time at the motel aligns with his Statement, but unfortunately that's where my luck ran out."

Bec picked up her notes and moved towards the window, unconsciously pacing as she reviewed the day's investigative outcomes.

"The motel is one of those 'leave the key in the room when you go' arrangements, so there's no way to know what time he left for certain. I had a thought that maybe I could check the odometer reading to confirm he'd travelled straight up and back, but that old F100 he drives is stuck on 279,000 clicks and hasn't worked for a while."

Bec took a breath and continued. "As it turns out,

it wouldn't have made much difference regardless. He stopped keeping mileage records after retirement, since it wasn't relevant for his taxes anymore." She shrugged. "So unfortunately, I wouldn't have had anything to compare it against anyway."

Liney chimed in, "It was still a good thought, and you did well to follow it up."

Bec tapped the biro thoughtfully on her notes again, before pulling out her chair and sitting back down. "It's not all bad news, anyway. There's a timestamped receipt for petrol purchased in North Adelaide on Saturday, which supports his Statement about when he left the city."

Kelly nodded. "It's just a pity about the motel check-out. It would have helped if we could definitively rule out the possibility that he made it back in time to kill his wife."

The room fell silent as each officer contemplated the limited evidence available.

"So, what we *do* have," Kelly summarised with a sigh, "is nothing. Except a victim stabbed in the back, in the dark, outside her own home – and a husband who technically could have made it home in time if he left the motel earlier than he said he did. Which we can't positively rule out, because of *course* there are no records available."

"Unfortunately, that's the whole of it, yeah." Bec's tone echoed Kelly's frustration. "I checked to see if there have been any break-ins in the surrounding areas and found nothing so far that hasn't already been reported."

Kelly rubbed at her eyes, which still felt gritty from standing in the dust storm. "Hopefully, the pathologist will find something to point us in the right direction. Did Sharpe say his wife wore a necklace? If there was one and it's missing, we need a description."

Bec said, "I followed-up on that. He said that if she was wearing a necklace it wouldn't have held any significant monetary value. She rarely wore jewellery. Or makeup. He did recall she had a simple silver cross on a chain she'd wear from time to time – we've checked, and it's not in her jewellery box – but he couldn't think of anything that would have made it worth stealing."

She paused for a second before adding, "Of course, just because we didn't find the cross, that doesn't mean that it's the chain that got stolen. She may have had additional jewellery her husband wasn't aware of. Just like she had makeup he wasn't aware of."

Kelly nodded. "That's what I keep coming back to, too. Lorraine was… well, let's say she didn't really do ornamentation. I've known the Sharpes – peripherally, admittedly – since I was a kid … and I have to say, the bold makeup just doesn't align with anything I've seen of her. And that's without even considering any fancier jewellery that she may or may not have been wearing."

Liney agreed. "And it's certainly odd for the middle of the night. So, what do we think? Any chance she was having an affair?"

Kelly threw up her hands in frustration. "Who knows? Maybe? The whole thing is out of character." She rubbed the back of her neck while she considered the matter. "But seriously, it's *Andamooka*. What are the odds she could carry on an affair without the whole town talking? Not even a whisper on the grapevine? You know how those old church ladies love their gossip."

Liney shrugged. "Could have been a first date?"

Bec muttered under her breath: *should've swiped left.*

Liney gave her a withering glare.

Kelly ignored the byplay. "I'll give Ray a few more hours to pull himself together and question him again. We have to be missing something."

Chazz fortuitously showed up at that moment to deliver the luncheon baguettes and more chilled water, providing an excuse to table the discussion for the moment. The officers ate in silence as they reviewed the notes and reports from the morning.

Bec swallowed the last mouthful of her lunch and leaned forward to pour another glass of water. "So, I was chatting with Izzy earlier, and she mentioned she's already had several enquiries about purchasing the Hamilton property. It's not even on the market yet, but you know what the grapevine's like around here. Anyway, what's interesting," Bec went on, "is that Ray Sharpe had talked to Izzy about the property. You know, wanting the asking price and that sort of thing?"

"In his case at least, it was probably just tyre-kicking, standard nosey neighbour stuff," Kelly offered. "He and Lorraine were pretty tight with the Hamiltons, after all." She tilted her head as a thought came to her. "Though, actually, he's fairly recently retired … he and Lorraine may have been looking for a project to fill in their time together. A seasonal Airbnb, maybe?"

"That would make sense," Bec agreed. "It's conveniently close. Easy to manage."

"Mmm-hmm. Well, I suspect Izzy will find the house to be slightly less in demand after today," Liney observed dryly, wiping her fingers with her napkin.

Bec considered Liney's statement with a tilt of her head before making an ambivalent gesture. "You'd certainly think so, but then again maybe not in this case. You know, it might even be a selling point," she added. "It being both a famous horror writer's family home *and* the scene of a murder, I mean."

Kelly raised a thoughtful eyebrow. "People can be surprisingly ghoulish," she allowed.

Bec nodded. "Plenty of people love mysteries – especially murder mysteries."

"Just wait," Liney predicted. "Before you know it, there'll be some entrepreneur running ghost tours out of Andamooka."

"Actually…" Bec started thoughtfully, "that could really take off. Have you heard about the *Burra Bakehouse's Daughter* tours being run out of the Burra Cemetery? I saw something on the news only a little while back. It's attracting a lot of visitors."

Kelly stretched, rolling a kink out of her shoulder with a slight grimace.

"As it happens," she offered, "the Andamooka cemeteries have some interesting history. The original cemetery from - oh, sometime back in the 1930's, I think – was literally built where a dead man fell." Noting Bec's obvious interest, she went on, "Being as the weather was hot and he'd been dead 3 days before they found him, they just up and started the cemetery on the spot rather than move him."

Bec wrinkled her nose and Liney chuckled.

"They're a pragmatic lot around here," Kelly

grinned.

After swiping her empty sandwich wrapper into the trash, she handed the wastepaper basket round for the others to dispose of their waste. Bec had pulled out her phone, and Kelly could see she was checking the Bureau of Meteorology's weather alerts.

"Any news on time of impact?" Liney asked, with an eye on the window. The sky outside had darkened noticeably since they'd stepped inside.

"Nothing good, I'm afraid" Bec said. "There's a priority warning up. We're going to get a drenching sometime in the next few hours. Definitely before this evening."

"Oh, and how *utterly* delightful that will be," Liney murmured sarcastically.

Kelly growled a 'hmph' of agreement.

Her mind whirled as she projected the likely fallout. As though the impact on her murder investigation wasn't enough, Kelvin was going to send the town into chaos. There would doubtless be flooding, with road closures to monitor and probably loss of electricity. And then, of course, people unable to get to work and bored at home usually drank too much alcohol or turned to drugs to fill in the time. *And then the fighting starts...*

"Oh, well," Liney said, pushing to her feet, "Let's do what we can before the storm hits."

Kelly's mobile vibrated against her hip. "Kelly Wells," she answered.

"Hey Kelly, this is Alex Starr. Shannon Evans asked me to follow up."

"Alex! Good to hear from you. Hang on a second, let me put you on speaker." Kelly placed the phone on the table in front of her and leaned in. "I'm here with Detective Brevet Sergeant Liney Deer and Detective Senior Constable Bec Heath. Liney, Bec, this is Alex Starr from Shannon's office."

There was a chorus of *hello* from the detectives and the same in response from Alex.

Kelly's pulse tripped into a faster rhythm. "Alex, I really hope you called to tell me Maxine Hamilton is right where she is supposed to be and that you spoke with her personally."

"I wish." Alex said with a sigh. "I spoke to her employer, a labour hire place. That's why it took so long, sorry - they had to chase up the shift supervisor. Hamilton's working as a casual at a wine packaging business." Alex took a breath and continued. "They confirmed she was at work on Friday as scheduled and had her rostered day off yesterday. But she was supposed to come to work today and didn't show. She's not answering her mobile, either. I called a detective in the Barossa and asked him to check out her place. No answer at the door, and her car's not in the driveway."

*Shit.* Kelly swore silently.

Alex went on, "The neighbours haven't seen her, but apparently that's not unusual. They generally only ever see her when she's out running or cycling. Her job includes rotating shifts, so they're used to her coming and going at odd hours and didn't notice when she left."

*Damn it, Maxine! What are you doing?!*

Before Kelly could ask, Alex went on to say, "I called the local hospitals to see if she'd had a vehicle accident or something. No one by the name of

Maxine Hamilton has been admitted in the past forty-eight hours. Also, there are no Jane Does matching her description currently under care or recently deceased." Alex paused, before noting "Obviously, none of this is evidence that she drove to Andamooka and committed your murder..."

Bec finished the sentence, "...but it's sure one heck of a coincidence. Yeah. Do you have a description of her car?"

"Sure do. Toyota Corolla sedan. Sky blue. 1992 model," Alex confirmed.

Kelly silently chastised herself as Bec wrote down the information: she should have thought to check that earlier. "Thanks, Alex, I appreciate you looking into the situation for me."

"No worries, Kelly. I'll ring you if I get any new information."

The call ended and Kelly exhaled a deep breath, looking grimly over the table at her colleagues.

Liney put down her biro as she finished making her notes from the conversation.

"You've got good rapport with Helen Hamilton from what I hear. It might pay to stick close to her. If Maxine's around, odds are high she'll head to her sister."

Kelly nodded. "I was just thinking the same thing." She picked up her mobile and started to scroll through her contact list before shaking her head. "I should do this in person. I'll head out to the Hamilton place and do an inspection."

Liney nodded, while Bec gave her a jaunty double thumbs-up.

It was in that moment, as Liney's brow furrowed

minutely at the junior officer's informality, that Kelly realised Bec had been deliberately provoking her tightly-wound senior officer in a range of tiny ways that wouldn't warrant a reprimand.

It brought back memories of her own days as a Constable dealing with staid senior officers, and she had to turn quickly to hide a smile. As she made to leave the room, Chazz stepped into the doorway.

"Hey, Chazz. I'm just about to head out. Did you need something?"

"Nope, not me. But I've got a call from *Elsbeth's Little Shop of Everything* on hold at the moment, and I told them I'd get an answer from you straight away. They're scheduled to make a delivery to the Hamilton place in Absalom Lane in Andamooka. Elsbeth wants to know if the road is still cordoned off before she heads out."

"Ahh, right. No, it's all clear now," Kelly confirmed, then hesitated. "I'm actually just about to head out that way. Do you want to let Elsbeth know I'll pick up the delivery and run it over for her?"

Chazz laughed. "She's going to be incredibly relieved you said that. Sounds like it's full-on at the store at the moment."

"I bet," Kelly said with a wry grin. She reached out and put her hand on Chazz's arm as her assistant made to speed off. "And Chazz, make sure you finish up on time today. That storm is going to be here this afternoon, and it's looking worse all the time."

Chazz rolled her eyes. "Yes, Mum," she drawled jokingly, before adding sincerely, "But seriously though, Kelly, be careful out on the roads, OK?"

Kelly nodded as she stepped out, pausing briefly at

her office to check the messages on her desk. Good: nothing that couldn't wait.

Grabbing her hat and keys, she headed over to *Elsbeth's Little Shop of Everything*. Elsbeth, the store's eponymous owner, waited for Kelly at the front entrance. She'd rolled a loaded cart out onto the verandah by the time Kelly pulled to a stop in the car park.

"Looks like that storm is going to be just as bad as they're saying," Elsbeth said, concern evident in her voice as she passed the first of three bags to Kelly. A wine carton sat on the trolley.

"It will. There's officers and SES going from door to door in Andamooka to check on the older residents," Kelly said. "We want to be sure everyone knows we're in for a bad one."

Elsbeth passed Kelly another bag. "I had to call in my entire team, including casual staff. Quite a few people in Roxby Downs and Andamooka have phoned in requesting deliveries." The store didn't make deliveries all the time – and mostly only to Andamooka – but in this kind of weather Elsbeth and her crew did all within their power to ensure those in the community who needed extra help had it.

Much of Roxby Down's adult population of nearly four thousand people was aged in their twenties through forties – fairly young and mostly in good health. Andamooka's population was less than a tenth of Roxby's, but the residents tended to be much older. Many were aged pensioners preferring the desert landscape - still mesmerized by opal, and too poor to move to a larger town with more services.

Kelly nodded approvingly towards Elsbeth. "Glad

to hear people are stocking up before Kelvin hits." She accepted the last of the three bags and shuffled it into position behind the front seat before accepting the only box in the order. The clinking within confirmed it was a box of wine and not pantry items in a recycled wine carton, and she shifted the passenger seat forward to accommodate the box safely on the floor behind it. "Let me or the station know if you run into any trouble or see anything out of place."

"You know I will." The older woman shook her head. "It's such a shame about Lorraine Sharpe. You got any leads yet?"

Elsbeth was a smart woman, building her own modest, independent empire despite competing with one of the supermarket giants. She also had a reputation for seeking out information.

Kelly gave her a direct look. "You know I can't comment on a current investigation," she stated bluntly, offering the rebuke in a neutral tone.

"I watched the breaking news report. You think whoever did this is still hanging around?"

*Nothing if not persistent. Still, a valid question considering the situation.*

"It's too early to be sure but we don't want to take any chances. We've put out an appeal to the community for help, along with a warning to be careful."

"Stuff like this just doesn't happen around here." Elsbeth seemed to catch herself on her last statement. "Not for a long time anyway."

Kelly nodded. "Yeah… it's been a long time." She closed the vehicle door. "Thanks, Elsbeth. I'll head out there right away."

"I heard she was back to sell her dad's place."

"It's time, I guess." Kelly couldn't blame Helen for wanting to let go of the past.

"You know, I read a couple of those books she wrote. Pretty scary stuff." Elsbeth looked shrewdly at Kelly. "Makes you wonder how a person could come up with something that twisted."

"I know what you mean. I feel the same about *Twilight*," Kelly said, dryly sarcastic.

Elsbeth continued on, ignoring the implicit warning in Kelly's tone. "It does make you wonder about the darkness hiding inside of people that seem like you and me. What really goes on inside people's heads."

Kelly squared her shoulders, facing the other woman front on.

*Can't take a hint, can you?*

Her tone, however, remained pleasantly neutral as she said patiently, "It's *fiction*, Elsbeth. After what she went through with her mother's murder, it's not surprising she understands what it feels like to be vulnerable and afraid."

"Guess so," Elsbeth agreed.

Kelly turned away and waved, stepping with a carefully cultivated air of detachment to the driver's side door, before tossing a casual wave to Elsbeth. Inwardly, she seethed.

People would come up with all sorts of scenarios to explain away the gruesome murder of a local, and the *'horror writer comes back home, kills neighbour'* theory was doubtless great gossip fodder - but Kelly didn't really expect that line of speculation to gain much traction. Too many people knew Helen. Knew her relationship with the Sharpes had only grown closer after the death of her mother and her sister's incarceration.

Kelly chewed her lip.

*Maxine, on the other hand...*

There was an alert out for Maxine's car for the region. If it was located, Kelly might have to issue a warning to the community to be on the lookout for Helen's sister.

*Once that happens, we're going to have a witch hunt on our hands*, she thought. Wincing at the thought, Kelly resolved that until there was some kind of proof Maxine had headed this way, she wasn't going to bring that kind of public inquisition down on Helen's shoulders.

As Kelly climbed back in her vehicle, her mobile vibrated again. "Kelly Wells."

"Hey... it's me." *Helen.*

Kelly immediately picked up the odd tone in her friend's voice. "Hey. Everything okay?"

"Honestly? I'm not sure. It's probably nothing, but with what's happened at the Sharpe's, I don't want to be too cavalier."

Tension rolled through Kelly. "I'm listening."

"I did some walking around the property a little while ago. I ended up at Sissi's house, way up the hill from here. Do you remember it?"

"Our secret hideaway?" Kelly cast her mind back in time. "I haven't been there in decades probably, but yeah, I remember where it is. Has something happened up there?"

Helen's voice was hesitant. "As I said, maybe it is nothing, but it looks like someone's been staying there. I found empty water bottles and food wrappers, still within their use-by dates. If that makes sense."

Kelly's tension ratcheted up a level. "I'm on my way. And Helen?"

"Yes?"

"You need to know... Maxine hasn't been seen since Friday. Be careful."

She could hear Helen's breathing speed up on the other end of the line.

"Stay put, Hels. I'm coming."

# CHAPTER NINE

**3.30pm Sunday, 18 February 2018**

Helen walked to the front window and checked to see if Kelly's Landcruiser was within sight. She felt stupid now for waiting to call Kelly until after she heard back from Melanie, but she'd hoped to have some confirmation of her sister's whereabouts.

Vexingly, Melanie hadn't been able to reach Maxine or her parole officer, though she'd been quick to add that this wasn't any evidence of wrongdoing: Maxine could be at work, or simply out to lunch with friends and had her phone turned off. Helen had clutched that to her like a lifeline.

Then Kelly had called, saying her sister may have dropped off the radar as early as Friday.

*Maxine, what have you done?*

Helen hugged her arms around herself.

*She played by the rules during her time in prison, and for more than a year after her release, and now suddenly she does this? Where is the logic?*

Her stomach sank as a new thought came to her.

Maxine's instruction that her family be excluded from communicating with her in prison had put them in a peculiar place, information-wise. As family to the *convicted criminal*, their link to her sister had been the lawyer's office, which dutifully carried out Maxine's instructions not to provide any news whatsoever. As the *victim's family*, however, the Attorney-General's Department had notified them of any change to Maxine's status as it pertained to her incarceration.

At the time, Helen's main feeling on the matter had been a profound sadness that the only information she received was due to her status as a victim of crime. Now, however, she realised a deeper ramification: if Maxine had ever been diagnosed with a mental illness, Helen wouldn't have been told. She had no way of knowing if her sister needed ongoing psychiatric or pharmaceutical intervention.

*…Maybe there seems to be no logic because there is no logic?*

Maxine had been declared fit to stand trial 20 years ago, but mental health care had come a long way in two decades.

Helen's hand flew to her mouth as she had a further realisation: she'd thought Maxine's decision to take on university qualifications in Communications during her imprisonment - with all the intense essays, research and thesis work that entailed - had been distinctly *uncharacteristic* of her energetic sibling … but was there a darker truth? Had it been the result of her finally getting a correct diagnosis and the treatment she required?

*Was she struggling her whole life? When she was booted from Uni the first time, should we have looked deeper for the reasons?*

A third thought, hard on the tail of the others, electrified her: since leaving the prison system, had Maxine seen a doctor, or even a counsellor? Was anyone monitoring her mental health, making sure any prescriptions were filled?

Helen checked the window again.

*Where are you, Kelly?*

The rain had started to fall in earnest. With a sudden change of wind direction, the blue chookie spun around hard with a reluctant, grinding squeal, and was now facing the other way. The wind speed was sending shimmers all through the wind vane.

Ex-tropical cyclone Kelvin had arrived.

Helen wasn't really worried about riding out the storm in her home. She had enough supplies to get by - though the additional supplies from Elsbeth would mark the difference between 'adequately' and 'comfortably'.

But what about whoever had been in Sissi's house?

*What if it's Maxine? What if she's cold and wet in that old house without electricity?*

The sleeping bag was ruined; she'd seen to that herself when she repurposed it for her escape. Worry suddenly swamped her, overriding the small part of her that said that even *if* Maxine was in Andamooka, she clearly didn't want anything from Helen.

*Unless she wants me dead.*

Helen blinked away the thought.

*There's no reason to believe that. She's never indicated anything of the sort.*

She bit her lip thoughtfully.

*Well, in as much as she's ever indicated anything, that is.*

But still.

Even during the worst of the aftermath of *that terrible day*, Maxine had never turned on her family with anger or threats. Maxine had insisted she was innocent, and Helen and her father had believed her, because the alternative made no sense.

*If anything, she was the one who was closest to Mum. Maxie adored her.*

Helen had always been happy to tag along with her dad on his trips to White Dam, to follow him about in the shed, to help with construction projects. It had been their mum who had taken Maxine to her sporting events and had organised cooking and crafting days during school holidays to channel her eldest daughter's energy productively.

Helen remembered coming back with her dad after one of those cooking days. The room had smelled sweetly of mixed spice and the deliciousness of fresh-baked biscuits. Her mum and Maxie had been midway through cleaning up the mess and had apparently turned it into some kind of game where each of them would try to sneakily steal a biscuit under the guise of 'cleaning', without the other seeing.

Helen couldn't prevent a soft chuckle at the memory of Maxie holding up empty hands to her mother as if to say, *"See?! Nothing to hide!"* while her mouth was stuffed tight with the evidence, cheeks bulging as she feigned wide-eyed innocence.

The memory was bittersweet; a beautiful moment, but it left the house emptier in its wake.

*Once this place is sold, there won't be any reason to come back.*

The thought churned her stomach.

What would it mean to live her life without Andamooka and everything it meant to her? Everything important in her life had started here: her bonds with family, Kelly ... even the wildly creative imagination that had spurred her career. All of it had been born under this desert sky.

She stared at her feet and blinked back sudden tears. When she again raised her eyes to the window, the familiar Landcruiser with its SA Police badging was pulling up close to the front door as though Helen's thoughts had summoned Kelly to banish her fears.

Helen watched as her friend climbed out of the Landcruiser. With one hand holding her Akubra hat in place, Kelly stalked across the yard and onto the verandah, rapping at the door as she stamped the mud free of her boots.

A smile pulled at Helen's lips as she opened the door. "The storm's not looking great," she observed, the words distinctly at odds with the warmth in her smile and eyes.

Kelly made a murmur of agreement as she stepped inside. Helen hurriedly closed the door behind her: the house wasn't designed for this type of weather, and the wind was blowing the heavy rain in under the verandah.

"It really isn't," Kelly agreed with a rueful grin, pulling off the Akubra and rubbing at her scalp. She shrugged out of her coat and placed it alongside her hat on the rack. "And, unfortunately, it's going to get a lot worse."

Kelly sighed as she rolled her shoulders, the war between fatigue and vigilance evident in every line of her body.

"Coffee?" Helen offered, starting to make a cup without waiting for the answer.

"Oh, god yes. *Please*."

Kelly leaned against the counter and rubbed her eyes before flicking her gaze out the window. "It's cooling down really quickly out there now," she observed.

As she poured two cups of the rich, dark brew, Helen pondered her recent insights about Maxine's possible mental health situation. She'd made some pretty major leaps of logic in the last ten minutes or so, and she debated whether to share them with Kelly. She didn't have any evidence, after all - and an allegation like that could be devastating to Maxine's presumption of innocence.

*But what if I'm right?*

"Please, sit down. Get comfy." Helen gestured to the lounge room with one hand as she passed Kelly her coffee with the other.

Kelly, cradling the mug like an offer of salvation, breathed in the rich aroma and sat, a smile of thankful appreciation beamed at Helen over the top of the mug. Helen, returning the smile, automatically took the armchair across from her and sagged into its comforting embrace.

Growing up in this house had been vastly different to her years in the city – not just the lifestyle, but in the basic accoutrements of home. Sydney apartments on her budget were notoriously small. She'd kitted-out her tiny apartment with sleek, stylish furnishings from IKEA and second-hand stores, restricting the colour palette to white and soft shades of grey to minimise visual clutter. She'd brought most of her furniture with her to Brisbane and hadn't really added to it since then. Her acquired style was minimalist, bordering on clinical.

The Andamooka house, for its part, was steeped in warm character and entirely eclectic, being concerned firstly with function, secondly with comfort, and lastly – if at all – with any regard to style or fashion. The kitchen still held the same stoneware and cast-iron cookware from when her parents were married - before the house had electricity, when cooking was done on a wood fire. The furnishings, too, were unchanged since her childhood: lots of dark wood and big florals. Knick-knacks and photos abounded. The couch and chairs were a little worse for wear but, Helen reflected, supremely comfortable.

"I'd like to have a look around Sissi's house," Kelly said, dragging Helen out of her musings. The sound of her rich voice was like a blanket of warmth – and much as Helen would have liked to chalk the effect up to the coffee, she hadn't taken so much as a sip.

"Kels, before you head up there… there's more you should know," Helen said, leaning forward. Haltingly at first, but with increasing confidence, she filled in her friend on the events of the day, including her improvised escape from the little room. Kelly, to her credit, listened without comment or judgment, although Helen could see the analysis going on behind her eyes.

"In retrospect," Helen finished, "I think it was mostly my own fear driving me – I let my imagination get out of control. But still… I'll honestly feel more at ease when you've had a look around. I *know* it seems silly, and I wouldn't normally be concerned, but with the murder and the dates on the chip packs being so recent …" She shrugged. "I had to tell you about it."

Kelly nodded, mulling over what she'd just been told. Her voice was free of inflection as she observed, "Sissi's shack is about halfway between your place and the Sharpes."

The contrived nonchalance might have fooled most people – even Helen, on a normal day – but with her own thoughts on high alert she couldn't miss the minute signs of her best friend's concern.

*I've known you most of my life, Kels. I can read you like a book. You're anxious. Disconcerted.*

"It's a pity about the dust storm," Kelly continued, "and now it's a rainstorm, any tracks will have blown or washed away." *But*, Kelly added to herself, if someone turns up again, *they'll be unable to avoid leaving tracks in the mud.*

"At least if he or she shows up again, we'll know." Helen uncannily voiced Kelly's thoughts, as she often did.

"It is quite likely that it's just kids," Kelly said, reassuringly, "but even so, with the timing…"

Helen had considered the possibility as well. "I'm crossing my fingers it turns out to be kids - it certainly wouldn't be the first time Sissi's has been used as a hangout. I'm just hoping it has nothing to do with Mrs Sharpe's murder."

Kelly nodded, sipped more coffee. Putting down her cup, she leaned forward, locking Helen's soft honey-brown eyes with her hazel ones.

"I'm thinking it might be better if you came into Roxby and stayed for a few days. Until we get a handle on the Sharpe murder."

A chill trickled through Helen. Kelly wouldn't make that suggestion lightly.

"I don't have a lot of time here, Kels. There's so much to do, and I have a deadline looming. I really need to stay and get this packing done."

She wasn't just fishing for information, although that was certainly part of it. The truth was, falling any further behind on her deadline would be a serious problem, and Helen was genuinely concerned about her ability to meet the date that had *already* been pushed out once at her request. She didn't want to beg for another extension - particularly with contract negotiations coming up after this book was turned in and accepted.

Kelly set her coffee mug on the table that fronted the lounge and rubbed a hand over her mouth, choosing her words carefully.

"So. About Maxine. I spoke to Shannon Evans – she's a police prosecutor I've worked with before. Shannon called a friend of hers, an investigator who lives in the Barossa.

"He went by Maxine's house, but it seems she hasn't been there for a couple of days. He also followed up with her employer – she finished her shift on Friday but didn't turn up for the one today. She had a rostered day off yesterday, so she could have gone missing anytime between Friday afternoon and this morning without anyone being the wiser.

"Maxine's Parole Officer has been advised, of course."

"Of course, yes." Helen's agreement was automatic, wooden, as she absorbed the additional information. "So, Maxine could be anywhere?"

Kelly nodded. Then she closed her eyes and shook her head.

When she opened her eyes once more, she said, "I hate putting this on you, but this isn't the time to play loose with the variables, and we can't pretend the risk isn't real. I can't fathom why Maxine would come back and do something like this, but it is a risk we can't take."

She looked at Helen, face stoic but her eyes pleading for Helen's understanding. "Helen, we *have* to consider Maxine a suspect until she has been located and cleared."

"I understand, truly," Helen said gently. "I'm sorry about the way I overreacted when you were here earlier. This is an emotional time for me, but I shouldn't have taken it out on you."

"I understand. We've been friends too long to doubt each other's motives".

Kelly had her there.

"So I hope you don't take it the wrong way," Kelly went on, "but it really might be best if you stay in town for a few days. You're welcome to stay at my place of course. Although," Kelly gave a dry chuckle, "Mum might ask you a million questions about the next book. She can't wait to get her hands on it."

"The next book is one of my problems," Helen admitted on a weary sigh. "I'm behind already. I can't afford not to stay on track at this point." She stared around the room, mentally cataloguing the work still left undone. "With everything I need to do to prepare the house for going on the market, I feel like I'm drowning. I guess what I'm asking, Kels is – *as a police officer*, are you saying I *need* to go to town or," she forced a lightly teasing note, "is this just my very protective friend looking out for me?"

Kelly narrowed her eyes, tapping the fingers of her right hand on the arm of the chair as she gave the question genuine thought. There was a heavy pause as she clearly battled with herself.

"More the second one," she admitted curtly, choosing honesty with obvious reluctance. "If you *weren't* my friend, I'd probably tell you to be cautious – lock the doors, don't answer without checking who's there, that kind of thing. We don't really have a reason to think anyone – including Maxine – would *specifically* want you harmed.

"But Helen," she stressed earnestly "*as your friend*, I'd feel happier knowing you were in Roxby Downs."

"Thanks, Kels." Helen pressed Kelly's gaze with her own. "But I'll be okay, really. Elsbeth should be delivering my order any time now. I'm all set. And," she added, holding up her hand in a rough approximation of the 'Scout's Honour' pledge, "you have my iron-clad guarantee I won't be answering the door to any strangers."

*Well, that's the answer I expected,* Kelly thought ruefully. *No point arguing; she'll just dig her heels in now she's made her mind up.*

"Speaking of your order - I almost forgot." Kelly stood. "I stopped by and picked it up since I was headed this way." At Helen's confused expression, Kelly explained, "Elsbeth called to confirm whether the road was open again, since we blocked it off this morning."

"Makes sense." Helen sat her nearly untouched coffee on the table next to her chair and pushed to her feet. "Better grab it while we're thinking of it."

Kelly held up a hand. "I've got it. No need for both of us to go out there. Plus," she added with a cheeky grin, "I'm conveniently *already* gross from all the wind, dust and rain earlier."

Before Helen could argue, Kelly strode out the door, shrugging on her coat as she went. In no time at all she had returned with two bags; Helen murmured her thanks as Kelly handed them over in the doorway before trekking back for the rest.

Helen stared at the rain-dampened plastic bags for a moment before she had the presence of mind to start putting things away.

*If Maxine is here, she wouldn't have known I was coming. She'd expect the house to be empty.*

Helen moved mechanically; her thoughts fixed on her sister.

*There are new locks on the doors, but she knows as well as I do how to coax the dodgy bathroom window open. So... would she really have set up at Sissi's? Wouldn't it make more sense to hide out in the house in comfort?*

She made a thoughtful 'hmm' as she put away the pantry items.

*She might have seen the new locks and wondered if there were security alarms inside.*

It made sense. Unfortunately.

As, too, did the possibility that Maxine had heard Helen intended to sell the house and decided to come, then lost her nerve when it came to facing her.

*But even if that's the case...where would she have*

*parked? Would she really hide at Sissi's when she could have just knocked on the door?*

This was Maxine's childhood home, the same as it was Helen's.

*Surely she knows me well enough to realise I'd never turn her out of her own home.*

But then, twenty years was a long time for anyone. And probably longer in prison. Maybe her sister didn't recognise her little sister in *Helen Hamilton, renowned author*, much as Helen couldn't find her big sister *Maxie in Maxine Hamilton, Communications Specialist*.

The sound of Kelly returning with the final bag and the wine carton spurred Helen into hurriedly shoving the last of the groceries away.

Kelly carefully settled the wine on the counter and lingered a few feet away for a moment before saying, "I'm going to check out Sissi's before the weather gets completely insane. Lock the door behind me, and don't let anyone in without calling me first." She reached out to put a hand on Helen's arm, ensuring she had her full attention. "We'll figure out what's next when I return, OK?"

Kelly half-expected an argument about locking the door, despite Helen's recent promise to do exactly that, but instead Helen nodded meekly.

*She's more concerned than she's letting on,* Kelly thought, jamming her hat on firmly. She stalked to the vehicle purposefully, head tilted slightly down against the storm.

Helen watched as her friend crossed the verandah and hauled herself into the 4WD. When the vehicle disappeared around the corner of the house, Helen closed the door and locked it.

Part of her wanted to pull on her boots and coat and go with Kelly. Instead, Helen stood vigil at the back door. Checked the lock again. Watched from behind the glass as Kelly's vehicle disappeared into the downpour, winding its way slowly up the hill on the gravel road.

The road was rapidly turning to ochre-brown slush. The rain was coming down much harder now, alternating between pelting downwards and being thrown into near-horizontal spears by the maddened winds.

But the weather, wild as it was, didn't scare her. What terrified her was what had blown in with this damned storm.

*Murder.* A woman was dead.

A woman she had known her entire life.

A woman her sister had every reason to want dead.

# CHAPTER TEN

**3.50pm Sunday, 18 February 2018**

Kelly pulled the brim of her Akubra down low to keep the water off her face. The wind had turned frenzied, and the temperature fallen dramatically, just in the short time she'd been at Helen's.

The timing of the storm could not have been worse.

Quite aside from the immediate fact that there was a murder to solve, she also had to ensure that both Ray Sharpe and Helen remained safe. Kelly couldn't shake the feeling that one or the other - or both - were still poised as targets in the killer's crosshairs.

Of course, she reminded herself, this assumed that the killer was still around. If the murder was - unlikely as it seemed - just an attempted robbery by a stranger passing through, then the killer was likely long gone.

But if Lorraine Sharpe's murder was about the past then the murderer was, in all probability, still here. And was probably Helen's sister.

*At least Mr Sharpe has an officer staying with him.*

Kelly sighed deeply, fingers drumming on the steering wheel in agitation.

*Please don't be here, Maxine. Please be starting your life over, finally getting everything you missed out on. Please don't make me arrest you.*

Back then, at fifteen, Kelly hadn't been especially interested in law enforcement as a career; it was just a convenient option that ticked the few boxes she had: variety, challenge, paid the bills. Most especially, it kept her within driving distance of her mother, Margaret.

Kelly had felt the need to look after Margaret after her diagnosis. Always feisty, Margaret had actively tried to discourage her daughter from making any career decisions based around her - she'd even tried to talk Kelly into following Helen. Even then, Margaret had understood how Kelly felt about her friend. *It seems sometimes like everybody did, except Helen.*

But Kelly had stayed in South Australia, watching from afar as Helen turned her dreams into a published reality. She was truly happy for Helen, despite how much she missed her. She'd learned to settle for Helen's rare visits.

It was difficult to believe how the time had passed. All their high school friends were in relationships – some were on their second marriage. Most of them had kids. Yet, both she and Helen were still single.

At only thirty-five, it wasn't like Kelly didn't still have plenty of time to build a future with someone. She'd certainly had opportunities; had them even now. Just not with the person she wanted.

As far as Kelly knew, Helen hadn't had any serious

relationships either. Kelly had often wondered if that meant Helen felt the same as she did – that the one for her was unreachable.

*Probably not*, she admitted to herself. Helen's first love had always been her writing. It was evident how much she loved her work. She probably hadn't even noticed the lack of a romantic relationship in her life.

It was, Kelly admitted to herself past the lump in her chest, entirely doubtful whether Helen even thought of Kelly outside of the times when she came home for the occasional visit.

*Still, I'm glad she's happy.*

Sissi's house came in to view in between the swipe of the windscreen wipers. Kelly pushed the vehicle cautiously forward, pressing into the wind and rain.

Parking as close as safely possible, Kelly cautiously entered the old building and checked each room. She noted where the ladder had been put down on the ground – *or slipped away from the wall*, she thought, reminding herself to be unbiased. Bending down, she moved her torch over the floor to try and determine whether the ladder had slid, but despite the numerous scuff marks in the dust on the floor, the wind buffeting through the broken windows made it impossible to determine whether there had been any distinct furrows prior to the storm. Shredded curtain fabric was strewn all about, flung by the wind.

Looking up, Kelly could immediately see where Helen had pulled out the mezzanine floorboards. Eyeing the sleeping bag hung precariously from above, Kelly was simultaneously impressed with her friend's ingenuity and horrified by the way she'd executed her plan. Even in the light of the torch it was obvious that Helen's improvised abseiling solution was a death trap waiting to happen. Repressing a shiver at the many ways Helen's escape could have gone tragically wrong, Kelly turned her attention back to the floor, scanning the room.

The evidence of Helen's precarious descent was obvious, but it looked to Kelly like more scuffled footprints were visible near the corners than would be accounted for by Helen's presence.

Someone *had* been out here with Helen; Kelly was sure of it.

*Were they still here when she left? Did they trap her and then leave, planning to return later once she was weakened?*

She took a shuddering breath.

*Or did they just abandon the house entirely, content to let the heat and dehydration take care of the problem for them?*

Kelly shook off the troubling thought as she scanned the scuffs in the dust with her torch.

Confident the ladder was solid enough, she repositioned it and climbed to the mezzanine floor, peering over the floorboards Helen had removed. She noted the table and chairs and the pillow, and then shifted her attention to the discarded food packaging and drink bottles.

The potato chip bags confirmed Helen's assertion that a visitor had been staying in the old house. Kelly took her time, sifting through the bags and bottles, and checked under the pillow. Nothing was hidden under the tabletop or the seats of the chairs.

Kelly shifted from her knees into a squatted crouch as she surveyed the old metal walls and ceiling. No new markings there.

She noticed, marked in one corner in childish penmanship '*Kelly*' and '*Helen*', and her heart twisted at the thought that this might be Helen's last visit. Once the house was sold, she'd have no reason to return.

Margaret, Kelly's mother, had told her more than once that she should share her feelings with her friend. Robert, Helen's father, had done the same: "*She'll find seventy ways to notice and describe how the light falls on a rock, Kelly, but she won't see what's under her nose. You'll have to open her eyes if you want her to think of you as anything more than a friend.*"

Remembering the moment, Kelly's thoughts echoed her wryly frustrated response at the time: "*Or become as interesting as a rock.*"

Her jaw clenched at the thought of all the opportunities she'd allowed to slip by over the years. She'd come close a couple of times, but always backed out at the last minute.

If it was just the possibility of being rejected romantically, she would have found the confidence – she was sure of that. Her fear wasn't that she'd lose a potential new relationship, but that she might lose everything she had now. There was a very real possibility that Helen would withdraw from Kelly's life completely if she thought their relationship had changed without her consent.

*Bob wasn't wrong, Kelly thought, she sees everything and nothing. She'll be blindsided.*

The possibility of losing everything was devastating. It just wasn't worth the risk.

Kelly pulled her phone from her vest and took a couple of photos of the items in situ on the mezzanine floor. There was no question someone had been here recently, but it wasn't entirely clear how much of the scuffled activity was Helen's work, and how much the unknown stranger.

Kelly reached for an evidence bag in her pocket. Selecting a soft drink bottle and a potato chip bag, she carefully stored both for future analysis.

After one final look around, she climbed down the ladder and headed out to the vehicle.

It was a slippery ride back down the hill to the Hamilton house - the wind surged against the back of the vehicle this time, making the pace uncertain and treacherous as the rain turned the dust into a mudslide.

When she finally exited the car back at Helen's, Kelly's boots were churning the mud.

*That's good. If anyone's been around while I'm gone there will be evidence,* she thought. The steady golden light of her torch beam moved in an arc around the house as she searched the perimeter.

Helen was watching for Kelly from the back door and flung it open as Kelly stamped the mud from her boots. Standing firmly on the tiled cement as the rain drummed against the galvanised iron on the roof, Kelly readied herself to confront her friend. *One more try,* she thought.

"Helen, *please* reconsider. Staying out here on your own is a bad idea."

"I'll be fine," Helen responded, tone straddling the line between reassuring and defensive.

Kelly automatically catalogued her friend's body language: *arms crossed; posture relaxed; chin up. She's made the decision to be stubborn, bloody well **knows** she's* *being stubborn, but she's had time to settle into it. Damn.*

Still, one more try couldn't hurt.

"You didn't sound fine earlier when you told me about what happened at Sissi's."

Kelly knew this was not a point that Helen would appreciate hearing, but it had to be said. The derelict house was a bit less than a kilometre from her back door, and someone had been holed up there very recently – very likely around the time of the murder. She needed to understand this was not the time for bravado.

"I was …disconcerted," Helen admitted, her shoulders squaring with the reluctant confession. "But I let my imagination run away with me. There's no reason to think anyone was lurking about in there."

"What about the ladder?"

Helen chewed her lip. "I don't really know what happened there. At the time I honestly thought it'd been moved, but I could easily have dislodged it when I climbed up to the mezzanine level." Helen's tone was uncertain, but became firmer as she added, "I definitely didn't see anyone there, though."

"What about the shed?" asked Kelly. "You're certain no one has been in there?"

"Almost certain. I was out there this morning and didn't see anyone or anything that would suggest so," Helen said, narrowing her eyes. "But you are welcome to look if you feel it is necessary."

*And there she goes, right on cue. Digging her heels in.*

"I'll request an officer be posted here with you to keep an eye on things," Kelly said, changing tack. "With the storm bringing the outdoor investigations to a halt, we have the workforce available."

Helen adamantly shook her head, her tone taking on a sharpened edge.

"Don't waste resources on me, Kelly. Your team is stretched thin enough and I can take care of myself. I'm not going out that door and I have no intention of allowing anyone to come through it. You should focus on your investigation, *Senior Sergeant*."

Well, that was plain enough. The determination on Helen's face and defiant crossing of her arms underscored her words. With a sigh, Kelly straightened her wet hair and jammed on her hat. "Well, I can't force you without arresting you, so I suppose I'll be on my way."

"I don't mean to sound ungrateful." Helen mustered an apologetic smile. "But as you said, as long as I'm sensible and keep myself indoors, there's no real reason to think I'm at risk. I truly do have a huge amount of work to get through – and obviously, your hands are more than full right now."

Before Kelly's brain could override the decision, she walked over to Helen and pulled her into a tight hug. "I just want you to be safe," she murmured over Helen's shoulder.

Helen hugged Kelly back. "I appreciate that." She drew away and searched Kelly's eyes. "Honestly, I truly do. But I've been thinking while you were at the shack."

She held up a finger. "First point: nobody knew I was here, not even you – there's no reason to think I've ever been at risk." Raising a second finger, she added, "Second point: *if* Maxine is here, *if* she's found out somehow that I'm here now too, I'm not afraid of her. She's never been a threat to me before, Kels. She always protected me, growing up."

Kelly wanted to believe in Maxine as strongly as Helen did, but her time in the police force had taught her a lot about the darkness buried inside people. "I hear you. Just... be careful, okay? If Maxine shows up at your door, think long and hard before you let her in."

"I will. Now go," Helen gently prodded Kelly towards the door, "before the roads get any worse."

Kelly glanced back at Helen one last time before striding through the rain to climb into the police vehicle. Helen walked inside and locked the door behind her. Watching from the window as Kelly drove away, she saw her friend wave goodbye.

Helen waved back, smiling.

Kelly drove off the property, fighting the instinct to question the judgment of both of them. *Decision's been made,* she thought, wrenching her thoughts back on track. *Right now, I have a murder to solve. The sooner that's done the sooner everyone's safe.*

When Kelly reached the top of Absalom Lane, she saw it was clearly impassable and circled around to get to Mihala Street; a right turn, and Kelly headed up the hill towards Miners Way to drive around the edge of town. The Sharpe place was in the opposite direction, around two kilometres or so away.

All the roads were gravel and already becoming slippery in the rain. With no hard shoulder to the road, it was swiftly becoming dangerous as the pouring rain obscured her vision, making it hard to work out where the edges lay. She hoped she didn't encounter any oncoming vehicles on the narrow road. Moving to the slick and muddy shoulder would require extreme caution.

As Kelly was passing the old Hoffmann place – empty, since the elderly couple had passed away – she instinctively slowed the vehicle to a stop, peering through the windscreen as the wipers tried to cope with the downpour. The rickety old house had been on the verge of falling in on itself for years now. With a thoughtful *hmm,* she carefully reversed to come alongside the driveway.

When Kelly and Helen had been kids, the Hoffmann's had lived there. After they passed away, the property had gone to a nephew in Broken Hill. The nephew had never come to collect any of their belongings, nor shown any interest in owning or maintaining the house. The Outback Communities Authority were still chasing him for years of unpaid taxes, Kelly recalled.

Nobody had a reason to come here, nobody lived in close proximity.

She tapped her fingers thoughtfully on the steering wheel. The deserted house had been checked by police earlier today, along with all other sheds or structures this close to the crime scene, but it wouldn't hurt to have another look now. Particularly considering it was this close to Helen's place and Sissi's old house.

*If anyone's been hiding close by, this weather will have driven them indoors.*

Mind made up; Kelly eased off the road into what had once been a narrow drive. The old house was close to the road, so she didn't have to go far. She climbed out of the vehicle and scanned the area. The drenching rain deadened all other sound as Kelly made her way to the stone and wood house.

*No tracks in the mud. That's a good sign.*

The front door was hanging open, probably from whoever had searched it earlier. The weathered door barely clung to the frame, captured only by a single hinge.

The house was simply-made with four main rooms, all stripped bare save for a few broken pieces here and there. The ceilings, lined with hemp sugar bags, sagged under the weight of old dust storms.

As her torch scanned the kitchen, Kelly noted that most of the cabinets had been torn out, and whatever other storage may once have existed – likely an icebox and meat-safe, from the age of the house - were long gone. Perhaps given away by the nephew, but more likely taken over the years and repurposed by pragmatic thieves as the house deteriorated. Even the heavy old butcher's block was gone.

Where the sink had been, there was just a water tap poking out of the wall and leading to the rainwater tank outside. *Forget 'everything but the kitchen sink' – they've taken off with that too,* Kelly thought, the irritation of an Officer of the Law warring with the amused respect of an Andamooka battler.

It *was* practically criminal to waste anything in the desert, after all.

Reassuringly, there was no indication that anyone had been inside since her officers had left. Dampness wafted in through the broken windows, creating a drift of moisture on the rammed dirt floor, but the only footprints freshly in the room were Kelly's.

The house didn't appear to have a lavatory, and she realised there was probably a bore-hole toilet somewhere out the back. Plenty of houses still had this style of primitive toilet on the property, basically a toilet seat set over a deep hole in the ground. It wasn't pleasant, but early residents hadn't been able afford to waste any precious water. Even now, despite modern plumbing having been introduced over time throughout the town, many of the old homes still had an old bore-hole dunny on the property.

She gave herself a reminder to check the toilet to see if it had been used recently. Assuming the basic outbuilding still stood at all, it wouldn't be located too far from the house.

*One room left*, she thought, stepping towards the second bedroom. At the doorframe, she stilled as her torch picked up the tell-tale glisten of water near the doorway - further into the room than the broken window would account for.

A quick scan was enough to tell her the room was empty now.

Stepping to the window, she peered out into the rain, her gaze immediately drawn to the fresh boot tracks beneath the window. Whoever had been there hadn't been gone long, and Kelly's eyes narrowed as she sought her prey. Mere seconds later, she was through the open window, feverishly tracking the footprints that the raging storm was obliterating before her eyes. Mobile phone already to her ear, she put in a call to Detective Senior Constable Heath.

"Hey, I was just about to call you," Bec said by way of a greeting.

"I'm at the old Hoffmann place," Kelly interrupted, speaking loudly over the pounding rain. "Someone's been here in the last few minutes." Reaching the edge of the property where the compacted ground gave way to gibber stones, she peered at the ground, looking for a trail.

"Sending help your way," Bec confirmed. "Stay on the line with me."

Kelly nodded agreement automatically. "I'm thinking whoever was here heard me pull up and took off out the bedroom window. They've headed out over the mullock heaps." Doggedly, she moved in a search pattern over the gibber area, alternately scanning the ground, and surveying the area around her. "Damn it! I've lost the trail," she cursed, turning all the way around. Rain drenched through her uniform to her skin.

"Ashley and Jett are on the way to your location," Bec advised. "You should stand down, Kelly, until you have backup."

Kelly remained as still as possible, moving nothing but her eyes from side to side, watching for the slightest movement. "Tell them I'm at the property line, behind the house…" she trailed off, her attention seized by the large general shed a few metres from the edge of the property. She pivoted in that direction. Whoever had fled the house when Kelly arrived could easily have circled back to the shed.

"I know that silence," Bec said sharply. "What's happening, Kelly?"

"I'm going into the old shed," Kelly spoke as quietly as she dared, not wanting to get the attention of a possible intruder but having to fight to be heard over the storm.

"It's still standing? In this wind? Be really careful, Kelly. We went through it earlier. Even at that point, before the storm hit, I honestly thought it would fall on top of us at any moment."

The blatant worry in Bec's voice didn't distract Kelly from her slow and deliberate progress as she stalked through the clinging mud and pouring rain. She didn't bother answering. While it was too much to hope for the element of surprise – there were more than enough gaps in the rusty corrugated iron walls for someone to have seen her heading towards them - she wasn't going to give an assailant any hints to her exact location either.

Kelly sidled up to the rear of the structure, the part closest to the property line. A couple of missing iron sheets allowed her to see inside. The roof had almost entirely collapsed, allowing in enough ambient light to make out general shapes without her torch. Water pooled across the mud floor inside. No tracks as best she could see. Kelly found a wider opening and ducked inside.

Kelly progressed cautiously through the building, rusty mining machinery creating a maze of blocks to her vision and path. Her gaze roved constantly over the ground and around the room, seeking any sign of human tracks or flickers of movement.

"I need to hear your voice, Kelly."

Kelly had almost forgotten she still had Bec on the line. "Nothing in the shed", she said, straightening up. "No sign anyone's been holed up long-term here or in the house, but someone has *definitely* passed through."

Kelly explained about Sissi's derelict house and what Helen found there. "Could have been a kid. Might have been a druggie," she said before Bec could suggest as much, "but seeing those tracks leading away from the Hoffmann house this close to our homicide scene makes me sceptical."

"Well, I have something else to make you doubt the kid or the druggie theory," Bec said, "I was just about to call you when you phoned me first."

Kelly set her back to the corrugated iron, stepping out of the direct force of the rain. Eyes alert for any movement towards the house and the property line, she switched the phone to her right hand as she slicked her hair back and wiped water from her forehead and eyes. "Oh? What's the news?"

"Elsbeth rang the station - she was rambling about some butch-looking woman coming into the shop. It took me a moment to get her calmed down so she could tell me who."

Kelly's eyes tracked the headlights of a 4WD lurching through the mud and rain. A once-white Landcruiser, liberally coated in muddy clay, pulled to a stop near the old house: seconds later, Ashley and Jett emerged. With the roads turning quickly into creeks, the two must have been close by.

Kelly turned her attention back to the phone call. "Jett and Ash have just pulled up. Go on."

"Elsbeth can't be positive, mind you," Bec warned. "She only saw her in profile... but she dug up a photo and showed it to the checkout operator who served the woman, and she's confident it was Maxine Hamilton."

"Mmm-hmm. And how recent was this photo of Elsbeth's?"

Kelly doubted anyone locally had seen Maxine Hamilton in twenty years. And Elsbeth had a tendency to inject herself into the centre of any story, as all of the local police knew.

"*Recent* recent," Bec confirmed, to Kelly's surprise. "It was from an article in the Port Augusta newspaper, back when she was released from prison. It seems she hasn't done much to change her appearance since, and the checkout operator was positive it was her."

Tension churned through Kelly's gut. It wasn't proof, not by a long shot. Witnesses were inclined to see what they wanted, or expected, to see - especially with an enthusiastic gossip like Elsbeth putting ideas in their head. It could have been someone else.

*There's no way I'm taking that risk.*

"I need to let Helen know about this," she snapped, thoughts travelling straight to her mouth as she spun towards the car.

With a self-directed grimace at her unplanned outburst, Kelly added calmly and professionally, "Bec, I'm going to head back to the Hamilton place. I'll get Ashley and Jett to look around here, make sure nobody's still lurking."

*Helen thinks she can take care of herself where Maxine's concerned, but I bet her mother thought the same thing.*

No one really knew what they would do when they came face-to-face with a killer.

Especially when it was someone you should be able to trust.

# CHAPTER ELEVEN

ABSALOM LANE, ANDAMOOKA, SOUTH AUSTRALIA

**4:30pm Sunday, 18 February 2018**

Helen poured the dregs of her last cup into the sink. *That's more than enough coffee for one day.* Her stomach gurgled sourly, punctuating the thought in agreement.

Refilling the cup with water, she headed back to the living room and peered out at the charcoal clouds curtaining the landscape. The teeming expanse of rain had seemingly vanished the rest of the world. Even the lights of the emergency services station in the distance were invisible through the downpour.

Craning her neck, she could see the creek bed between the neighbouring property boundary and Christmas Hill Road, usually bone-dry, was already starting to swirl with run-off.

The drop in the outside temperature permeated the glass, making Helen shiver.

*How ludicrous. I'm in the desert, mid-Summer, and all I*

*want right now is a cardigan*, she thought with a mix of irritation and amusement.

She recalled there'd been news on the radio that a warm front was following behind Kelvin. *When that heat hits, I'll probably wish the storm was back. With all this water about it's going to be putridly humid.*

But on the plus side, all the waterholes would come to life – for a while at least. It was always spectacular when that happened.

She couldn't remember, exactly, when she'd last seen the outback thrown into that vivid, joyful grandeur, but she distinctly recalled her disappointment when the photo prints had come back. That bitter sense of regret that if only she'd had a better camera – or better skills – she might have properly captured the vibrant glory of those red-and-black Sturt Desert Peas and yellow-white poached egg daisies cascading over the red sand dunes, or the sheer exuberance of the birds flocking to Lake Torrens to feast on the tiny shrimp.

She looked thoughtfully at her phone; the camera integrated into it was leagues ahead of the old point-and-click she'd had all those years ago.

*If only I can stay a while longer...* but even as the thought crossed her mind, she knew it was futile. Ultimately, there were too many things to do: she had to keep her momentum going. It didn't allow time to stop and smell the roses.

*Or photograph the wildflowers, as the case may be.*

With a small sigh of regret, she turned her mind to practical matters. While the electricity supply was fairly reliable, Helen knew she had to be serious about preparing for a potential power outage. Her little hire car certainly couldn't manage the roads.

Going through a mental check list, she ticked off the essentials.

*Enough food for a few days: check.* Mostly tins and boxed cereal. Powdered milk as a back-up when the carton in the fridge ran out. Nothing to inspire the senses, but she certainly wouldn't starve.

*Fresh water.* She'd brought in a supply of bottled water - but if that ran out, the rainwater tanks would be full. *Check.*

*Coffee: check.* As long as the power stayed on, she'd be able to caffeinate.

*And of course, wine,* Helen thought with a smirk, *since it's socially acceptable to drink alone when the sky is literally falling. Check.*

On that note, she poured herself a glass and started in earnest on the sorting and packing.

The collection of photo albums and keepsakes were first on her agenda, and time flew by as she worked her way through three small and two medium size boxes, stopping occasionally to smile or laugh at the memories captured on film.

Standing and stretching, she realised that the previously frenzied fury of the rain on the roof had turned hypnotically soothing as the wind started dying down. She hadn't noticed when it happened, but now it made her wonder how the world outside was faring.

Wandering over to the window, Helen was surprised to see a Landcruiser with police branding lurch to a stop outside. The driver was obscured by the rain and dazzling headlights, so Helen was both relieved and confused on seeing her best friend step from the vehicle.

Curious, she stepped to the back door and opened it wide for Kelly to come into the foyer. Water rippled over the tiles as it streamed from Kelly's coat and hat, but the wind had died down enough that the rain no longer flung itself inside the house along with her.

Hanging up Kelly's coat, she half-turned her head and asked, "Don't take this the wrong way – I'm glad to see you – but why are you back so soon?"

Kelly locked the door behind her and scanned the room before meeting Helen's gaze.

Helen's stomach sank. Something else had happened.

*Please don't let it be another murder.*

Kelly removed her Akubra hat, setting it aside. "You haven't heard from Maxine, have you?"

A frown tugged at Helen's brow. *This again?!*

"What? No. I've already told you this. You said she didn't show up for work but that's the last I heard." A thought occurred to her. "Has she contacted you?"

"No." Kelly looked uncharacteristically uncertain. "But it's possible she's been in Roxby Downs. Someone's come forward and identified her from a newspaper photo from last year."

Helen remembered the photo, taken on her sister's release from prison, as well as the accompanying article. It was the first time she had seen her sister's face in twenty years. She'd looked so much like their father: good looking, square jaw. Same hair and eyes.

Helen blinked the memory away.

"You think they're right. That Maxie's here." A mixture of anticipation and uncertainty churned Helen's stomach. She didn't know whether to be afraid or cautiously optimistic.

"I… look, Hels." Kelly locked eyes with her friend. "I'll be honest: it's more of a gut feel than anything else, but …" she shrugged.

"I need coffee. Or alcohol. Or both." Helen scowled at the coffee maker, the closest victim for the unease roiling through her. "Why has nobody made coffee wine?"

Caught off-guard, Kelly laughed. "Because it'd be gross? I think you want Kahlua."

"Christ, I want *something.*" Helen had pulled her braid over her shoulder and was unravelling it with her fingers. She flung an agitated smile her friend's way. "Kahlua, huh? Maybe it's time to learn to love cocktails."

While the rest of her brain caught up on the latest revelation, she moved automatically into hosting mode. "Sorry, Kels, I didn't even offer you anything. I know you're on duty… would you like water, or actually" her bit her lip on a mischievous smile, "it looks like you have enough of that. Perhaps coffee?"

"Thanks, but I'm good for the moment." She paused. "I was going to check on Ray, but given the news, I don't really want to leave you here alone."

There it was. Kelly's refusal to believe that Helen could take care of herself.

*That*, at least, was familiar.

"I get that you won't come into Roxby Downs with me," Kelly continued, *"believe me,* I get it. So I'm staying here with you." Kelly's tone and posture had shifted; no longer uncertain, she seemed somehow larger than before as she paced over to the rack and got her coat again. "I just need to check in at the Sharpe's place first. And I don't want to leave you here on your own with this new development, so," Kelly's tone brooked no argument, "you're coming with me."

*Are you serious?!*

Helen had never known Kelly to be so unyielding, but the sheer determination in her friend's hazel eyes warned her she was deadly serious. Half a dozen arguments raced to the tip of Helen's tongue and died there, unspoken.

Helen was as surprised as Kelly when the words that eventually came out were, "...All right. Give me a sec to get changed."

She rushed to the bedroom to haul on some jeans. She grabbed a pair of her dad's thick work socks: a bit large, but they'd do. Back to the foyer, and Helen automatically checked for spiders before pushing her feet into the walking boots by the back door.

Kelly, in the meantime, had pulled Helen's old yellow raincoat from its hook, shaken it out, and inspected it for insects. Helen pulled it on, positioning the hood over her head.

*Ready as I'll ever be, I guess.*

She locked the door on the way out, popping the key into the lock box.

"Watch out - it's sticky out here!" Kelly's warning came just in time, as Helen felt her boots sink into the mud. The steady rain clattered against her head and shoulders, protected by the bright yellow raincoat with the Wonder Woman design from her teen years.

*Good thing it's still in decent condition after all those years in storage.* Her mouth quirked in amusement. *Wouldn't want anyone thinking I looked stupid or anything.*

At least there wouldn't be many people out and

about.

*Except Kelly.*

Helen glanced at the woman who opened the passenger side of the police Landcruiser. She settled into the seat and fastened her safety belt. Thinking.

*Kelly won't find any real rest until this storm is over. Neither will her team.*

She'd known Kelly and her crew would do all within their power to see that the residents were safe: that was just a fact she accepted, same as the rising of the sun each day. It simply was.

She was only now realising what it actually *meant*.

Her father had frequently enthused about what a great community worker Kelly was: volunteering with Roxby Downs and Andamooka youth groups, leading the motorcycle riders' Christmas Toy Run, and participating in NAIDOC celebrations every May.

The region was home to four Aboriginal groups: Kokatha, Barngarla, Kuyani and Adnyamathanha. Kelly always made time to chat with the Elders - checking in and being a friend, not just an authority figure. She'd done a lot, her father had told her, to strengthen relationships between the residents of the area and the traditional owners.

Just by being herself.

Helen stared at Kelly's profile as she slid behind the wheel. Kelly's dark hair was shorter than ever, trimmed around her ears. Long black lashes framed striking hazel eyes.

*"Why in the world aren't you in a relationship?"*

The thought darted out of her mouth before she could intercept it. Helen could have bitten off her tongue. Heat rushed up her neck and she stiffened up, staring straight ahead once more.

"I could ask you the same thing." Thankfully, Kelly didn't seem to have taken offence; the rebuttal was delivered with a casual smirk, gaze still on the boggy road.

"Too busy." Helen reflexively replied: too curtly, too dismissively. With an internal growl of exasperation, she flung her head against the head rest and silently ranted at herself. There were many reasons why she remained single and being busy wasn't at the top of the list.

*Could you have answered any more coldly?*

The resounding silence from Kelly didn't help.

Finally, Kelly said, "OK." There was a pause of a few seconds before she added, teasingly, "I'd like to retract the question, Your Honour."

Gratefully accepting the conversational escape hatch, Helen leaned forward and changed the subject. "Ray and Lorraine always used to pop around to Dad's when I visited. I can't remember the last time I visited them at home." Her brow furrowed as she cast her mind back. "It'd have to have been in high school, I reckon."

Four Nations Road wound over the original mullock heaps up towards Miner's Way. As a child, Helen had simply wandered cross-country to visit the Sharpes - in dry weather it was actually quicker than driving.

Kelly peered through the pounding rain, her already cautious pace slowing down as she spied the property entrance. "You'll get a chance to see how your memory stacks up in a sec," she said, pulling the Landcruiser into the Sharpe's driveway, "I have to check in with the officer onsite to make sure the property is safely secured".

A dark blue Commodore sedan with police insignia sat in the boggy driveway a few metres from the house. Idling the Landcruiser, Kelly phoned the officer on scene; a few moments later a silhouetted figure emerged from the house and gave them a casual wave as he verbally confirmed everything was fine.

Reassured that all was as it should be, Kelly turned the vehicle around and headed back to the road.

Helen looked back at the house. "I'm surprised you were able to convince Mr Sharpe to leave long enough to investigate, let alone move out temporarily," she observed. She recalled him telling her how he'd trucked his home all the way from Woomera on a semi-trailer across the sand dunes along the old Andamooka Road.

He'd built his life with Lorraine in this house. Her things were here.

Helen knew only too well how the weight of a loved one lingered in the home they'd made. More than a year after his death, she still sensed her father's essence in the house he'd built.

Kelly interrupted Helen's reverie as she turned the vehicle out of the driveway, "We were able to isolate him in the bedroom until the crime scene technicians were done, but it was difficult to convince him to leave the house except to follow his wife to Roxby Downs.

"When we explained that Lorraine would have to go to Adelaide, he eventually agreed to go to a holiday shack we negotiated for him. But he wasn't happy about it." Kelly steered carefully along the slippery road. "Can't blame him, really."

"You mean he doesn't have anyone left?" Helen asked. "What about the sister in Iron Knob?"

"He didn't want to leave Andamooka. Bronwyn – one of our constables – told me the sister spoke to him on the phone but was too afraid to drive to him through this storm." Kelly glanced across at Helen. "Which, honestly, is for the best, much as I hate to say it. At her age, and in this weather? The risks outweigh the benefits to either of them."

Helen understood. "There's never a good time to die," she said, staring out the windshield at the water streaming across the surface. "But there are certainly *worse* times."

"No kidding."

Kelly drove the police vehicle across the boggy ground, following the road back around to Christmas Hill Road and out to Trealor Road, where the row of holiday shacks was located.

"So what's with these holiday shacks, anyway?" Helen asked. "Are they new? Last time I was here, I don't recall anything like that out this way."

"Oh, they're not new – not by a long shot." Kelly flicked a glance across at Helen. "You remember the old ones, for the opal miners? Some local entrepreneur decided they'd be great for AirBnB and brought them up to code again." She smirked, adding, "Although, maybe I should clarify, *for the benefit of the Sydney girl...*"

"That's Brisbane girl to you, missy!" Helen interjected in faux outrage.

A chuckle. "Sorry! As I was saying, *Brisbane* girl, when I say 'AirBnB', they're probably not what you're thinking." Kelly's eyes crinkled in amusement. "Let's just say, I don't think they'll end up in *Home Beautiful* any time soon."

As they pulled up, Helen was forced to admit there might be some truth to the Sydney – *Brisbane, dammit!* - thing: she had definitely pitched her expectations too high.

Up to code, the units might be, but they were a long way from luxurious. Her eye roamed over the outside, cataloguing: galvanised iron walls and roof, screened-in porch with what looked like a barbeque area. She suspected the interior wouldn't do anything to belie the view from the outside.

A police vehicle was parked on the gravel driveway right in front of the shack. The driveway continued around the back of the unit: Ray Sharpe's vehicle would be back there, more protected from the storm.

Helen dithered internally over whether to come inside or not.

Personally, she felt she owed it to Mr Sharpe to offer her condolences. He and his wife had been good neighbours and friends to her family for as long as she could remember.

Warring with that, however, was concern that Kelly's officers might think she was unprofessional if she allowed a civilian onto a police-managed site – even if it wasn't an actual crime scene. She knew Kelly had overcome a lot of barriers to get where she was, and she'd worked hard to earn the trust and respect of her team. Helen would hate to jeopardise her friend's hard-won status for anything so frivolous as a personal errand.

Then Kelly was at the passenger door, offering her hand.

Helen's face lit up in a beam of pure joy and affection that went straight to Kelly's heart like an electric shock. She sucked in a tiny gasp of air; a reaction that thankfully went unnoticed in the rain. *I don't know what I did, but I'd do it again a thousand times for that look.* She couldn't help the smile that bloomed on her own face as they walked to the shack together.

A uniformed constable met them at the porch with a friendly wave. The kitchen light was behind her, placing her face in shadow and turning the windblown hair that escaped her sensible bun into a halo of burnished gold.

Helen's first glance past the constable and through the doorway confirmed that the interior would generously be described as 'functional'. A towel was laid across the threshold to sop up any muddy water that had tracked in.

"Please, come on through. It's no day to be outside." The constable's voice was low and calming, reminding Helen incongruously of the way early childhood educators spoke. It tugged at her memory. Perhaps they'd met before?

Once they were all inside, the constable locked the door, smoothing her hair down as she turned to smile warmly at Helen. The smile was clearly genuine, dispelling any lingering notion that Helen was unwelcome here. It, along with the woman's large doe-like eyes – strangely soft and beautiful in an otherwise ruggedly plain face - triggered a strong sense of recognition.

*I'm **sure** I know you.*

Glancing at the woman's name tag, Helen stilled as she made the connection. It came back to her with a stabbing of pain. No wonder she hadn't remembered. She hadn't wanted to.

*She's the one that found Dad after the accident. Constable King.*

Robert Hamilton had been on a ladder repairing a piece of roofing iron on the house. He'd fallen, hit his head, and died of exposure to the elements before he was found. The guilt Helen had felt at the time twisted deep in her heart. She'd been on a book tour and hadn't taken the time to call that evening.

Her mind whirled. Seeing Constable King again brought back a host of horrible memories, but the woman herself had been nothing but supportive. Had they met in any other circumstance, she would have been delighted to see her again.

*Kelly picked the perfect person to look after a grieving widower*, she acknowledged.

Reaching deep within herself she forced a smile, channelling sincere gratitude in lieu of pleasure. "Constable King, I don't know if I ever properly thanked you for how kind you were when..." she stumbled a little over the words, "... when I was here last year."

"Helen, it's good to see you again. How have you been?" The constable's expressive eyes told Helen that the question was genuine. "Oh, and please, call me Bronwyn."

Before Helen could answer, Ray Sharpe materialised in the doorway that led into kitchen, as though summoned by hearing her name.

"Helen?" His voice wavered, uncertain.

He started to move towards her for a hug, like he did when she was young, before suddenly pulling himself up. Helen breached the gap for both of them, stepping forward to give him a quick hug and a murmured, *"Mr Sharpe. I'm so sorry."*

Sharpe returned the hug, eyes glittering with unshed tears, before turning his attention to Kelly. "Officer."

"Mr Sharpe, I wanted to check once more, before the roads become completely impassable," Kelly said. "Are you *certain* you won't stay with a friend here in Andamooka?"

Sharpe shook his head. "I'm not leaving. I'm okay here now. I know the storm is causing issues for your investigation, but all I want is for you to find out who killed Lorraine." His words were for Kelly, but his gaze was on Helen.

Helen's heart ached for the man. His wife had been so nice. Every holiday after her mother was gone, she'd brought homemade cookies to Helen and her father. She opened her mouth to tell him how much Lorraine had meant to her, but he cut her off.

"You know," he said to her, his steel blue eyes strangely cold, "my wife was murdered around the same time you showed up. I've been thinking about that all day. I just can't see it as a coincidence."

"Mr Sharpe, I understand you're..." Kelly was responding to the man's unexpected comment, but Helen's brain couldn't assimilate the words. Instead, poleaxed, she could only stare at the man who had known her since she was born.

*How can you think I would ever hurt Lorraine?*

Maybe he thought it was Maxine. It would be logical to assume she'd have some knowledge of her sister's whereabouts.

"Mr Sharpe... I swear, I haven't seen my sister," she said, the words bursting out of her and interrupting whatever Kelly was saying. "Not in twenty years, honestly. We haven't spoken in all that time. Whatever you're thinking, you're wrong."

"Like my Lorraine was wrong when your mother was murdered?" he countered, his voice rising with fury. "That bitch sister of yours called her a liar!"

Helen, eyes wide and brimming with concern and confusion, was frozen in disbelief. Thankfully, Kelly stepped between them, severing the searing glare that held her transfixed.

"Mr Sharpe, you're emotional right now. You're not thinking clearly. Helen hasn't hurt anyone."

"I've read her books!" he shouted. "Seems to me she's got all sorts of evil thoughts in that head of hers."

The force of his words had Helen backing up a step. Her hands twitched as she fought the instinct telling her to raise them to ward off a blow. *It's Mr Sharpe. He'd never hurt you. He's just an emotional wreck right now. He doesn't mean any of it.*

"We're going to head out now," Kelly said, firmly redirecting the conversation. "Mr Sharpe. Listen to what Constable King says. We *will* get through this storm, and back to what needs to be done as quickly as possible."

Sharpe stamped out of the room. Helen stared after him, unable to think of anything to say.

Kelly turned to her. "I'm sorry. I should have

anticipated he might react this way. They were married for much of their lives. He's going to be all over the place for a while… he's still in shock."

Feeling sad and defeated, Helen felt there was nothing to do but shake her head.

"I just wanted… it's okay. It doesn't matter." She raised her eyes to Kelly's. "It's okay. I'll go wait in the vehicle."

Kelly held up a hand. "Give me a minute and we'll go together. I just need to speak with Bronwyn a moment."

"I'll follow you out," the constable offered.

Helen was already through the door before Kelly had finished pulling on her coat. The three of them stood on the small front porch in silence for a moment, before Kelly squared her shoulders and stalked out into the rain, Helen following behind.

Kelly held her door while Helen climbed into the passenger seat. "I'll just be a minute," she said. Helen watched through the rain-blurred passenger window as Kelly sloshed back to the front porch and carried on a conversation that seemed to be mostly one-sided.

*Probably filling her in on the news about Maxine.*

Helen shifted her gaze, stared unseeingly out the windscreen.

*I can't go through this again.*

She exhaled a foggy breath, recognising that the thought had been entirely selfish. *Mr Sharpe didn't want his wife to be murdered, either,* she reprimanded herself.

The two officers broke the huddle. Constable King went back indoors, and Kelly climbed into the driver's seat.

"Sorry about that," she said as she started the engine and attempted to clear the fogged-up windscreen with the air-conditioner on high.

"It's okay. You had to bring her up to date about Maxine."

"That, for starters" Kelly agreed, "but there's also the fact that someone was definitely lurking out at the old Hoffmann place. I'm concerned it's the same person that was at Sissi's place."

Kelly didn't add, "Maxine."

She didn't have to.

# CHAPTER TWELVE

**6:00pm Sunday, 18 February 2018**

The few fraught minutes it took to drive to Helen's house elapsed in silence.

Kelly parked; Helen moved to leave but was restrained by Kelly's gentle hand on her shoulder.

"You can't let his words get to you. Whatever happened to Lorraine Sharpe, you had nothing to do with it."

"Too bad you and I are probably the only ones who believe that." Helen forced the door open against the force of the wind and bolted from the vehicle, battling the rain to reach the porch.

*It's going to be just like last time all over again.*

She punched in the access code and unlocked the door without looking back. Kelly, sensing her need to collect herself, came in slightly behind her.

"It will be dark within the next half an hour," Kelly observed, hanging her coat on the hook in the foyer and pulling off her boots. "Will you be okay if the power goes off?"

"Yep," said Helen. "All sorted earlier."

"Good. Don't argue about this: I'm staying."

"It might surprise you," Helen said, wearily - *and God knows I'm surprising myself* - "but I'm not going to argue." She stared out the window. History seemed determined to repeat itself, and that chilled her to the bone, but she forced a smile for Kelly. "You win this time."

Helen removed her boots, placing them next to Kelly's in the foyer. She shivered. The raincoat had done an admirable job, but her socks were soaked through. "I'll be right back," she said, and padded down the hall.

Bypassing her bedroom, she raided her father's bureau for two pairs of his thick work socks. Returning to the kitchen, she caught Kelly's eye and gently lobbed a pair in her direction. "They'll be a bit big, but they're really comfy," she affirmed, smiling, before pulling on her pair.

Kelly switched out her socks in record time. "Oh, that's immensely better", she agreed, before adding with a hopeful look "I wouldn't say no to a cup of coffee if you're making?"

"I do believe I can make that happen," Helen said, with a small smirk. "Give me five minutes."

By the time the cozy fragrance of coffee filled the air, Helen couldn't resist having a cup herself, despite being confident she'd had too much caffeine already. She passed one to Kelly and cradled the other in her fingers.

Kelly leaned a hip against the counter. "So, what

is it that you do up in the big city… you know, when you're not *too busy*?"

Helen laughed. She couldn't help herself. She should have known Kelly wouldn't let the comment go. "Hey, it takes a lot of time to do research for my work!"

"Looking up best axe-murdering techniques on Google? That should get you on a few watch lists," Kelly observed.

Helen snorted. "Oh, I'm sure I'm on more than a few lists now …but you'd be surprised. It's mostly more prosaic than that."

She took a sip of coffee, her gaze turning thoughtful.

"The thing you learn surprisingly quickly is that 'suspension of disbelief' is a really funny thing. For the sake of the story, a reader will extend a free pass to the idea that a demon-possessed axe-wielding clown in combat boots can move around a wood-floored attic silently. But," her eyes widened dramatically "should you be so foolish as to describe the killer's dog in passing as having *dropped* ears when the breed clearly has *folded* ears…"

Shuddering in mock horror, Helen put the cup down and looked her friend firmly in the eyes. "Quiz me about the difference. I *dare* you."

Kelly laughed, holding up her hands in surrender. "Happy to trust you on this one, I think."

Helen chuckled, and Kelly was pleased to note that some of the tension had dropped from her shoulders. "Other than all the research though, it's pretty much standard stuff that fills up everyone's days." Her mouth quirked in a half-smile. "Despite what Dad would have everyone believe; I do *occasionally* make my way outside to catch up with friends. I also have regular lunches with colleagues. And reporters, sometimes – even the occasional blogger. And then there's all the obligatory reading or speaking engagement and the tours." Helen shrugged. "And then I work. *A lot.*" She shot her friend a rueful look. "I should be working now."

Kelly raised an eyebrow. "If 'interrupted by murder' isn't a valid excuse for delay, I can't imagine what it would take," she said dryly.

Helen half-choked on her coffee as a sudden laugh escaped her. "I hadn't thought of it that way."

Kelly sipped her coffee, looking over the raised mug and locking Helen's honey-brown eyes with her own green-flecked hazel. "No boyfriend? Girlfriend? Significant other?"

Kelly realised her voice had been a shade north of casual; Helen, thankfully, hadn't seemed to notice. Instead, Helen circled the edge of the coffee mug with her hands then shook her head. "I go on a date every so often, but nothing serious."

Kelly stared at Helen for a long moment. Helen steeled herself against the shiver of awareness she felt under that gaze. It was too late at this point to blame the cold.

"You're beautiful. You're successful – hell, you're a *celebrity*. How can you not be inundated with people wanting to spend time with you?"

Now Helen really laughed. She extended her hand to shake. "Pleased to meet you: I'm Helen. You might remember me from my hit records, *'just one minute while I finish this chapter'* and *'hang on, I'm in the middle of something'* and everyone's favourite, *'I'm grumpy* because my characters aren't doing what I want them to'. Trust me, I'm not inundated with dinner invitations." She grinned. "At least, not more than once."

"Hard to believe." Kelly said, with an airy hand gesture. "I've always found it rather charming."

She placed her mug on the counter and stared at Helen as if she'd asked a question and was anticipating Helen's answer. Rather than give Kelly the chance, Helen asked her own.

"What about you? You're still single. I suppose you're *too busy* as well."

Kelly grabbed her coffee mug and swallowed a gulp. "I never date the same woman more than a couple of times."

Helen raised her eyebrows. "I'm sure you don't mean that the way it sounds."

Kelly blinked then shook her head. "No, I mean … I had a 'friends with benefits' arrangement go *excruciatingly* sideways." She winced at the memory. "Now I'm more careful to make sure they know where I stand."

"I see." Helen nodded sagely. "So, you *are* inundated with intimate dinner invitations."

Kelly laughed, and quoted Helen: "Not more than once."

Extending her own hand, she said brightly, "Hi Helen, I'm Kelly. *You* might recognise *me* from my chart-topping tunes: *'sorry I have to go, I'm on call'*, *'I'll try not to wake you when I get back from Port Augusta'*, and that perennial golden oldie, *'I know I said we'd go out, but I really need time alone to decompress'*.

"So no, I'm not having to beat romantic prospects away with sticks." Her face became serious. "But even if I were, it wouldn't matter. I never got over the one who got away."

Helen's heart kicked into a faster rhythm, and she had to turn away.

*Does she mean me? Probably not.* She went to the sink and poured out the rest of her coffee. *Surely not. I'd know, wouldn't I?*

"I've had far too much of this already. I'll never sleep tonight."

*I hope I'd know.*

When Helen started to move away from the sink, Kelly stepped in beside her with her own mug. Helen could feel the heat from Kelly's body. The tension between them sparked with new potency. Those hazel eyes rested on Helen with a weight that made it hard to breathe.

Kelly's mobile vibrated.

There was a hitch of hesitation, then Kelly reached for the phone, checked the screen, and stepped away.

Helen managed a too-shallow breath. She closed her eyes and gathered her wits. They had been friends for so long... they'd shared everything until she moved away. Even on her visits to her father, Kelly had always made time to take her for coffee and to sit around talking, catching up.

*This doesn't feel like friendship.*

This felt like far more. As if they'd passed through some invisible barrier that separated the warmth and familiarity they'd always shared, from something hot and fierce...and visceral.

Her father's advice echoed in her mind. *Don't put your heart on hold for work.*

He'd always hoped she'd find someone to spend

her life with. He'd repeatedly encouraged her to look around with open eyes and see the opportunities life had put right in front of her.

As a college student Helen had been alternately amused and irritated by his persistent optimism on the subject. She had serious career plans and those plans did not involve coming back to Andamooka to spend the rest of her life in the Outback. She'd needed to get away from this place. Away from the memories... from the way people had looked at her even long after *that terrible day.*

*He told me to open my eyes to what I had here. I thought he meant I should live in Andamooka.*

*Did he mean Kelly?*

Kelly came back into the kitchen, face clean of whatever might be on her mind. The sound of the electric pump hummed under the sound of the steady rain falling on the roof as she rinsed her mug, filled it with water and drank it down.

Despite her best efforts, Helen watched Kelly's hand, throat and lips as Kelly lowered the mug to the sink next to hers.

Helen blinked to clear her head.

"That phone call... is everything okay?" If there had been another sighting of Maxine, she would like to know.

"All quiet so far. The two constables didn't find anything at the Hoffmann property," Kelly began, rightly guessing Helen's first interest. "I'm expecting a lot more calls over the next few hours; my team is focussing on keeping people safe as the storm sweeps through. There'll be periodic phone calls all the way through." She tapped the pocket where her phone resided. "I'm just hoping we don't get any accidents or people going missing. The locals are pretty savvy and mostly know to stay put and ride out the storm, but there's always one or two too drunk, or too new to the outback…"

A haunted look flicked across Kelly's eyes; gone before Helen could be sure she'd seen it. "Thankfully," Kelly followed-up smoothly, "there are SES volunteers on the job, so we should have enough hands on deck if we need them." She leaned back with a smile. "All of which goes to say: *I don't need to be anywhere in a hurry.* Shall we sort out something to eat, and you can tell me a bit about your latest project?"

"That sounds like a plan," Helen said, glad that the unnerving tension seemed to have seeped away for the moment. "I should point out, you promised you'd bring pizza next time you called in." she teased Kelly, "Fortunately, I have one in the freezer from today's delivery."

Kelly raised an eyebrow. "Well, I did bring the groceries so *technically*….? No?" She chuckled as Helen crossed her arms in implicit rejection. "Oh, well – in that case, let me make it up to you by tackling the very important job of preheating the oven." Kelly ostentatiously fiddled with the dials, making the task look immensely more difficult than it was.

Helen laughed at her antics, feeling a little of the unfamiliar tension slip away.

Leaning together against the countertop while the pizza reheated, Helen told Kelly about her latest project.

"… main problem I'm having isn't the plot itself – I'm actually loving the way the hero from the very first book ends up a villain, and the villain ends up exonerated. It totally makes sense in context, and I've got a whole bunch of Easter eggs scattered through the first couple of novels that suddenly pay off. It should, honestly, be the best book yet.

"My problem is with the journey – how he gets there. It's like, the ideas in my head, and the words on the page just aren't meshing." Helen bit her bottom lip, brow furrowed. "I know how it should work, but it feels like I'm doing info-dumps instead of telling a story." She paused for a sip of wine and noted that Kelly appeared to be enthralled. It was an unexpectedly warm feeling, and Helen felt the tension from earlier rising again.

"Anyway," she finished hurriedly, "I was really hoping to spend a few hours at least every day, just putting words to paper. If I can progress the plot along, I think I can sort out the rough edges and rewrite the dialogue once I'm back in Brissie. I'm even thinking about begging a favour of a friend-of-a-friend who's a psychologist and seeing if she'll run an eye over the key points to see if they gel for her. But enough about me – tell me more about your mum's craft success!"

Helen smiled encouragingly as she poured herself another glass of wine.

Having changed the topic to a neutral third party, Helen felt the atmosphere become less charged as Kelly took over the storytelling. When the pizza was finished, Helen opened the second bottle of wine and they moved into the living room. Kelly sat on the sofa, and Helen nestled into her mother's chair.

"Since I've missed every class reunion, why don't you catch me up on all the gossip? Assuming you're in the loop these days, of course."

"About once a month," Kelly responded in the driest possible tone, "my mother informs me of what every classmate we had is doing." At Helen's confused expression, Kelly elaborated, "It's her way of reminding me that I'm not married and have not provided her with any grandchildren." She rolled her eyes with a small growl of irritation and resignation.

Helen laughed as much from Kelly's expression as from her mother's persistence.

"Anyway," Kelly sighed, "it's safe to say I can bring you up to speed." For the next hour, the conversation meandered companionably around topics of who was married and who had children, who was divorced, and who had moved away.

Helen reflected that it was a little depressing in one sense, but mostly it was funny and real and familiar. Eventually, she laughed and put up her hands in mock surrender.

"Good grief," she said, "social media has nothing on Margaret Wells. She's told you all that?!"

Kelly chuckled. "She's probably told me a lot more; I honestly filter out as much as I can without making it obvious. Seriously, though, Mum should be a gossip columnist."

Then the trip down memory lane really began.

As she sipped her wine, Helen couldn't remember when she'd laughed so much.

Still technically 'on call' for work, Kelly was stuck drinking water. Didn't matter. Helen had consumed enough wine for them both, just listening to Kelly talk. Watching Kelly's lips as she spoke. Relishing the way Kelly's eyes lit up whenever she talked about some of the more memorable times they had shared.

Before Helen knew it, she was the one talking, and Kelly was doing the watching and listening.

That was the moment… the moment Helen saw in Kelly's eyes what she believed deep inside.

There would never be a serious relationship or a special someone for either of them.

Because Kelly was here, and Helen was there, and this bond between them refused to be severed by time or distance.

Instead, it grew stronger and stretched into new territory.

# INTERLUDE

# ABC WEATHER NEWS, KIMBERLEY REGION

BROOME, WESTERN AUSTRALIA

**5:00pm Sunday 18 February 2018**

Ryleigh Stone fumed silently; jaw clenched in spite of the pleasantly neutral expression schooling her face. Beneath the surface, she was beating and clawing at the walls, shrieking in impotent fury.

From the knees up, Ryleigh was dressed immaculately in a stylish teal dress, artfully chosen: the high collar would keep the oldies from writing Letters to the Editor, meanwhile the clinging fabric highlighted every curve for the viewers who still had a pulse.

Beneath the dress, she'd surrendered to practical footwear. There were times when fashion had to take a back seat to pragmatism, and standing in inch-deep mud was definitely one of those times. The camera would keep the heavy Wellington boots – on loan from a local resident – out of the public eye.

She was waiting, seemingly patiently, just outside

the entrance to Broome's historical Hop'n'Broom Brewery. The old brew house had been reimagined as a working microbrewery-cum-tourist attraction paying homage to the historical place of women in the brewing industry. Now, however, the once-stylish signage lay twisted against the wall, dragged back from where it had been carelessly flung by ex-tropical cyclone Kelvin.

*Ex-cyclone*, she thought, sourly. *Drops a bombshell, then fucks off into the sunset. Standard 'Ex' behaviour.*

In every direction, the view was much the same: palm fronds and huge tropical leaves ripped from trees to form a mosaic layer on the flooded streets; metalwork fences warped and crumpled; mango trees uprooted and tossed into backyard swimming pools. Sheets of roofing iron had been hurled through the air like blades. Vehicles lay askew in the street, pushed by water and wind out of their parking bays. Cars were pinned beneath trees toppled by the gale.

*Good god, what a mess*, Ryleigh thought, looking around.

Workers were doing everything possible to clear the roads and restore power. Guests from nearby hotels were gathered at the Hop'n'Broom where a generator was powering the twinkling lights and refrigerators. In typical resilient Aussie style, a local DJ was cranking out high-energy tunes to raise the spirits of exhausted volunteers.

*Probably not the most sensible use for that generator, but it's definitely helping keep people moving,* she thought. *And volunteers working in the background makes it more relatable. Increases the 'human interest' angle.*

Ryleigh didn't mind having an audience. She'd

had a change of clothes and freshened her makeup since her last broadcast. She was good to go. She just wished they'd sort out the cameras already, so she could go back to her hotel room and maybe scream into a pillow for a while.

Two topics warred for priority on her rage scale, and both of them had to do with *Kelly Bloody Wells*.

It was one thing that the relationship with Kelly hadn't worked out: Ryleigh had made her peace with that. She had moved on. She'd even been feeling optimistic about the future, overall.

And she might still be feeling that way, if not for two tiny, itty-bitty things.

The first had arisen – some would say 'inevitably' – from the fact that she was currently stuck in a share accommodation situation rather than in her own space. Following her unexpected job opportunity, Ryleigh had been more than happy to flee the scene of her failed relationship with Kelly and move interstate. Her sister, Tiffany, lived close enough and offered to let her move in. Ryleigh's job kept her on the road fairly often, so she really just needed a base of operations more than a residence.

And it had been fine, for the most part, sharing a space with her sister and her sister's pointless fiancé, Fernando …a man so utterly mediocre in every discernible way that Ryleigh had internally renamed him 'Blando'.

Obviously, living with Tiff and Blando wasn't *exactly* how she'd hoped her life would pan out, but Ryleigh had taken the opportunity to save some money and get her feet under her again. It had even been a bonding opportunity in many ways, and the two sisters had finally buried the hatchet over Tiffany's predatory hunting of Ryleigh's boyfriends back in high school and university.

*The past is the past*, Ryleigh had thought, *and Tiff's stepped up for me now, when I need her*.

However, the last few days had seen that illusion of familial bliss shattered like a rotten egg thrown at a windscreen. And it hadn't come from any of the provocations she'd anticipated.

Astonishingly, it wasn't Tiff's self-absorption, astonishing ego, and penchant for dealing out backhanded compliments.

It wasn't Tiff's continual insistence that her own job – modelling *pearls*, for goodness' sake – was not only more glamorous than her sister's (unfortunately arguable in present circumstances, given Ryleigh's current *haute couture* ensemble included borrowed boots ankle-deep in slurry) but – *but!* - that her job was also much more *important* as well.

Ryleigh turned her head with studied casualness, expression pleasant, tiny smile in place on her mouth. Only her normally deep chestnut eyes, currently throwing to amber as her pupils narrowed with sparkling rage, gave any hint of the towering rage within.

It

Wasn't

Even

The fact

that the only reason Tiff had such a blindingly fatuous 'career' in the first place was because Blando was financing her from whatever dreary thing it was he did in banking, rather than any hard-won effort or actual talent on her part.

No. Ryleigh had predicted all that. Had built her walls high and hard against it all.

*Reflect and deflect, let none of it stick.*

She was so confident in her ability to wave away Tiff's usual barbs and arrows that she was caught completely off-guard when her sister abruptly launched the conversational equivalent of a WMD during the worst of the cyclone.

Tiff's *'liaison'* with Kelly.

The lobbing of that news had rocked Blando nearly as much as Ryleigh.

Even so, Ryleigh had been prepared to talk to Kelly and ascertain the truth of the matter first. Tiff wasn't above stirring the pot for the sheet drama of it, and she was far from a reliable narrator. And so Ryleigh had, once the shock wore off, approached the situation very reasonably, she thought: a simple request to Kelly for confirmation – or denial - of the allegation.

A torrent of unanswered texts and calls later, and Ryleigh wasn't feeling *reasonable* anymore.

Eventually, since Kelly hadn't returned the calls to her mobile, Ryleigh had rung the Roxby police station. Kelly was out, so she'd spoken briefly with Morgan Fowler, one of the young constables.

In the space of perhaps forty seconds of conversation from Morgan, Ryleigh had been made aware that: Kelly had just left the office headed for the Hamilton house; Helen Hamilton was in town and might be a future murder victim; and there'd been a homicide in Andamooka.

In that order.

*It's quite a lot to unpack, really.*

The thought charitably crossed her mind that she should probably let Kelly know that her young constable was a bit of a gossip.

*But then again, I wouldn't have heard anything otherwise, so hmm.. yeah nah.*

Ryleigh, of course, knew of Helen Hamilton, though she'd never met the woman. She'd heard, from more than one person who knew the two, that there were suspicions of something more than friendship between them.

*So... are we protecting a potential victim, there, Kelly? Or cozying up with an old flame?*

Oh, well, Kelly had made it abundantly clear she wasn't interested in a relationship.

*And screw you, Tiff, she didn't want you for more than a night either.*

It wasn't much comfort, but there was a certain bitter satisfaction in the thought.

Despite feeling like she'd been punched in the gut, Ryleigh was willing herself to let the whole thing go. It had taken quite a bit of therapy and a lot of self-help books, but she hadn't dragged herself out of that depression just to let her sister pull her back down again.

*You can't change the past, all you can do is choose how you want to learn from it in the future. I misread the relationship; that was on me... although Kelly sure as hell never tried to clarify... and if her standards are low enough to sleep with my sister –* an uncontrollable snarl flicked across her face; instinctively she disguised the reaction by brushing her hand in front of her face as though a fly had startled her - *then I'm lucky to be rid of her.*

Look forward, not back. Deep breaths. Ignore the knife twisting away in your gut.

*But a murder happens right smack dab in your bloody town, Kelly, and you can't even be arsed to send a text?! It was fine for me to get shoved to the side every time **your** work came first, but heaven forbid you give a flying fuck about helping **my** career. I could have been reporting on a **murder** instead of this stupid fucking storm if you'd spared 30 fucking seconds to give me a heads up…*

Breathe. Smile. The storm is national news.

*Head in the game, come on. I'm getting major face time across the country for this. Reporting on some dead old biddy from some pissy little outback town – probably drunken domestic violence, whothefuck knows… it wouldn't have done as much for my career as Kelvin.*

Be grateful for what you've got. Work with what you have.

*But Kelly could have at least told me about it. She owed me that fucking much.*

"And we're live in," her camera operator announced, "three, two, one."

Ryleigh sparkled to life like a fairy tale.

"Kelvin has certainly lived up to his promise, friends," she said, gesturing behind her at the devastated streets.

*Tilt the head a little: concern, care; flash the smile; bring you all closer…come and see.*

"Two days ago, the Department of Fire and Emergency Services warned of the possible threat to lives and homes as Severe Tropical Cyclone Kelvin approached Broome.

"People were warned to remain inside and shelter in

the strongest part of their homes or at the evacuation centre, away from doors and windows, and to keep emergency kits with them. We braced for the worst.

"Then the cyclone crossed the coast near Anna Plains Station, along Eighty Mile Beach with sustained winds of one hundred and fifty kilometres per hour. The damage has been devastating. As you can see behind me, significant property damage has occurred in Broome.

"Luckily, no loss of life has been reported."

*Except in Andamooka.*

Focus.

*Smile of relief for lives saved; pause one beat. Widen eyes.*

"Severe Tropical Cyclone Kelvin delivered a record annual rainfall total of 1506.0 mm – yes, that's more than a metre and a half of rain - despite being less than two months into the calendar year. There are reports the Great Northern Highway has suffered infrastructure damage due to the heavy rainfall and flooding."

*Lean towards camera. Earnest intent. Hear me. **See me.***

"This means the Kimberley and Pilbara regions are now cut off from the rest of Australia by road. Please - do not attempt the roads, and do not risk the flood waters."

Ryleigh pressed her hand to her chest.

*Gravitas. Sincerity. A plea for others.*

"I urge you to stay tuned for further updates. This is Ryleigh Stone in Broome. Back to you in the studio, Gabrielle."

***Fucking nailed it.***

Hopefully the studio executives were paying attention.

*Now, why won't Kelly return my calls?*

# PART 2

# CHAPTER THIRTEEN

## ABSALOM LANE, ANDAMOOKA, SOUTH AUSTRALIA

**11.30pm Sunday, 18 February 2018**

Kelly leaned up and forward, throwing aside the soft blanket, and listened. Rain fell heavily on the corrugated iron roof. The old house creaked and groaned beneath the lash of the windstorm.

She checked her mobile, ignoring Ryleigh's stream of missed calls and text messages.

*No problems the team haven't handled. Excellent. Hopefully a good sign.*

She checked the time: nearly midnight. The weather report had indicated that the worst would be over by noon tomorrow, but for now the howling storm continued unabated. The house complained with another uneasy groan.

Kelly rubbed the back of her neck and listened to the cry of the wind. The sheer force of the wind and rain would be playing havoc right across the region. Serious damage was on the cards... hopefully it would be limited to property, not people. Although even then, there were those who couldn't afford insurance. A storm like this could ruin them.

*But **things** can be replaced; **people** can't.*

Kelly stood, stretching, feeling nearly as creaky as the house. She was surprised she'd managed nearly two hours of uneasy sleep cramped up on the couch.

Helen had decided to call it a night early. She'd gone to her room by nine, which had come as somewhat of a relief to Kelly. She'd been on the verge of confessing the renewed feelings churning inside her.

*Am I crazy? It seemed like maybe Helen felt the same.*

Kelly shook her head, ran her hands through her short hair. Exhaled on a sigh.

She searched for news about Helen on the internet far more often than was healthy, and one thing was clear: they'd grown up as equals, but they were far from equal now. Kelly was a regional copper, and Helen – well, Helen was famous. An exciting international life, legions of adoring fans.

*Do I even have anything to offer?*

Squaring her jaw, Kelly put the thought from her head and turned her attention to the text messages and phone calls that Ryleigh had fired off from Broome, scrolling backwards as she went.

*I'm in the middle of a murder **and** a major destructive storm event, and you're sniffing around for a story. Typical Ry.*

The thought was mixed irritation and affection. Despite the way their relationship had ended, Kelly maintained fondness for Ryleigh. She was nakedly ambitious, but beneath that smoothly polished façade she was complicated in interesting ways. It was just a pity Kelly hadn't been smart enough to keep things on a purely platonic level, like with Chazz.

*Uh-oh.*

She was getting towards the earlier texts now. And it looked like Ryleigh had just found out about Kelly sleeping with her sister. There was only one possible source for that information.

*Jesus, Tiffany, you really are a twisted, evil bitch.*

It was because of Ryleigh and Tiffany that Kelly had learned extreme caution in her dating life.

She'd genuinely thought that Ryleigh understood they were 'friends with benefits' – but in retrospect, it was obvious to Kelly how the time they'd spent together had been superficial on her side but seemed far more meaningful for Ryleigh.

*But then, hindsight is always 20/20,* she thought darkly.

Kelly's days were full-on with work and commitments - constantly busy, surrounded by people. Ryleigh, though, had been studying full-time at home through Universities Online. In her limited spare time, she developed, edited, and pitched local interest pieces to the networks. She was fully focused and determined to do whatever it took to break her into television news.

From Kelly's perspective, time spent with Ryleigh was a fun way to relax at the end of an evening - but for Ryleigh, things were very different. Kelly was Ryleigh's only direct social and emotional contact for days or even weeks at a time.

They were experiencing the same relationship through very different lenses.

But even in a 'friends with benefits' arrangement,

there would have been nothing that could have compelled Kelly to knowingly sleep with Ryleigh's sister. The idea repelled her on every level

Kelly still felt self-revulsion when she thought back on that time.

People in the outback tended to be more conservative. It was hard enough being a woman in community policing, and harder still since her sexuality had become grist for the rumour mill. Judging eyes constantly assessed her: was she being *too friendly* with another woman? Was there something illicit going on? Even if she'd wanted a serious relationship – and she very much hadn't – few women would find life lived under a microscope to be a fair trade-off for Kelly's affections.

Even without the constant scrutiny, dating anyone from within the tight-knit community came with inherent capacity for widespread blowback if the relationship failed. Not just an angry ex to deal with: their whole family - and possibly entire sections of the community - could get involved. There was no way Kelly was risking that kind of social and career suicide for anything short of true love.

Kelly had met Tiffany outside the police station as she was finishing up her shift. Much later, of course, it was obvious it had been a set-up. She had no idea who, or what, Tiffany was - but Tiffany must have known all about her.

She'd said she was visiting. A tourist. Long blonde hair, crystal blue eyes. Movie-star elegance in every move. Just a stranger, passing through.

Perhaps Kelly could suggest some things to see... some things to do?

Kelly couldn't repress a shudder. She'd been used, and too stupid or blind to see it.

*Or too arrogant,* she thought, not for the first time. *Too sure of myself.*

A police officer conned by one of the oldest and simplest tricks in the book.

The moment when Kelly had finally understood the whole twisted situation, she had instinctively revolted, bringing the whole relationship with Ryleigh crashing down.

*I screwed up how I did that, too,* she thought with a wince.

For Ryleigh, the death of the relationship she'd believed she was in had come as a bolt out of the blue. And Kelly had been too ashamed to give her the whole story. She'd stuck to the truth – that she'd never seen Ryleigh that way, that the relationship had no future - but it hadn't been *all* of the truth.

Not by a long shot.

She still wasn't sure if omitting the full story had been cowardice on her part, or whether it was the desire to minimise harm to Ryleigh, who'd been made a victim twice-over without knowing.

*A bit of both, perhaps.*

*She'll be furious now. And hurt. Resentful. And she has every right. I cut the legs out from under her, and it wasn't her fault.*

*I screwed up. I couldn't have spent another day with her, not once I knew how she really felt about me. Not knowing what I'd done.*

*But I handled it awfully.*

And now the cat was out of the bag. She'd have to ring Ryleigh back at some point, but that kind of discussion warranted more than a basic text or a couple of minutes jammed in while her attention was diverted by current events. She owed her a proper conversation, and the chance to vent.

She owed her honesty.

Having resolved to call Ryleigh on her next day off, Kelly rolled her shoulders, re-tucked her shirt, and switched on her torch.

The house that Robert Hamilton had built by hand was a bit of a maze, with rock steps cemented in place at varying levels to accommodate the sloping site. Helen might be able to navigate the home in the dark, but for Kelly the darkness turned the variable-height stairs into an obstacle course.

Padding carefully in her socks, she quietly headed away from the main living area, towards the newer section of the house. The bathroom was simple: just a shower – baths being an expensive luxury in the outback – a single handbasin, and modern, plumbed toilet.

Washing her hands over the basin, Kelly reflected on the home that craftmanship and determination had built.

At its core, the house was basic. It was practical. Built-on year after year, expanding to fit the family, the house was eccentric in many ways, though extremely functional for all of that. Some of the stones in the wall were impressively large, their retrieval from the ancient riverbeds a testament to Robert Hamilton's grit and imagination.

Ruth, Helen's mother, had softened the hard edges of the rock walls with her watercolours depicting local wildflowers. Here in the bathroom, the theme was a medley of white and yellow poached egg daisies peeping through red and black Sturt Desert Peas. Set behind glass in natural wood frames, the paintings glowed against the rock in the torchlight.

She found herself staring at the rocks, their shapes and grains distorted by light and shadows. In the low light it was easy to imagine Ruth's drawings as a kind of cave painting, capturing the things that were important to her life upon the walls. Recording them there for her children, and her children's children.

The house wasn't a glorious construct, but looking at it through the eyes of an adult – *Bob would have been younger than me when he started this project*, she realised with a start - she was filled with respect for the character it took to build this home: stone by stone, day by day, relentlessly pushing back in the face of the unforgiving desert.

Looking at her reflection, Kelly noticed a dirt smudge near her hairline and splashed a little water on her face to clean it, rubbing the excess through her hair to dry her hands before padding back out to the hall.

This section of the house had additional roof insulation and was noticeably quieter in the storm. Having become used to the loud creaks, snaps and groans in the lounge room, the comparative quiet was almost a little eerie in the low torchlight.

From a security perspective, the number of external doors bothered her. She quietly checked each one carefully on her way back to the kitchen. All locked, as expected, but she couldn't lose the sense of unease that she had overlooked something important.

Back in the kitchen, Kelly switched off her torch

and turned on the overhead light.

*A fresh cup of coffee wouldn't go astray*, she thought, helping herself to Helen's supply.

As the brew process got underway, she walked to the other end of the kitchen, looking out to the carport. Nothing moving. The lonely spotlight above the Emergency Services Station was barely visible through the rain, but the fact it could be seen at all suggested the storm had died down a little.

Or perhaps she was just being hopeful.

Kelly hadn't heard a peep from Helen's room. With any luck she was still asleep, but the total lack of any sound was disconcerting: Helen had a tendency to snore and was a fidgety, restless sleeper - as Kelly knew all too well, from the many sleepovers they'd had over the years growing up.

*Maybe I should check?*

As soundlessly as possible, Kelly padded along the cement floors again. Maxine's room was up a couple of stone steps, and then Helen's room was further along on the right.

Before Kelly could analyse her actions, she opened Maxine's door and switched on the light, blinking to adjust her eyes.

Everything looked the same as it had when nineteen-year-old Maxine Hamilton lived here. Celebrity athletic posters on the wall. Headphones still lying on the bed. Trophies on the shelf above the bed reminded Kelly that Maxine had been a talented athlete all through high school.

Kelly frowned, surveyed the trophies again. There was a gap.

*Where's that cricket bat Maxine used in her final season?*

The coach had it engraved with the year and the score and mounted it on a plaque. The plaque was there, but no cricket bat.

Kelly made a mental note to ask Helen if she'd noticed anything missing. She turned off the light and moved on to Helen's room, quietly opening the door.

Kelly knew the space beyond that door as well as her own room at home.

As the door creaked open, despite Kelly's best efforts at silence, Helen made a sound - not quite a squeal, but something of that order. There was a sound of shuffling movement and the side lamp switched on, revealing that Helen had scrambled further up the bed, away from the door.

"Oh, god, I'm sorry! I didn't mean to wake you!" Kelly burst out, cursing her bad judgment. "I woke up and your room was really quiet. I was just checking-in to see that you were okay."

Helen had relaxed as soon as it became obvious the shape in the doorway wasn't a potential murderer.

"You didn't wake me...that was probably the rain. I've been half-dozing for a while, thinking about Maxine. Then I thought I smelled coffee, which got me thinking about whether I wanted one enough to get up or not."

As Helen spoke, Kelly's gaze drifted to her lips then dropped down to the nightshirt she wore. Helen had never been the pyjama or nightgown type. Nothing frilly. Just a big old comfy t-shirt. Nothing fancy.

Helen swung her bare legs over the side of her bed and stood, breasts swaying gently as she rubbed her eyes and stretched. Kelly blinked, jerked her attention upward.

"Is everything okay?" Helen asked, stepping over to the door and peering outwards.

"Yeah." Kelly rasped, her mouth suddenly dry. "Everything's good." *Everything except my ability to keep my head on straight.* "I've got the coffee machine warmed up."

"Well, that settles it. Come on, I'll join you."

Helen turned back to her bed. A moment of confusion kept Kelly from moving, as her mental gears spun without engaging.

*Join me... in bed?*

Helen retrieved a robe from the foot of the bed, pulling it on as she headed back to the doorway. Woodenly, Kelly walked back to the door and followed her friend.

*Kitchen.*

*Coffee.*

*Yes.*

Kelly cleared her throat as she scrambled for a neutral topic. "Do you ever wake up in the middle of the night with an idea for one of your stories?"

Helen yawned hugely before nodding. "Way too often. I get an idea and can't sleep until I get it down. It used to wreak havoc with my day job. It's a good thing I get to write on my own schedule now."

Kelly followed Helen to the kitchen. Her fingers itched to reach out and touch Helen's tousled hair. All day it had been in a loose braid; now it fell around her shoulders, flowing down her back in waves that made Kelly think of caramel and treacle. Silky, glossy...tempting.

*Jesus, woman, you're in your thirties, not some hormonal*

*teen. Get it together,* she admonished herself.

In the kitchen Helen poured the coffee, unconsciously making a happy humming sound as she did so. Kelly's heart did a tiny flip.

Noticing Helen's eyes turning towards the scene outside, she asked the obvious question: "Are you concerned Maxine is going to show up?"

Helen cradled her coffee mug in both hands, brow furrowing as she considered Kelly's question.

"Honestly...no. Not so much that. Mostly I'm worried I've been wrong about her all this time." Helen's eyes were troubled. "Kels, I've never doubted she was innocent. Not until now."

The possibility had crossed Kelly's mind more than once since this morning.

"It's possible we'll never know for sure," she replied gently.

"But what if she was the one who... what if Mum..."

"Let's not go there right now," Kelly said, holding up a hand. "One crisis at a time, hey?"

Helen huffed a humourless laugh and nodded, taking another sip of coffee.

Thinking of the missing cricket bat, Kelly changed the subject. "Have you noticed anything missing in the house?"

Helen shook her head, then stopped mid shake.

"Actually, yes. Mum's opals," she said, looking around thoughtfully. "I'm sure they're around here somewhere, but I haven't found them yet."

She set her cup down on the counter, the action like a punctuation mark. Her eyes met Kelly's and there was raw pain in them.

"Kels, I can't stop thinking about the way Mr

Sharpe looked at me. That absolute *hatred*. Those things he said." She flinched, remembering. "He's known me my whole life. How can he believe, even for a second…?"

Kelly put her arm around Helen's shoulders in a quick half-hug.

"He doesn't; not really. He just lost his wife. He's not thinking clearly. He's looking for anything to make sense of the situation." She met Helen's eyes with assurance. "Trust me. It happens, even when it's natural causes. Some people turn inwards, others lash out. But it's not really aimed at you, it's aimed at death for taking their loved one from them."

"I understand that on a logical level, but part of me feels like I deserve it." Helen had raised the cup to her lips, but put it down again without drinking, her gaze far away. "Maybe because deep down I know Maxine may have been involved."

Kelly wished she could find the right words to comfort Helen, but there were none that would ease the painful possibility that her sister might be a murderer. She hoped what she was about to ask wouldn't make matters worse.

"Did you or your father remove or change anything in…" Kelly's mobile vibrated before she could finish the question. "One sec," she said, holding up a finger as she pulled the mobile from its holster. Liney's name and image flashed on the screen.

*Detective calling instead of constable. This can't be good.*

"What's happened?" she asked, rather than her usual greeting.

There was the tiniest of pauses as the Detective Brevet Sergeant weighed her response. "Nothing,

I hope," Liney replied slowly, "but Bronwyn King didn't make her last check-in. I've called her three times on her radio and twice on the mobile. She's not answering. I thought about sending someone out to follow up, but with the dangerous conditions it'd take some serious time to get there."

"You're right." Dread congealed in Kelly's gut. "I can get over there a whole lot faster."

"Call me when you reach the shack," Liney said, "and stay on the line. If anything has happened to the old man or Bronwyn, I need you to stay safe."

As Kelly opened her mouth to reply, Liney added heavily, "It's bad out there, Kelly, really bad. We've been lucky so far that people are staying in, but that could change anytime and it's going to be chaos when it does. The roads are incredibly dangerous right now."

Liney wasn't telling Kelly anything she didn't know. The white sandy clay called 'kopi', discarded by opal miners, was widely used as cheap fill for road building despite being notoriously slippery and boggy when wet.

What concerned her more was what Liney didn't say. Kelly recognised the careful tone of a manager who doesn't want to alarm any subordinates within earshot.

"Heading out straight away, Liney. Call you when I get there."

Kelly ended the call and slid her mobile back into her pocket. "I have to go to Treloar Road and check on things. Bronwyn isn't picking up her mobile or radio. I need to make sure she and Mr Sharpe are okay."

The slight catch in Helen's breath warned Kelly

that Helen feared the worst.

Helen banged her mug on the counter. "Give me two minutes, I'll go with you."

"You can't come this time." When Helen would have argued, Kelly held up her hand, her expression grave. "I don't have time to debate this. I need you to do exactly what I say."

"All right." Helen pulled the lapels of the robe closer to her throat. "Tell me what you want me to do."

"I need you to get dressed. Shoes, jacket, the works. Then I need you to sit here in the kitchen, keep the doors locked, and wait." She took a deep breath. "Helen, if anything happens and you need to leave in a hurry, I want you ready with everything on you. Wallet, keys, phone. Because if you need to go, you can't come back. For anything. Not until it's safe." Her gaze was piercing. "Do you understand?"

Helen shivered, clearly understanding Kelly's intent. "I do." She nodded sharply, then sprinted for the bedroom. Kelly pulled on her boots, then the utility belt. By the time her coat was on and zipped to her throat, Helen was back in the kitchen, boots on and coat in hand. With uncharacteristic obedience, she settled in her mother's chair; raincoat on one side, and the barbeque fork on the other.

"Where's your phone?"

Helen tugged it from her pocket and put it in front of her. "Fully charged. I have my wallet and keys, too."

"Good." Kelly reached for her hat, put it on her head and resisted the impulse to go to Helen. She'd only do something she might regret, like pull her into a hug and kiss her.

"Lock the door behind me," she said, stepping out into the night.

"Kelly."

Kelly looked back at Helen, who stood rigidly by the door.

"Be careful. When this is over, we have things to talk about."

Kelly nodded, tightness in her throat. "You do the same."

Kelly strode away without looking back, shoulders braced against the wind and rain. Yanking open the door, she pulled herself into the Landcruiser.

Helen, watching from the kitchen window, raised a hand in a half-wave, knowing it wouldn't be seen but needing the gesture.

Headlights madly refracting off the curtain of raindrops, the Landcruiser carefully negotiated the driveway exit and headed out towards the shack on Treloar Road.

Helen watched until the storm swallowed it from view.

# CHAPTER FOURTEEN

TRELOAR ROAD, ANDAMOOKA, SOUTH AUSTRALIA

**12:15 am Monday, 19 February 2018**

Kelly cautiously travelled from Christmas Hill Road, left into Dunstan Road, and left again into Treloar Road. It was nearly impossible to see where the roadside ended and the flooding erosion gullies began, and she cautiously hugged the approximate centre of the road as best she could.

She almost missed the turn into the shack's driveway.

The spotlights were next to useless in the heavy rain, and headlights couldn't penetrate the mullock heaps and gullies, but she could see enough to know that if there was trouble, it hadn't driven in: any vehicle would leave deep ruts in the cloggy ground.

As Kelly pulled closer to the gravelled clearing where the shack stood, Constable King's assigned Holden Commodore sedan came into view. The motor was running, headlights on.

The sense of unease that had plagued Kelly since waking ratcheted up to high alert: the driver's side door had been left open, rain pelting in.

She turned off the engine of her Landcruiser and powered down the window to listen. Rain. Motor running.

Nothing else.

Kelly shoved her flashlight into her utility belt, eased out of the vehicle, left the door ajar rather than risk the noise of closing it. She switched on the torch and began the march through the mud. Listening intently, scanning the area left to right, right to left, over and over as she slowly moved forward.

She saw the blood before she saw the body laying between the cabin and the car.

*Oh no. No no no.*

Kelly moved closer, crouched down next to the form that had been her friend and colleague. Fury and loss tore through Kelly. Bronwyn King's unseeing eyes stared into the storm. Blood filled the front of her uniform; a crimson stream flowed with the rain onto the ground.

Kelly rose to her full height and turned all the way around, watching for movement, listening for sound.

She no longer felt the rain. The cold. No longer cared as the wind whipped the rain into blades around her, stinging her eyes. All she felt was powerful rage wrapped around a core of emptiness, and a driving need to avenge Bronwyn's senseless death.

Had the assailant appeared in that moment, Kelly might have killed them where they stood. But no one appeared in her line of sight. Rain continued to fall heavily.

Kelly started forward again, moving toward the porch. Treading as stealthily as possible across boggy ground, she eased up the porch and headed to the door.

It was ajar.

The last ounce of hope fled her with the bitter taste of bile.

With Bronwyn dead, the likelihood that Ray Sharpe was still alive was little to none.

*Bronwyn would never open the door without checking first. What was it that drew her outside?*

Kelly pushed the door inward. Shadows pressed in from all sides, smothering the room. Smoothing her hand over the switch did not bring results.

*Power's off...would that have drawn her out? No, she wouldn't leave a potential victim behind to check the fuse box. If anything, the power going out would raise her guard, not lower it.*

There was no sound inside other than the pounding rain on the roof.

Kelly entered the house and closed the door to prevent anyone coming in behind her.

Or escaping.

Torch extended; she cast its beam around the room with one hand while calling Liney on her phone with the other.

"Bronwyn King is dead." Kelly didn't waste time with salutations. Her voice was huskier than usual, but still clear. Her mind was spinning too fast for the emotions flooding her body to keep up. "The shack's unlocked and open. Power's out; may have been cut. I'll check once I'm done in here."

If Sharpe was also dead, as Kelly suspected, it was

far too easy to predict the next victim. She gritted her teeth. *I should never have left Helen alone.*

"Backup is on the way," Liney confirmed. "I'll get formal notifications started."

"Send the first car to the Hamilton house for Helen. She's alone."

For a second, Kelly thought Liney was about to argue, but after a brief pause her clipped voice said, "Okay". A quick conversation followed in the background via police radio, before Liney returned to the phone call with confirmation: "Done."

Moving slowly and methodically through the house, Kelly woodenly responded to Liney's questions in between her own commentary as she checked the small shack.

Living room and kitchen windows. *None broken, none ajar.*

Muddy clay clumps plopped from Kelly's boots like so much wet confetti. It was easy to see where she had checked each window just by following her clay trail. But hers were the only footprints to be seen. There were no other signs anyone had entered the house.

Back door: locked. *Whoever came in, had to be by the front door. Where are the footprints?*

And where the hell was Ray Sharpe... or his body?

Kelly checked the coat closet and bathroom, then each of the two bedrooms, methodically clearing room to room.

Finally, Kelly said, "Ray Sharpe is gone. No evidence of a struggle."

The reality that the killer had stayed around after murdering Lorraine Sharpe confirmed that the killer knew the Sharpe family and had one or more reasons to want them dead.

The only person Kelly knew with that kind of motive was Maxine Hamilton.

*Damn it.*

She took a deep breath and straightened her shoulders. "I want an urgent alert out for Maxine Hamilton. If she's here, I want to find her." The alert on Maxine's car had garnered no results.

"Will do." Pause. "Kelly, watch your back."

"Doing my best," she said in lieu of farewell.

*Fuck this. Fuck all of this.*

Kelly cancelled the call as she moved cautiously back along the hall, heart thundering. As she reached the living room doorway, she scrolled down for Helen's number.

*I need to warn her.*

The blow that slammed into the back of Kelly's head sent her hurtling forward, her mobile flying from her hand and across the floor. Her fingers instinctively tightened on the butt of the torch. Pain reverberated through her skull as she attempted to scramble to her feet.

Before she could steady herself, another blow landed. Pinpricks of light flashed in her field of vision.

She slumped face down on the hardwood floor.

As her vision receded, she could see the blurred outline of boots coming into view, but she couldn't move... couldn't raise her head or turn her eyes to look upward.

A cricket bat thumped to the floor next to Kelly's head.

Kelly tried to speak, but the darkness overtook her

before her lips could form the words.

# CHAPTER FIFTEEN

## ABSALOM LANE, ANDAMOOKA, SOUTH AUSTRALIA

**1.40am Monday, 19 February 2018**

Helen checked the time again. Her nerves were jumping. Surely Kelly had made it to the Sharpe's place by now. She'd been gone more than an hour. If everything was okay, why hadn't she heard anything? The delay could only mean trouble.

She looked around the room. The rain continued to hammer on the roof. It was a deafening reminder of the passing of time. She had to do something.

Stand.

Pace.

Check her inventory again. *Jeans: phone, keys, wallet. Jacket: water bottle, muesli bar, gloves. Boots: securely laced.*

Sit.

Repeat.

Pushing to her feet, barbeque fork in hand, she took a breath and looked outside. The rain flew at the window, plastering itself to the glass so intensely she could barely see. The moon and stars were blocked by the thick, swirling cloud cover.

She checked the locks again even though she vividly recalled setting them when Kelly left.

Worry and frustration rising, she walked back to the kitchen. Checked the lock on the back door, then peered out the glass portion of the door. The small Hyundai she'd rented in Adelaide was barely visible under the carport.

Staring out at the darkness, Helen thought about the tension that had simmered between them tonight. Admittedly, there had been moments when they were younger, and even occasionally when she visited, where she felt an unexpected spark or flash of warmth... a tug of *more than friends*. But nothing on this level. This attraction was undeniable. Impossible to label as anything else. The pull was deep, strong.

Was it because they'd both turned thirty-five this year? Most of the others from their childhood had families, or at least had been married.

*Is it just biology? Hormones telling me that time's running out to start a family?*

She'd never really believed in that sort of thing. Sure, she quite enjoyed kids, but she hadn't put a lot of thought into having one of her own.

*My books keep me up at all hours and steal all my attention. I'd be a terrible mother.*

She shook off a sudden mental image of her child on fire while she sat nearby, absorbed in her computer screen. *Not now, honey, mummy's writing.*

Yep, terrible mother material.

Helen leaned her head against the window. The

cold coming through the pane reminded her to snap out of it. Staying vigilant was essential. No drifting off in thought.

Rather than continue waiting for Kelly to call her, she tucked the barbeque fork under her arm and called Kelly. Kelly kept her mobile on silent, so she wasn't going to interrupt anything or give away her position if...

Not going there.

Four rings and the call went to voicemail.

Helen swore and poked at the screen to end the call.

What was the number for police attendance calls in South Australia? One three one... triple something. No point wasting time. She couldn't remember. She navigated to the internet and entered the information to find the number.

Her heart thumped harder and harder. Something was wrong. Kelly would have returned her call by now if she could.

Helen thought about her rental car. Too small. Although the front wheel drive could be good in slippery conditions, it wasn't made for the volume of water or the depth of mud on these unsealed roads. The possibility of ending up in a gully or getting bogged just getting out of the driveway was far more likely.

Dialling the number, Helen tried to tell herself she was worrying for no reason.

*You do this kind of stress fake-out to characters all the time.*

She should be accustomed to the tension.

But this was real.

"South Australia Police."

Relief trickled through Helen at hearing the official voice. "This is Helen Hamilton. I'm in Andamooka…"

"Hold on, please."

The line went on hold and Helen snapped her mouth shut.

*Well, hell.*

Helen paced the floor. No doubt emergency calls related to the storm were coming in and she would, of course, have to wait behind those. This wasn't an emergency… she hoped.

Worry gnawed at her. What was taking so long? She looked at the screen to ensure the call was still connected. Any sense of calm she'd felt when the call was answered vanished, her pulse accelerating with each passing second.

Hanging up and calling again wouldn't help unless she went the triple zero emergency route this time. Tying up that line was not appropriate… yet.

*Calm down. Breathe. Think.*

She closed her eyes and told her heart to slow its pounding.

If her father were here, he would tell her there was nothing to worry about until the trouble was in front of her. He always said, "Don't borrow trouble, it'll come along in its own time."

*I need you, Dad.*

She wished she had a number for Maxine. Maybe if she called, Maxine would answer. She was sure that if she could only hear her sister's voice, she would know. No matter that four years separated them in age, she and Maxine had always been close.

*A killer wouldn't have protected and saved me the way Maxie did when we were kids. She could never hurt me.*

The memory of speaking in public on that very subject nudged her. Helen had told audiences at more than one of her readings that the villain could never be all bad: he or she must possess at least one relatable or redeeming quality if the character was going to touch the reader in a similar manner as the protagonist.

*That's the kind of thinking that will get you dead. Real-life killers don't have to be consistent. They don't necessarily have weaknesses you can exploit.*

*More importantly, they don't see themselves as the villains; they think they're the protagonist.*

A tap at the door jerked her attention back to the present, and Helen rushed to the window. The sight of the SAPOL hi-vis coat had relief soaring through her. But it was Kelly's distinctive hat that had her setting the barbeque fork aside and reaching for the door, just as the dispatch office reconnected.

"Ms Hamilton, I need you to…" the dispatcher's voice echoed in her ear.

"Never mind," she blurted, hanging up and tucking the phone into her pocket as she unlocked the door and yanked it open.

"At last! I was getting worried."

Kelly raised her head, the wide brim of her hat coming up to reveal her face.

Not Kelly.

*Maxine.*

Helen reached for the barbeque fork. Her sister grabbed it first.

Helen drew back two steps. "Where's Kelly?"

The fact that Maxine had on Kelly's hat and coat tore at her heart. As Maxine stepped inside, she saw the Police Landcruiser idling outside. Kelly's vehicle.

Fury blasted away the softer emotions. "What did you do, Maxine?"

Maxine slammed the door behind her, held the barbeque fork in her hands but didn't point it at Helen. "I came to save you."

Defeat sank inside Helen. "What's happened to Kelly?"

"She's hurt."

Fear rammed into Helen's chest. "What did you do to her?"

"I didn't do anything to Kelly. I used her phone to call triple zero and left the line open so they could trace the call. Then I grabbed her hat and came looking for you. I knew you'd never open the door otherwise, and I need you to listen to what I have to say." Her sister grabbed her by the shoulder. "We have to go, Helen. You're not safe."

"You're wearing her hat and her coat. And driving her Landcruiser. What did you do?!"

Helen's shout ended up strangled as a flood of adrenaline spiked through her. Hyperventilating, she felt like she was drowning, gasping for breath. She needed to do something. *Kelly could be dying.* Part of her wanted to tear into Maxine, but there wasn't time.

"Where. Is. She." She gasped out the words. Her eyes locked her sister with a sudden seething outrage.

Maxine shook her head. Her eyes were wide with fear, or insanity, or maybe both.

"I needed to be sure you'd open the door. The jacket was on the couch in the place on Treloar Road. I took it. I think it belonged to the dead constable."

Dead constable? Was Maxine referring to Bronwyn

King? Cold washed over Helen in ripples of apprehension. "Oh my god, did you kill her? Where's Mr Sharpe?"

"Helen!" Maxine practically shouted, "You have to come with me! Now."

"I need to get to Kelly." Helen squared her shoulders and glared into the chocolate-brown eyes that were so much darker than hers. Their father's eyes. Maxine had the square jaw, straight nose, and tall, muscular frame of their father. Helen, as her father had told her so often, was the spitting image of their mother, Ruth.

"Stab me or get out of my way."

"Kelly isn't dead. Believe me. But we must get out of here. Now."

"Why?" Helen folded her arms over her chest. "Why would I listen to anything you have to say? I believed in you once, Maxine. I won't make that mistake again."

Maxine looked confused. Uncertain what to do next. Her body was practically vibrating with restrained action.

"You stole Mum's opals, didn't you?!"

Maxine blinked at the non-sequitur. "What are you talking about?"

"How did you get into the house?" Helen's eyes were darting around the room, trying to figure how her sister had previously gained entry.

*Of course, she would have learned to pick locks in prison.*

Maxine shook her head. "No, no. I didn't get here until just on dark. I came as soon as I heard what happened. I haven't been in this house since…"

Maxine's expression shifted from confused and anxious to *nothing*; Helen felt like she was looking at a mannequin come to life as her sister shut down in front of her.

"I saw the stuff you left in Sissi's house," Helen accused.

She could see Maxine open her mouth for more denials and cut her off.

"Just stop! Stop lying!" Helen demanded. "Get out of my way! I'm taking the Landcruiser and going to find Kelly."

Maxine's lips formed a grim line. "You have to come with me, Helen. I need to protect you. It's the only way we'll make it through this."

Helen held up her hands. "I don't trust anything you say. I'm not going anywhere with you." Helen reached for her mobile in her pocket. "I'm calling for help."

Maxine turned the business end of the barbeque fork toward Helen. Helen's hand fell to her side. Maxine's face was now suffused with anger and determination.

"Listen, you stubborn bitch. I don't have time for this shit. Put on your coat and do what I tell you," Maxine snarled.

Helen got it now. Either Helen was going to be Maxine's ticket out of here or she had plans to kill her. If the latter was Maxine's intent, why didn't she just do it?

"I don't know what you think you're doing, but if Kelly dies," Helen warned, "I will kill you." The hard words coming straight from her heart shook Helen, and from the look of surprise in Maxine's eyes, her sister as well. Not once in Helen's life had she ever wanted to physically harm anyone. Even when the whole world thought Maxine had murdered their mother, she had only wanted to help her sister.

The flash of surprise in Maxine's eyes shifted back to anger. "Just shut up. Shut up and listen. I couldn't save Dad, but I'm damned sure going to save you whether you want me to or not."

Nothing Maxine said made sense to Helen. A fresh wave of fear poured through Helen. "What are you talking about?"

"Dad. I hadn't been released yet." Maxine drew in a harsh breath. "When I heard, I knew what had really happened."

"Dad fell off the ladder doing repairs to the house, Maxine. The police investigated. It was a horrible accident."

Maxine moved her head frantically from side to side, eyes wild. "No! No! He didn't. That's just what he wanted you to think."

Any lingering hopes she'd had that Maxine was sane were dashed in that moment, and Helen knew she'd slipped over the ledge into paranoid psychosis. Maybe she had years ago, and Helen just hadn't wanted to see it.

"You're not making sense. How could you possibly know anything about Dad's death?"

Would Maxine stab her with the barbeque fork if she made a run for the back door? With her boots on, she just might have a chance.

"Dad wrote to me the day before he died. I didn't get the letter until days later, and then it was too late."

That didn't seem likely. "Dad was still writing to you?"

Maxine shook her head wildly. "He hadn't written

to me in years. When I got a letter after hearing that he was dead, I was freaked out, so I read it instead of sending it back.

"He wanted me to know that he still believed in me. He said he'd never stopped loving me. But Helen," she said, her eyes boring into her sister's, "the day he wrote the letter, he'd learned something new about Mum's death. He was going to investigate it. He said I shouldn't get my hopes up and I should wait until I heard from him again. But," Maxine's words caught in her mouth in a way that seemed like genuine grief, "by the time I received his letter it didn't matter anymore."

*Impossible. If Dad had any new ideas, we'd have talked them through together. He wouldn't fire off a letter to Maxine after all this time.*

"So if Dad had all this new information," Helen accused, "why didn't he tell me?" Her voice gained volume and passion as long-buried resentment came to the fore. "More to the point, why didn't you get in touch with me when you read his letter, instead of just blowing off the funeral and leaving me to bury our father alone?!"

"Because *he was already dead*, Helen! And still I didn't have any more evidence than I did when I went to prison. What would you have done if I'd written to you? Assumed I'd finally flipped my lid?"

Maxine ducked her head, her free hand making a fist. "If I went to the guards, they'd say I was making something out of nothing. Accuse me of conspiracy theories. I'd end up with a black mark on my record, and Helen, I've tried so hard. *So hard.* So, I waited. Don't you understand?"

Maxine's eyes were wild, pleading. "I was already too late. I had less than a year and then I'd probably be released. I'd waited nineteen years. What was one more year?" Her eyes glittered with madness or unshed tears.

Helen held up her hands, pushing out at her sister.

"I'm leaving, Maxine. But not with you."

Maxine's face turned as hard as stone, her eyes going flat. She lifted the barbeque fork.

"One way or the other, Helen, you *are* going with me."

# CHAPTER SIXTEEN

**1.40am Monday, 19 February 2018**

Pain burst in her skull.

Kelly's eyes opened slowly. She blinked, struggled to bring things into focus. Jumbled memories poured through her head, making it ache even more.

She groggily turned towards the only source of sound.

*Door is open.*

The storm rode the wind into the room.

Snapshots of memory.

*Blood in the water. Bronwyn dead.*

She jerked.

**Helen.**

Kelly pushed her hands to the floor and tried to push herself upward. The room spun; her arms trembled. She closed her eyes against a fresh wave of pain.

*Got to get up.*

Deep breath. Kelly tried again. Made it to her knees, panting, then staggered to her feet. For a time that may have been seconds or minutes – or hours, for all she knew - she held the position, swaying like a drunken brawler on a Friday night binge. Willing the world to stop spinning.

Once the floor had subsided to a gentle sway, Kelly cautiously turned around, surveying the room.

*Need backup.*

Kelly instinctively reached for the radio on her shoulder. Fumbled. Couldn't find it.

*Gone.* Her thoughts moved sluggishly. *Stolen?*

Instinctively, she reached for her mobile. The slow-motion memory of the mobile flying from her hand and sliding across the floor had her scanning the room.

*There.*

Kelly spotted it in the corner near the single lounge chair, and slowly made her way to where it lay. She braced one hand against the wall to bend down and pick up the damned thing.

It vibrated in her hand. Liney's face flashed on the screen.

"Liney," she started, before clearing her throat. She blinked a couple of times as her vision blurred with another round and round of the room.

"Kelly! Thank god! I thought you were dead."

Kelly licked her lips. "Not far off," she rasped. Her gut roiled with the need to vomit.

"Backup just turned into Miners Way. Opal Creek is absolutely flooded. We had to send a vehicle across from the Borefield Road."

"Liney." Kelly coughed and swallowed. She paused

for a breath and said more clearly, "Liney. I've been attacked. My radio was stolen."

To her own ears, her voice pitched and roiled in time with her stomach.

Half a heartbeat and Liney responded.

"I'll get Bec on it. Are you ok? Are you safe now?"

"I am heading to Helen's." Kelly replied, enunciating each word with uncharacteristically clipped diction in her attempt at clarity.

"Be cautious."

Kelly started toward the front door; her legs rubbery beneath her, the room swaying with her motion. At the station, Liney listened in rising fear as Kelly's voice abruptly switched from clipped and professional to slurred and mournful. "Couldn' find Ray Sharpe. He's prob'ly dead, and's my fault. Like Bronwyn. I let them down."

In the tiny pause that came with Liney's horrified silence, Kelly realised that she had said that out loud. With a heroic effort, she articulated precisely, "Tell everyone. To keep. An eye out. For Maxine Hamilton."

"Will do. But Kelly, *you have to stay there*. You're hurt."

"Shure," Kelly ventured, before backing up and trying again: "Sure. Okay."

Kelly ended the call without saying more, shoving the mobile away in her pocket.

*Hat.*

She looked blearily to where she'd woken on the floor, didn't see it.

*No time.*

Kelly shuffled across the porch and down the steps as quickly as she dared. The rain pelted her, landing like blows. Kelly halted. Stumbled. Blinked owlishly at the space where her car had been as her mind tried to take in this new information.

*Need a car.*

Kelly turned to Constable King's Holden Commodore, its engine still idling. Unwisely turning straight towards the headlights. The bright beams pierced her eyes, driving daggers into her brain. She doubled over and vomited up the coffee she'd consumed earlier.

*Definitely concussion,* she thought through the pounding in her head as it violently protested the sudden motion. Strangely, though, her thoughts seemed a little clearer.

Kelly's gaze lowered to where Bronwyn had fallen. Nausea roiled through her, not entirely from the concussion, as she made her way to where the body lay in the mud. The rain rolled down her friend's face like tears.

*Can't contaminate the crime scene.*

*But Helen's in danger.*

*No good choices.*

Steeling herself, Kelly leaned over Bronwyn's body and into the car. Instead of pulling the keys from the ignition, she pressed the button to unlock the passenger door then popped the car's boot. Staggering to the back of the car, Kelly pulled a body bag from the highway policing emergency sack.

Breathing carefully, she took a moment to strengthen herself before snicking open the passenger door and returning to Bronwyn's body.

"I'm so sorry, Bron. So sorry."

She crouched down, spread the body bag, and

rolled the body onto the rectangular sheet, working steadily and methodically – pausing only to dry heave when she saw the wound at the back of the constable's head. She zipped the edges of the body bag together with difficulty as another wave of nausea and dizziness rolled over her. Several efforts were required to get her arms underneath the body bag and lift it.

Kelly pushed to her feet, the weight of her friend's body making her sway. One slow, staggering step at a time, murmuring apologies like a litany, Kelly made her way to the back-passenger door. Hefting it open with her hip, she placed Bronwyn's body, in the bag, across the back seat.

Kelly leaned her head against the roof of the vehicle. "This is the best I can do for now, Bron."

*Please forgive me.*

Kelly closed the passenger door and got in the driver's seat, breathing heavily as she steeled herself for the next part.

The Commodore was an interceptor vehicle designed for high-speed pursuit on sealed roads. Low-slung and superfast on the highway, it was a terrible choice for the ruts and slippery clay. Had things gone to plan, the car would have remained at the shack with the officer on duty, only returning to Roxby once the roads were passable again.

It was going to be beyond difficult to manoeuvre in the slush without ending up bogged or sliding off into a ditch…or worse.

Kelly made a slow loop around the backyard, using the headlights as spotlights. No sign of anyone else down in the mud.

*Did she take him with her? Why? None of this makes sense.*

Kelly eased along the drive, taking it slower than she wanted to. If she ended up in a gully, she'd be stuck for sure, and every minute wasted could cost lives.

Thankfully, her thoughts were coming clearer now, and with that clarity she knew: Ray Sharpe was almost certainly dead. At best, he might still be alive as a hostage to lure Helen.

*I'd sacrifice him a million times if it'd save Helen.*

The thought was unworthy of a police officer, but she couldn't deny the truth of it.

Kelly reached the end of Treloar Road and slowly, so slowly, negotiated the right turn into Dunstan Drive before easing onto Christmas Hill Road. She groaned in dismay at the state of the road. It was going to take a miracle to get to the Hamilton house in time.

*Or at all.*

A traitorous thought, quickly smothered.

Six minutes ticked past on the digital clock on the dash before she reached the turn to the Hamilton property. Kelly's frustration ramped higher and higher, and it took every ounce of strength she possessed not to floor the accelerator. The car made slow, steady progress and Kelly screamed internally as the seconds ticked by.

The rain cleared momentarily. Across the gully she glimpsed her own Landcruiser at Helen's house and sucked in a breath of pure terror.

The moment of shock and inattention cost her dearly. The Commodore lurched to the right, fishtailing wildly before sliding sideways into a shallow gully on the wrong side of the road.

Struggling out, Kelly flicked on the hazard lights to alert the dispatched officers, then trekked down the centre of the road as best she could on foot, cursing her stupidity. A few minutes later, as she waded through thigh-high floodwaters in the gully, she realised with certainty that the Commodore could never have made this crossing.

Approaching the Hamilton place, she could just make out Helen's little rental, her father's truck and the Landcruiser. The Landcruiser's lights and engine were both off; whoever had taken it had no expectation of leaving quickly.

Kelly edged around the vehicle, using it as camouflage from the house as she moved closer. The pounding in her chest blocked the sound of the rain.

The silence from the house worried her more than if she'd been able to hear screams.

Indentations in the mud leading to the house were partially submerged in the sludge created by the intense rain. The tracks Kelly had made leaving the house had been swallowed by the rain, but these others – the tracks of her assailant - were still easy enough to see.

*It can't have been too long.*

She wasn't sure if the thought was wishful thinking.

*Please let her be alright.*

She lumbered to the entrance, pressing her back to the wall by the front door as she took a moment to brace herself.

Thankfully her vision had returned to normal on the drive from the shack, and her balance had improved on the final walk to the house. She still had a headache strong enough to make her feel nauseated, but at least she could think again. Could see again.

Her heart made a silent prayer that she'd stay that way long enough to face whatever was inside. If Helen was already dead – she squeezed her eyes shut and banished the thought.

*Please don't let me be too late.*

# CHAPTER SEVENTEEN

**2.00 am Monday, 19 February 2018**

Helen desperately wished she'd hidden her mobile phone in one of her boots. Her sister had been quick to take the phone from her, tossing it into the mud as they reached the upward slope of the hill.

She berated herself for her stupidity: she'd even included a similar scenario in one of her books. But put on the spot, in real life? She'd turned into the kind of victim she destroyed in her novels.

*My characters are smarter than I am*, she thought with self-directed fury.

"Keep moving."

The admonishment came at just the wrong time: instead of complying, Helen stopped dead, stubbornly refusing to play the victim any longer.

The tines of the barbeque fork nudged her in the back. Ignoring the warning jab, Helen turned around and stared belligerently at Maxine. The rain was easing considerably.

"Why should I? If you're going to stab me, come on."

Helen did her best to balance her weight on the slippery ground. If Maxine leapt at her, she'd go down fighting.

*I'm not playing your game anymore.*

Maxine's eyes narrowed. "I promise, Helen. When we get to Sissi's house, I will explain everything."

"Why not now?" Helen lifted her chin and glared at Maxine.

Maxine took a breath, looked around. "Sissi's house is safer. A good lookout. No one can sneak up on us."

Exasperated, Helen tapped her temple, baiting her sister. "Kelly knows about Sissi's house! I showed her the evidence you left behind. We both know you were hiding there. That's the first place Kelly will look when she comes for you."

Maxine's face momentarily glitched with an emotion Helen couldn't identify, then she shook her head slowly. "Helen. *Please*." Her voice was subdued, almost anguished. "I can't watch out for us and fight with you at the same time. I know what I'm doing, but it's complicated. I need to know we're safe before we get into it."

Maxine's expression was haunted. "I didn't kill Mum. I didn't kill Mrs Sharpe. Please believe me."

Against her better judgment, Helen found herself responding to the plea. Whether by the grace of insanity, or from some core of *Maxie* that still existed inside Maxine, she sounded sincere.

Her eyes begged Helen for trust.

"Do you really expect me to believe you, Maxine?"

Helen said, more gently than she intended. One thing had become clear: whatever fantasy her sister was following, she didn't see Helen as an enemy. And Helen couldn't find it in herself to treat her as one, either.

*Oh, Maxie, what has life done to you?*

Helen's shoulders slumped as the fight leached out of her all at once.

"All right. I'll go with you to Sissi's house, but I want you to lower the barbeque fork. You trip, and you might end up stabbing me whether that's your intent or not."

Maxine closed her eyes briefly in relief and lowered the barbeque fork. True to her word, Helen turned around and trudged forward. There was still a distance to go, and the rain had made the hillside extremely slippery.

"Please. Just … just tell me if Kelly's okay." Helen choked out, without looking back. She blinked back tears.

"She was breathing, I promise. It was dark, but I didn't see any blood near her. And the emergency services will be there by now."

They were both huffing and heaving for breath as they struggled up the steep slippery clay slope to Sissi's house. The rain had eased to a drenching spray with smaller droplets.

Staggering to a halt at the entrance to the house, Helen stared at the dark façade as if seeing it for the first time.

*I always hid from my life out here.*

Fitting, in a way, that things had come full circle.

"Did you… Maxine, did you hurt Kelly?" Helen

ground out. Fearing, but needing, the answer.

At the same time, Maxine said, "You go in ahead, Helen."

Helen balked at the door.

"Answer my question first. Did you hurt Kelly?"

Visibly suppressing her need to rush, Maxine gently turned Helen's head to look her directly in her eyes. Helen was transported back in time by the tortured anguish and sincerity in that gaze.

Maxine's response was unequivocal.

"I. Would. Never."

In that moment, Helen knew that whatever the reality, her sister genuinely hadn't intended any harm to come to Kelly. The realisation was bleak, but strangely comforting, nonetheless.

*She's not evil. She's sick, but she's not evil. She's not a murderer in her heart.*

With that realisation came another.

*She truly hasn't brought me here to kill me. That's not her intention.*

Helen's eyes searched her sister's face, seeking wicked intent and finding none.

*It might still happen if things go wrong…but that's not her plan. There might be a chance to escape.*

Throwing a quick glance over her shoulder at the shadowy desert scrub behind them both, Maxine made a shooing motion with her hands.

"Now go! *Hurry!*" she hissed, nudging Helen with the barbeque fork.

The darkness did not stop the two of them from readily navigating the old house to the loft room. As Helen climbed the rickety ladder, she gritted her teeth, steeling herself for action.

Whatever her sister had planned– and whether she believed was telling the truth or not – Helen wasn't taking any chances. There was no telling how long this period of lucidity would last.

*This is my chance to take control.*

Helen scrambled onto the floorboards, avoiding the hole she had made, and eased her way to the far side. The creak of the ladder told her Maxine was coming up as promised.

Helen grabbed one of the little chairs her father had made and readied to do whatever she could to protect herself.

Maxine had always been the athletic one; Helen had been bookish, soft. The past twenty years had only made the differences more starkly apparent.

*I need to surprise her, or she'll easily overpower me.*

Maxine's hands reached the top of the ladder, the gleaming points of the barbeque fork pointing skywards. It would have been easy to brace against the wall and kick the ladder backwards, but the memory of her father's death flashed in her mind, stilling her movement as she realised that the move could kill her sister.

*No. Not at that cost.*

Helen just wanted to stop Maxine from hurting her or anyone else. She braced herself for attack.

Maxine hoisted herself the rest of the way up - looking not at Helen, but back down the ladder as she clambered onto the rough wooden floor.

The knowledge that her sister clearly didn't see her as any kind of threat was as insulting as it was liberating.

Launching herself forward, Helen slammed the

chair into Maxine's left shoulder. By luck more than skill, the chair clipped her sister's head, the leg snapping off as it sent Maxine staggering to the right. The barbeque fork flew out of her hand and spun across the floor.

Maxine's head turned to follow the path of the fork and she scrambled away towards it. With her sister distracted and her back turned, Helen dove at her in a tackle.

Adrenaline sharpened Helen's focus to laser-like precision while stretching time to a slow-motion moment. She could see how and where her attack would land. Knew that it would stun and possibly cripple her sister.

*Stay strong, Kelly. I'm coming.*

# CHAPTER EIGHTEEN

## ABSALOM LANE, ANDAMOOKA, SOUTH AUSTRALIA

**2:30am Monday, 19 February 2018**

With her left hand, Kelly reached out and twisted the doorknob: unlocked, it turned without hesitation. She shoved the door open and held her ground to the count of three.

No sound. No movement.

Kelly slipped through the open doorway. Her gaze moved across the foyer.

Clear.

No overturned furniture. Nothing broken. She scanned the floor for blood. Trying to listen past the pounding in her head, she couldn't detect any voices, or even sounds of breathing.

*Fuck.*

"Helen!" Her voice echoed in the silence.

Kelly quietly stepped towards the kitchen, trailing muddy water and lumps of clay behind her.

"Helen!" she cried, hoarsely, as fear clawed at her

throat.

The room was clear. Again, nothing overturned, nothing broken. No blood.

No mud.

*Did they drag her out? Did they clean up?*

Kelly lurched through the lounge room, her thighs rubbing in the wet uniform, head throbbing in time with her heart. Head swimming, she frantically searched room to room.

A staggering lance of pain in her head had her leaning against the wall, blinded for a moment by agony. Acutely aware of how vulnerable she was.

She stumbled back to the kitchen and leaned on the counter. Her gut roiled and cramped. She leaned over the sink as a wave of nausea washed over her, but there was nothing left to bring up. Shakily, Kelly poured a glass of water; rinsed and swished, rinsed and swished. Cautiously took a couple of sips before a warning spike of nausea drove her to put the glass aside.

She looked through the window. Helen's rental was still there. Beyond it was another vehicle towards the shed. Kelly couldn't be certain, but it didn't look like Ray Sharpe's vehicle.

*Think.* **Think.**

The house was empty. She needed to have another look around outside. It seemed as if the rain might be letting up.

*Backup should be here soon.*

With two or more officers they could cover far more ground.

Kelly was at the front door when her mobile vibrated. She snatched it up, hoping against hope it was Helen, but her hopes were dashed as *Dr Rosemary McGregor* flashed on the screen.

"Kelly Wells," she said, eyes roving over the landscape in front of her.

"Kelly, it's Rosie. I've received some interesting news about Lorraine Sharpe."

"You can't have heard from Adelaide already?" Kelly thought it unlikely; the lab didn't generally operate seven days a week.

"Believe it or not!" Rosemary sounded as surprised as Kelly felt. "Tiger McAuley was catching up on paperwork when the body was brought in. She stayed on to do the autopsy, and when she ran the tox screen, things got interesting. Either Lorraine Sharpe planned to take her own life, or someone forced her to swallow a fatal dose of benzodiazepines."

Kelly startled at the unexpected information. "Were they hers?"

"We'll have to confirm, but I think it's likely. I checked her medical record, and Garry Guthrie prescribed Valium six years ago. But Kelly, that's our answer to why there was less blood at the scene than we expected… she was almost dead when she was stabbed. Her heart was still beating, but barely."

"Why bother to stab a dying woman?"

The question was a rhetorical one: in this situation, Kelly knew the answer.

*Because it's personal.*

Still, it seemed unnecessary to force the woman to take pills to render her immobile and then stab her. Maxine was presumably still athletic, and she was nearly half the woman's age.

*Why not just clobber her with that damn cricket bat she*

*hit me with, and be done with it?*

The scenario begged another question.

*Why didn't Maxine kill me? Why leave without finishing the job?*

*Is it because I'm outside whatever fantasy feud she's carrying on? Is she sane enough to recognise the difference?*

"Thanks for the update, Rosie. I'll get back to you."

# CHAPTER NINETEEN

**2:30 am Monday, 19 February 2018**

Had Helen been fighting someone like herself, her adrenaline-fuelled tackle would have led to a moment she'd forever remember with awe.

Maxine, however, was an altogether different beast. Her sister's instincts and peripheral vision had been formed by adolescent team sports, then relentlessly honed through two decades in prison.

Maxine twisted mid-movement; her hands came up, fingers winding around Helen's throat. With awe and overwhelming despair, Helen felt first-hand the difference in their physical skills, as Maxine slammed Helen onto her back on the floor almost effortlessly.

"Don't. Move," Maxine growled in Helen's face. "I swear, if you do…"

"You'll what? Kill me?" Helen's eyes filled with tears, the futility of her situation finally sinking in along with her failure to overpower her sister. "Why bother bringing me here if you were only going to kill me anyway?"

"I'm setting a trap," Maxine snarled as she released Helen. Maxine retrieved the barbeque fork and got to her feet. "Get up," she snapped.

Helen didn't bother. Instead, she crawled to the very back of the space and huddled there. "Talk." She said, dully. "Tell me whatever it is you think I need to hear. I want this over."

Maxine stood in the dark silence for a bit.

Helen waited, locked up in anguish for Kelly.

*I never found the courage to tell you how I felt. Now you'll never know.*

"Like I said before and during the trial," Maxine began, her voice a husky low rumble in the night, "I came home from school and found Mum on the ground bleeding. I tried to help her, but it was too late. The next thing I knew, Mrs Sharpe was standing there screaming at me. She rushed toward me and pushed me away. She said at the trial that's when she got the blood on her. But that's not true. She already had the blood on her."

And there it was. A claim the police had already investigated and found to be unsubstantiated.

"You did your time, Maxine." She said, emotional exhaustion leeching into her voice. "Why did you come back? You violated your parole leaving the Barossa and…" Helen couldn't say the rest, but her thoughts carried on regardless: *you killed an old woman, just to get even.*

Helen felt sick.

"I violated the terms of my parole *to protect you.*"

Oh, yeah, Helen had forgotten that ridiculous plot

detail of this ongoing saga.

"Uh-huh. And let me guess. You didn't have time to bring Dad's letter with you?"

"I did. I have it here."

Maxine's answer jolted Helen out of her fugue state; against her will, she found herself aching to believe her sister.

Fabric rustled as Maxine dug in her pocket.

"I don't have a flashlight, but here it is." Maxine thrust an envelope at Helen.

"Well, that's convenient." Helen tucked it into her raincoat pocket. "I guess I'll have to read it when I get home. Assuming I'm still alive."

Maxine exhaled a big breath.

"Dad figured something out, Helen. He said so in his letter. He didn't say what, but the very next day he was dead. That has to tell you something!"

"That we are cursed? Have the worst luck? He fell off a ladder, Maxine. He wasn't murdered." Helen shivered as the low temperature finally filtered through her wet outerwear and absorbed into her bones.

The silence that followed had Helen hugging her knees to her chest.

*Did I push her too far? What will she do if she snaps?*

"Dad would never make a mistake like that," Maxine argued. "He'd painted that house plenty of times. Painted other people's houses. He'd done all kinds of maintenance and never - not once – did he fall. He was careful, always."

There was a shuffling noise as Maxine leaned forward.

"Helen, I think it was made to look that way. There

wasn't an autopsy. No-one even investigated the possibility."

Maxine's words made Helen uncomfortable. She was right about their father; he'd never fallen before. Not even a near miss.

*What if she's on to something?* The thought was desperate, crazy. And yet...

"But who would have done this? And more importantly - why?" Helen demanded, determined not to be swayed without some sort of tangible evidence besides a letter she couldn't read.

Maxine's voice was soft in the darkness. "I thought it was Mrs Sharpe at first."

Helen couldn't help scoffing at the ludicrous idea. "You are kidding, right? The woman was tiny! Maybe five two or five three. How could she possibly kill a full-grown man without a weapon? You know, like a gun? Not to mention, why in the world would she want to?"

"I said, 'at first'," Maxine snapped. "Then, when she ended up dead, I knew it was *him*. Mr Sharpe. That's why I rushed home to protect you."

*This is beyond insane.*

"**He's** convinced it was **you**, Maxine! He looked at me with sheer hatred when I told him how sorry I was to hear about his wife. He was devastated."

"But who else could it have been? It's him, I know it."

Helen felt the last of her hope shrivel and die.

Maxine had no evidence. No reason to think their father's death was anything more than a tragic accident. No reason to think Mr Sharpe had anything to do with either death. Nothing. Just the delusions of a sad, sick mind still reliving the horror of 20 years ago.

Maxine had violated her parole for nothing.

Maxine had done whatever the hell she had done since coming back to Andamooka for nothing.

It was all so tragic. So horrible. So … pointless.

Helen blinked away tears and moved towards the ladder. "I'm going to find Kelly."

She was nearly at the opening where the ladder waited when Maxine stopped her.

"I can't let you go out there. He'll kill you. We must wait for him to come to us. There are too many doors in our place. Too easy to separate us. We *must* stay together."

"Why would you want to protect me?" Helen demanded. "All those years you refused to see us. Returned our letters. Why would you do that and then pretend to come back here to *protect* me like this?"

"I didn't want either of you to be hurt any more than you already had been," Maxine said quietly. "Nobody believed me. But that woman had already killed Mum. What would they do to cover up the murder if you or Dad started sniffing around?"

Maxine's voice was mesmerising in its anguish, filled with an ancient despair that battered at Helen's disbelief. "I was the only one who knew, and I couldn't protect you. And if you kept poking away at her story, it could get you both killed."

Maxine brushed at her eyes. "I couldn't save Mum. I arrived too late, after she'd already… I couldn't save her, Helen. I *tried* to save her." Her voice cracked as she added, "But if I let you keep digging, you and

Dad could get killed. And it would be my fault."

Helen wanted to believe Maxine. She really did.

*She believes everything she's saying. She's suffered so much. But I don't think she'll hurt me.*

Helen reached out and touched her sister on the arm.

"I'm going, Maxine," she said, gently. "If you mean what you say, then come with me and protect me. Help me prove your story."

Maxine's shoulders were slumped in defeat.

Helen started down the ladder, pausing only to grab one of the broken chair legs on her way down.

"For defence. If you're right," she said.

Maxine didn't raise her head to acknowledge either Helen's words or action, seemingly too far gone in her own misery to care.

Helen's feet were on the ground before Maxine started her way slowly down.

Maybe Helen could get Maxine back to the house. If Kelly were able, she would be looking for her.

*Please let Kelly be okay.*

Helen backed away from the ladder as Maxine lowered her feet to the ground.

A cold, latex-gloved hand grabbed Helen by the throat and yanked her backward. Helen yelped as a gun pressed into her temple. She couldn't see her captor.

She could see her sister, though.

The gleam in Maxine's eye had turned cold. The shadows reshaped her face, hardening the strong planes of her cheeks and jawline. Her expression was flat. She looked hard. Feral.

Deadly.

*This is the face of someone who could kill.*

"What took you so long?!" Maxine barked to the stranger holding Helen.

Helen felt overwhelming despair rise up from within.

This was so much worse than anything she'd imagined.

*She's got a partner. That's why nothing added up. There's two of them.*

The devastation Helen felt in that moment eclipsed everything else, even her own danger.

Helen's assailant snarled directly in her ear, "Drop it."

The chair leg Helen had taken as an impromptu weapon clattered to the ground from nerveless fingers.

She felt herself going into shock.

Time seemed to stop.

Her thoughts spun, unable to gain traction, as her brain digested and recognised the raised voice.

*Ray Sharpe.*

This couldn't be right. Why would the two of them team up together? She couldn't restrain the whimper that escaped her: not of fear, but of absolute and total confusion.

*Maxine and Ray?!*

Ray Sharpe had always been like family. Maxine *was* family.

There was no way this made sense.

None of it made sense.

# CHAPTER TWENTY

**2:40 am Monday, 19 February 2018**

Kelly's mobile vibrated again before she could tuck it back into her pocket.

*Liney.*

"Where's that backup?" Kelly heard the snap in her voice but chose not to apologise. Whatever else was going on, she needed help here. Now.

"Stuck, sorry," Liney said. "We've tried multiple routes. There are trees floating down the creek, and all access through Opal Creek Boulevard and Borefield Road has been cut off by washaways."

Kelly instinctively made to rub the back of her head in frustration, before dropping her hand with a hiss of remembered pain right before encountering the wound.

*What the hell else can happen?*

Liney continued, "We've got a work-around - the SES trucks are headed out with some officers on board. That's the good news. Unfortunately, it's going to be about half an hour before they get to the Hamilton place."

*Great,* Kelly thought sourly.

Liney went on, "Also, Doctor McGregor rang with an interesting update."

"Mm-hmm. I just had a call from her. Listen, I'm at the Hamilton house now."

She heard Liney's startled breath. "What? You were supposed to stay - "

Kelly bulldozed on, ignoring the interruption. "There's no sign of anyone, and no indication of a struggle. Whoever put me down, took my radio and my Landcruiser and drove it here. I had to drive Bronwyn's patrol car. I've left it on Christmas Hill Road with the hazard lights on. Bronwyn's body," her voice caught a little, "is in a body bag on the back seat. I haven't found anyone – alive or otherwise – yet. There's another vehicle out behind the house, and I don't think I recognise it. I'm going to check it out now."

"Kelly, wait. Backup will be there soon."

Kelly pinched the bridge of her nose.

"Liney, a murderer drove here in *my stolen vehicle,* and now Helen is gone. *Soon* isn't soon enough." Recognising that she was taking out her frustration unfairly, Kelly added in a gentler tone, "I'll be careful. But you know this can't wait."

One of Liney's more appealing qualities was her ability to recognise the inevitable.

"I wish you'd hold out for backup, but I understand. Be careful. Check in again as soon as you can."

"Will do. Bye, Liney. And thanks."

Kelly hadn't seen any vehicular tracks other than her own out front, so she headed for the back door. If Maxine had taken Helen, they couldn't go far without transport.

Outside, Kelly pulled her flashlight from her utility belt and scanned the mud around Helen's rental car. Tracks from the far side of the yard cut across the landscape and ended next to Helen's car.

The blue car near the shed was a puzzle, quickly solved: a quick check of her mobile screen showed the make, model, and colour of the vehicle matched Maxine's.

Kelly dashed off a quick text to Liney with the news.

Desperation fuelled her forward; she started a grid pattern, looking for tracks... blood... anything that would give her a direction.

They had to be here...

Somewhere.

More than anything, Kelly needed Helen to be alive.

# CHAPTER TWENTY-ONE

**2:50 am Monday, 19 February 2018**

"What took you so long?" Maxine's words echoed in Helen's head, unbinding her from any sense of reality.

When Helen's assailant – *Ray Sharpe,* she recognised distantly – had snarled directly in her ear, "Drop it," she'd released her improvised weapon before her brain had even fully caught up with the instruction.

She was adrift in a warped reality where nothing made sense.

*Maxine and Ray?*

She barely registered when Sharpe repeated the instruction, jerking her closer against his body. "I said, drop it! Now!"

Felt nothing but that dull, woolly confusion.

*Already dropped it.*

Helen's eyes rested dully on the chair leg, where it had fallen to the ground. Thoughts flipped through her mind, too fleeting to grasp, and she found that she didn't even care. Mostly, she just felt sad that she'd destroyed the chair – *the chair Dad built, and Mum painted* - for nothing.

Then Maxine tossed the barbeque fork to the floor. The action broke through Helen's self-imposed retreat from reality with a clatter that sounded like hope.

"I knew you'd be back to finish the job, you fucking bastard," Maxine snarled. "You're not taking anyone else from me."

Helen raised her eyes to her sister, hope rising like the dawn.

*You were telling the truth the whole time.*

For a moment, the sheer joy and relief of knowing her sister hadn't betrayed her – hadn't betrayed *anyone* – overrode everything.

Ray Sharpe laughed bitterly. "You won't miss her because you'll be dead too."

Helen rode out the wave of new shock. She inhaled deeply. She had to do something.

"Kelly is on her way," she lied. "She'll be here any minute."

Sharpe's laughter was mocking this time. "Kelly's dead, you stupid cow. And when the police finally do arrive, they'll find that your crazy sister has killed you and then herself."

The last walls of Helen's disbelief crumbled to dust. Behind it, far in the distance but inexorable, rose a tsunami of rage and hatred for the man in front of her. She began to tremble: adrenaline, not fear.

"Maxine was telling the truth all along, wasn't she?"

Helen's voice was hollow, empty. But cold fury

was seeping in to fill the gaps.

"You, of all people, should know the truth is whatever you want it to be," Sharpe countered. "Sometimes the story changes and you have to improvise."

Helen's eyes narrowed to slits.

"You. Murdered. My mother."

"No." The old man uttered the single syllable with a mixture of agony and anger. "I loved her."

"You *slaughtered* her." Helen growled.

Sharpe's denial was adamant. "I would *never* have hurt her. Never." Helen felt the shudder in his chest. Felt his head shake from side to side. "I would have done anything for Ruth. She was the love of my life. My heart."

Helen was shaking with adrenaline and fury. Visions of clawing Sharpe's eyes out. Of finding a knife and doing to him what had been done to their mother. But the sincerity in his voice jarred her, cutting through her towering rage... before the meaning of his words sank in.

*You what?!* Helen wanted to scream the words, but her breath had been stolen from her by the sheer audacity of the statement.

Not so Maxine.

"But she didn't love you," Maxine said calmly. "She loved our father. She would never have looked at anyone else."

"He was nothing but a waster, an obstacle," Sharpe sneered with undisguised loathing. "I could wait. I would have waited the rest of my life, content to see her from time to time. Hear her voice. Relish her touch when her hand brushed mine."

His words turned Helen's stomach.

"But you decided you couldn't, and you killed her instead," Helen suggested, following Maxine's lead. "If you couldn't have her, no one could."

His hand clamped harder around Helen's throat, making her gag.

"*Lorraine* killed her."

Helen froze, the pressure on her throat no longer important.

"Your wife killed our mother?" The words were Helen's, but she didn't recognise them.

"She was jealous. She knew how I felt. I tried to hide it, but it was impossible."

Maxine stepped forward, stopping only when Sharpe jabbed the gun harder against Helen's head.

"You knew it was her and you let me go to jail for it?"

"I was devastated. I couldn't think straight for months," Ray Sharpe argued. "Lorraine was all I had left. I couldn't lose her too. Anything was better than being alone."

"I was a child! My *sister* was a child! Anything was better than *you* being alone?! *We lost our mother*!" Maxine's voice was a scream of loss and fury. "You filthy, foul, evil bastards! You both kept going to church, you fucking hypocrites! So fucking pious, while one of you was a murderer and the other covered it up. *She* killed *my mother*, and *you* sent *me* to rot in jail?!" Finishing the sentence on a screech, Maxine appeared to have exhausted her capacity for coherent thought and began calling him every vile name in her vocabulary.

The more Maxine shouted, the faster the man

holding Helen breathed, as if the ugly words were pushing the oxygen from his lungs faster than he could fill them. The rasp of his respiration brushed against Helen's hair. He was shaken to the core.

*Good. Now to keep him that way. Remind him what he's done.*

"You said you couldn't be alone," Helen said, cutting off her sister's tirade. "Why kill Lorraine now? She was still all you had. Aren't you going to be lonely without her?"

"It was the dementia. The confusion started a little over a year ago. Lorraine couldn't remember things that happened five minutes before. She kept getting confused. She said something to your father that had him demanding answers from me about Ruth. I knew he'd just keep digging until he figured out how much I had loved Ruth and what happened when she died. I had no choice but to kill him."

Helen's knees almost buckled. She'd truly believed that much was an accident.

She steadied herself, struggled to keep the discussion going.

"Kelly said Dad fell off a ladder. Kelly would never lie to me." Ray Sharpe had to be lying.

"I made it look that way."

"He died. Slowly. In the heat." Helen forced the words out past the bile that rose up in her throat.

Sharpe wasn't moved. "Yeah," he said. "The constable who showed up was completely convinced. Problem solved. She's dead now too, so that's that."

White hot rage blasted against Helen's chest. She wasn't sure if she was going to throw up, faint, or explode with the emotions coursing through her.

Sharpe carried on, his tone bizarrely conversational. "Lorraine just kept getting worse. The more the disease dragged her into the past, the bigger liability she became. When I found out from Elsbeth you were coming back to pack up the house, I knew I had to do something."

Now that he'd started talking, Ray Sharpe seemed determined to get everything out. Unburden himself.

*I am not your fucking confessional, you twisted fuck.*

"It was perfect timing. I knew Kelly would find some way to blame Maxine for yours and Lorraine's murders. Knowing the codes to your new locks, I was able to get into the house and take that cricket bat from Maxine's room. I was going to use it on Lorraine. But then I got home, and she'd taken the pills..." his eyes were crazed, filled with grief and twisted anger "but like everything else that Lorraine did in her life, she wasn't quite thorough enough."

Revulsion boiled through Helen.

"Kelly won't be fooled by any of this," she asserted bluntly. "You can't think for an instant she'll just let this go."

Sharpe laughed. "Kelly's not in a position to do anything. I took care of her."

"You're wrong," Maxine spoke up, taking another step towards them, "I was there after. Kelly was still breathing. I called the ambulance. She'll get better, and she *will* find you." Her voice was a confident snarl. "Kelly's not old-school like the cops when our mother was killed. You both got lucky then. But Kelly won't stop digging until she finds the truth."

"Stop right there," Sharpe ordered. Maxine finished the forward step and came to a halt, bringing her arms up. Hands open and empty.

Sharpe shrugged his left shoulder, and something dropped to the ground. "I'll let you go first so you don't have to watch your sister die. Whatever you think, I'm not completely heartless." His voice was bizarrely cheerful as he instructed, "There's a rope in that pack. Fix yourself a hanging noose, Maxine. Today's the day you're going to end your suffering."

"I won't let you hurt her," Maxine warned, moving yet another step toward them.

"You can't stop me," Ray Sharpe said calmly. "I've planned everything out. In this weather it will be hard to tell who went first. Course, I'll make sure the gun has your prints on it."

He grinned darkly. "And I don't care how good you think Kelly Wells is, she won't figure it out. Oh, we all know about her and Helen here," he said, yanking Helen into him in a twisted parody of a hug. "Unnatural, both of them. But it's going to help me," he chuckled, "because Wells will be devastated that she couldn't stop this tragedy. So busy blaming herself, she'll never see past it."

*We're both going to die here,* Helen realised.

In that moment, she knew what she had to do. She sagged against Sharpe's body, the very picture of a woman without hope.

"Go ahead, Maxine," Helen urged. "There's no point fighting the inevitable. You go first."

Maxine stared at Helen for a long moment, before nodding slowly. Reaching forward, she made as if to pick up the bag, only to dart past the pair of them at the last moment. Swinging around the corner, she disappeared in the darkness.

"Stop, you bitch!" Sharpe instinctively shifted his body towards Helen's fleeing sister.

In that moment, Helen jerked out of his hold, whipped around and pushed him as hard as she could, sending him flying face-first onto the floor of Sissi's house.

Helen took off in the direction her sister had disappeared. Racing out of the house, she slithered down the hill, hoping she wouldn't break any bones.

Ray Sharpe's shouted warnings echoed around the hills. A gunshot reverberated, harsh in the darkness.

Helen kept going.

# CHAPTER TWENTY-TWO

**3.15am Monday, 19 February 2018**

Backup had arrived at the Hamilton home, in the form of two of the SES' enormous emergency trucks. To Kelly's immense gratitude and relief, Senior Constables Harry Flugelman and Gerry Chadowski, Constables Sheila Roberts, Morgan Fowler, Ashley Zone and Jett Bullock - all of her remaining team – had arrived to provide her with search-and-rescue support.

It was very much against protocol … especially since the team was in a shift rotation throughout the storm crisis, which meant some of them were *definitely* off-duty.

But Kelly couldn't bring herself to care about protocol.

Her team was there, together.

*Maybe we have a chance now.*

The looks on their faces and evidence of hastily-scrubbed tears revealed they'd already heard about Bronwyn. As soon as the team had assembled with Kelly, Sheila and Morgan had quietly stepped up and offered to move Bronwyn's body from the highway patrol car to one of the SES vehicles for transport to the small morgue at Roxby downs.

Kelly knew it wasn't the most urgent priority but agreed without hesitation. The knowledge that her friend was sprawled like so much discarded luggage across the back seat of the Commodore did not sit well with her – and her officers, she knew, would feel better and stronger once they'd done what they could to honour their teammate.

One of the SES vehicles had completed a multi-point turn to face the truck back up the driveway and waited. As soon as permission had been granted, the constables re-entered the SES truck and headed slowly up the driveway to retrieve their fallen colleague.

Kelly made a mental note to thank the driver later for their compassion.

Kelly's next step was to send Ashley and Jett out to the shack on the second SES vehicle. She couldn't remember if she'd even shut the shack door on her way out, and it galled her to think that she may have contributed to contamination of the scene – even if she was concussed at the time. She had resigned herself to the fact that it was unlikely they would find the old man alive, but at least they could secure the scene as much as possible from further damage from the pounding storm.

That left Kelly with her most senior officers to carry out a grid search of the area surrounding the Hamilton house. In particular, she was relieved to have Harry with her – his attention to detail was remarkable, as he'd recently proven during a team building exercise to one of Andamooka's fossil fields. In this wild weather, Harry's eagle-eyed perception could literally mean the difference between life and death.

Kelly was still a little unsteady on her feet and couldn't shake the pounding headache, but she refused to sit by while Helen was missing. She was more than thirty metres from the house when she heard shouting in the distance. It was hard to pinpoint the location through the howling wind, but it seemed to be coming from further up the hill.

"Harry! Gerry! With me!" The beam of her flashlight guiding her, she ran towards the distant noise. The senior constables fanned out and did the same, keeping pace about ten metres out on either side of her, ensuring none of them got separated by chance.

A gun shot exploded across the hills, and she ran harder, lurching across the uneven ground. Her right knee buckled as the soft ground gave way, and she hissed with the pain. Her head pounded, but she scrambled to her feet and kept moving.

"Kelly!" Harry's shout came from her left: he'd spotted movement – a human figure, running. As one, the officers turned in pursuit, Harry in the lead.

When Harry was within a few long strides of the fleeing figure, the person suddenly stopped in place, yelling and waving his arms frantically.

"She took her! She's going to kill her!"

Male. Strained, hoarse voice.

Harry caught up to him and turned him to the moonlight just in time for Kelly, arriving seconds later, to identify the figure clearly.

*Ray Sharpe. How are you alive?!*

That question would have to wait. "Who took her?" Kelly demanded.

Sharpe gasped for breath. "Max...ine...She's taking... Helen... to the creek. She's going... to drown her."

Ray Sharpe shook his head and started to wail hysterically, his words not making sense.

"Are you injured?" Kelly demanded.

Sharpe trembled uncontrollably, though whether from fear or the cold temperature, Kelly couldn't be sure.

"Are. You. Injured?" she repeated, slowly and clearly, needing him to pay attention.

Sharpe's head wagged side to side. "No. No. I'm fine. You have to go save her." His eyes were wild as he grabbed at Kelly's coat in desperation. "She's got a gun!"

Harry's deep bass rumbled, "I've got him, Kelly." He'd moved his hand from Sharpe's coat to his arm, kindly helping the older gentleman stand upright.

"Right. Mr Sharpe, Senior Constable Flugelman is going to take you back to the Hamilton house, OK?"

Without waiting for an answer, she turned to her attention to each of her team in turn.

"Harry: get him warmed up and take his statement. Gerry: you and I are in pursuit. You follow the erosion gully; I'll head directly to the creek."

A nod from both officers and the team separated.

Kelly headed for Opal Creek. It cut across the town and was flooding through the main street. Her heart beat faster and faster, her head spinning with urgency and contradictions.

Where'd Maxine get a gun? If she had one all along, why drug and stab Mrs Sharpe? If she's got a gun, why would she want to drown Helen?

*Is she even heading for the creek, or did she say that to throw Mr Sharpe off the scent?*

A memory tickled at the edge of her mind. Kelly suddenly recalled one of the many late-night discussions she'd had with Helen during sleepovers at the Hamilton house. They'd been talking about whether Maxine could have killed her mother, and Helen had mentioned several times that even when she'd been an annoying little kid tagging along behind her big sister, Maxine had never bullied her or pushed her around. She'd also said Maxine had saved her...

*Fuck.*

*Maxine saved her from drowning.*

It made sense, in a horrible way.

*She's trying to 'correct' her history. First remove the woman that put her in jail, then un-save her sister...*

*And she has a gun.*

*Oh god.*

Kelly might have no other choice but to take Maxine down.

Movement in the distance on the right snagged her attention - a flash of light against darkness.

Not a flashlight.

Not reflective lettering.

Yellow coat.

*Helen!*

It was too hard to tell in the downpour if she was on her own. Kelly restrained the urge to call out to her: if she'd evaded Maxine, Kelly didn't want to give away her position.

And if the two were still together, the less warning Maxine had, the better.

Kelly pushed her body harder, lunged through an erosion gully, and slid down an embankment. If she could just catch up with Helen before Maxine got her, she might be able to avoid a violent confrontation.

A bush rattled and a few rocks were dislodged to her left.

Another figure rushing in the same direction as Helen whizzed past Kelly's line of sight.

Kelly altered course to intersect with her new target. It had to be Maxine.

The new figure looked back; saw her. Powered forward, grabbed the one in front.

A scream split the air.

*Helen!*

"Stay right there, Kelly!" Maxine's voice was sharp.

Kelly almost went face-down in the mud as she pulled to a halt on the muddy ground. She kept her torch lowered, not wanting Maxine to feel more threatened than she already did... yet. She strained to see the weapon... not visible.

"Let Helen go, Maxine, and we'll figure this out."

Kelly felt a moment of immense gratitude for the training that allowed her to keep her voice steady and calm despite her turmoil.

Maxine laughed, a mixture of dark humour and despair.

"If I let Helen go, you'll end up shooting me and then they'll win. Again."

At the same time, Helen cried out, "Kelly! Thank

god you're alive!"

Helen's voice was pure relief, and Kelly's heart leapt as she realised her friend had feared for her as much as she'd feared for Helen.

The next words out of Helen's mouth, however, were not what Kelly expected.

"Please. Listen to Maxine," Helen went on. "You're not thinking clearly, or you wouldn't be doing this."

Kelly couldn't see Helen's eyes or face well enough to read her emotional state, but her voice… there was definite stress, but also an underlying confidence that told Kelly that Helen had something in mind. Some kind of plan.

She could play along.

"I won't shoot you, Maxine," Kelly assured her. "You have my word."

It was an easy promise: Kelly didn't even have pepper spray, and she wasn't carrying her gun. But Maxine didn't have to know that.

"You know me, Maxine. You remember me. You know I won't lie to you."

She could hear hushed discussion between Helen and Maxine, and Maxine's shoulders started to relax. Kelly felt the first glimmer of true hope she'd had all evening.

The sound of backup arriving could not have come at a worse time. Instantly, Maxine's silhouette was fully alert, all trust vanished.

"Tell them to stay back," Maxine cautioned, her voice calmer than Kelly expected.

"Kelly, please," Helen urged, "you have to listen to Maxine. She's telling the truth."

Kelly took a shuddering breath.

"Hold your position," she ordered the officers.

*Whatever you're doing, Helen, you'd better be right. I'll never forgive myself if you're wrong.*

She shifted her attention to Maxine, holding tightly to Helen.

"You don't need Helen to protect you. I won't allow this situation to go wrong."

Maxine let out a laugh that was almost a sob. "The last police officer I trusted made me spend half my life in prison."

"Wait," Helen begged them both. There was another murmur of conversation, and Helen pulled free from her sister's hold. Kelly braced herself to launch between Helen and Maxine as Helen stepped forward.

"Wait! Kelly, no!"

Helen held up her hands. Rather than run, Helen stood in front of Maxine, arms spread in an attempt to shield her.

"I'll hear Maxine out," Kelly promised Helen. "Just let me do this the right way."

*With handcuffs.*

Damn it! Helen needed to move aside.

"It's not Maxine," Helen cried. "It never was. Lorraine Sharpe was the one." A sob tore past her lips. "Maxine has been telling the truth all along."

Taking a deep breath and hoping like hell she wasn't making a mistake, Kelly glanced over one shoulder, then the other. "Lower your weapons."

The two officers did as she ordered.

Helen looked back at her sister, said something that Kelly couldn't make out. Every second ticked off like the countdown to an explosion.

"Maxine is telling the truth," Helen said to Kelly.

Then, turning to her sister, she urged her, "You can trust Kelly."

Helen started plodding through the mud toward Kelly. Maxine stayed where she was, stance alert and ready for action.

Forcing herself to look beyond her friend, Kelly kept eyes on Maxine, alert for treachery. "Put your weapon down, Maxine. I promise we'll figure this out."

Helen stopped where she was, only a couple of metres out, and held up her hands again.

"Maxine doesn't have a weapon. Ray Sharpe has a gun. He was going to kill us back there." She choked a sob. "Kelly. He killed Dad. Left him to suffer."

Kelly didn't have to question Helen about the statement; sincerity and tragic outrage were woven through her voice in a way that couldn't be feigned. She might not understand the story yet, but she had no doubt that Helen was telling the truth.

*Oh, Jesus. And Harry took him in.*

"Sheila," she called to the officer on her right, "Get these two up to Sissi's house for the time being. Be cautious. Report to Liney before you leave this position and check in again when you get to the house."

Kelly turned to the officer on her left, "Morgan, you're with me. We're going back to the Hamilton place. Harry took Sharpe there."

Constable Morgan Fowler gave a sharp nod.

"Be careful, Kelly," Helen begged. She repeated her earlier warning: "He has a gun."

Kelly held Helen's gaze a moment longer, before

sweeping her into a brief but tight hug, hoping Helen understood what she wasn't saying. Pulling away, she nodded, and started back to the house with the constable in tow.

Kelly had never known Ray Sharpe to own a gun. He was certainly not on the Firearms Register. If he was armed with a handgun, then he'd taken it from someone.

*Bronwyn's gun.*

Her stomach turned once, before rising rage overpowered it, bringing a burst of adrenaline. She made it to the house boundary in record time, Constable Fowler right behind her.

The first thing Kelly noticed was a vehicle missing from the front of the house. Helen's little rental car was there, as well as Robert Hamilton's truck. The old blue car registered to Maxine was visible out by the shed.

But her Landcruiser was gone.

The second thing she noticed was the reflection off a high-visibility vest in the shadow of the house. Terror propelled another burst of adrenaline in her veins as she raced over to where her senior sergeant lay sprawled in the shadow near the house, his khaki uniform blending with the muddy sludge.

*No no no no no. No, Harry. No.*

Emotional flashbacks to finding Bronwyn hours before rocked through her.

Kelly fell to Harry's side and checked his carotid pulse as Morgan radioed for emergency medical aid.

*Still alive. Still alive.*

One shot. Lower torso.

"Hang on, Harry. Hang on." Panicking, Kelly

tried to lift the large man into her arms, but even the adrenaline rushing through her body was not enough to move her giant senior constable. Morgan rushed to her aid.

"Slow down, Kelly. We've got this. You know your way around here. Go and get towels."

Kelly spun off into the house.

Together, they worked quickly to apply pressure to the wound with wadded towels. Additional towels sheltered Harry from the direct rain.

When she was confident they had stabilised him as best as possible, Kelly stood up.

Morgan, though young, had proven herself level-headed in this crisis – *more level-headed than me*, Kelly thought, remembering how she'd panicked during her flashback to Bronwyn – and Kelly knew Harry would be in safe hands with her.

"Take care of him, Morgan. I'm going after Sharpe."

Morgan nodded, continuing to apply pressure to the wound. "I've got this. Be careful, Kelly. That old man seems determined to take as many with him as possible before he goes down."

Kelly gave Morgan a nod. "Report with an update to Liney, will you?"

Kelly was running, slipping and sliding along the driveway when she spotted Helen, Maxine and Sheila emerging through the misty darkness. She noted they were near the flooding erosion gully running down from Mihala Street, headed towards Sissi's house.

At least that was something to be grateful for in this damned mess. Helen was safe.

Kelly barrelled down the drive with her torch, following the tracks rutted into the mud as she descended the hill from Absalom Lane. The rain had slowed to a heavy mist. Kelly phoned dispatch and put out an alert for Ray Sharpe and the missing police vehicle.

She'd barely turned off the phone as she steadied her progress through the mud when she reached the T-junction on Christmas Hill Road. The missing Landcruiser came into view further down the hill on the left.

Kelly hurried as best she could in the mud with the rain misting her vision, her rib cage heaving. Her torch bobbed indicating her progress, pounding in rhythm with her unsteady stride.

The Landcruiser sat in the middle of the road, brake lights glaring. Kelly stood in the rutted mud behind the Landcruiser. Her chest huffed with the effort to be calm.

The headlights illuminated the heaving flood waters, the two-metre flood water marker at the Opal Creek crossing completely submerged or washed way.

She sent a quick text to verify her position with Liney.

Kelly strode warily forward and approached the driver's side with caution, her torch extended and steady. A murdered officer, a murdered elderly woman, a gravely wounded officer, all within twenty-four hours.

Whatever Ray Sharpe was doing, he hadn't moved. Brakes were still engaged.

Besides Helen's father, who else had this man murdered?

Rage roaring through her, Kelly jerked the driver's

side door open.

Sharpe turned his head, his hand pressed to his abdomen, blood oozing between his fingers.

"Oh, no. You're not getting out of it that easy, you bastard."

With those words, Kelly called in the incident and did what she could to help until the emergency services crew arrived.

# CHAPTER TWENTY-THREE

**10.30am Monday, 19 February 2018**

Helen waited in Kelly's office. She had never been so exhausted, grateful, hurt and angry in her life. All those years of separation, pain and disappointment had been for nothing.

Maxine was innocent.

Detectives Brevet Sergeant Liney Deer and Senior Constable Bec Heath had interviewed and taken a statement from her and Maxine separately. Now the team was at the hospital interviewing Ray Sharpe.

They'd had to wait until after his surgery.

Helen huddled in the chair. She'd been given clean, dry clothes to change into, but doubted she'd feel warm and rested until she'd had a long hot bath and about a hundred hours of sleep.

The door opened and Helen looked up, expecting Kelly with news. Instead, it was Maxine.

She studied Maxine's face, so familiar and yet so

alien to her. She hadn't seen her sister in twenty years. Her jaw was leaner, squarer now. Her shoulders had broadened, and her tall frame was more muscular.

Helen smiled, patting the seat beside her. "You doing okay, Maxie?"

Maxine sat down in the proffered chair and appeared to think about the question for a moment. "I … I think so?" She looked around, still clearly on edge in the police station. "I'll let you know when all the shock wears off."

"Fair enough," Helen replied. She reached for her sister's hand. After a moment's hesitation, Maxine grasped it back.

They sat together in silence for a while, too exhausted and emotionally battered for words to flow. Both wrapped in their own thoughts.

Nearly half of Maxine's life had been stolen from her, and Helen desperately wished she could go back in time and undo everything that had led to her sister's incarceration.

*If I could, I'd write you a better story, Maxie. You deserved so much more out of life.*

There were, however, some things she could do.

"I've been thinking," Helen said. "We should go ahead with selling the house and the mining equipment. You can take the money and buy a home – well, you'll have a deposit at least." She squeezed her sister's hand gently. "Dad would want you to have it. You've paid so much already…too much. I don't want you suffering financially or any other way from this point forward."

Maxine stared at Helen for a long time before she spoke. Gently, she unlinked their hands, and ran her fingers through her hair with a sigh. "That wouldn't be right. What happened wasn't your fault. You shouldn't be trying to shoulder the burden of making it right. It happened. We can't change history."

"I don't need the money, Maxie. My career is going well. I'm good. I want you to have the freedom to make a home. Or start a business. Or whatever it is you *want* to do." She looked her sister directly in the eyes. "You deserve a new start. One on your terms."

Maxine laughed, a soft, low sound. "I'm thankful the truth has finally come out, but I missed a lot, Helen. I can't get that back. Money, university, none of that really matters."

Helen's eyes filled with sympathetic tears, knowing what her sister meant. Huskily, she said, "You might not have been here, Maxie, but you were *always* in his thoughts – in *our* thoughts."

Seeing her sister starting to look uncomfortable with the emotional weight of the conversation, Helen tried to lighten the mood. Leaning over like she was imparting a secret, she said, "Hey. You could always come visit me in Brisbane. I have a pretty sweet apartment, sis."

Maxine made a small chuff of amusement, before searching Helen's eyes for another of those long moments. "Are you sure you want to go back to Brisbane?"

Helen startled. "Of course. Why would you ask?" Guilt that maybe Maxine might want to spend time together plagued her instantly. "But I can stay a while if you like. I really could use your help going through things at the house."

Maxine laughed out loud this time. "Not for me, or

any that," she said, shaking her head. "For you and Kelly."

Before she could try to stop it, heat rushed up Helen's throat. "We'll always be friends, but…"

Maxine shook her head. "*Come on*, Helen. I've seen the way Kelly looks at you. I saw it when we were young. Kelly has spent her whole life in love with you."

Helen opened her mouth to deny it, but her sister held up a palm.

"Stop right there, Hels." Maxine gave her a withering look. "Don't tell me you don't feel the same. You thought I was there to kill you and *still* didn't give a damn about anything other than Kelly."

Before Helen was forced to respond, the door opened again. Kelly stepped through, closing the door behind her. Rounding her desk, she collapsed into her chair.

"This has been a very," she said, pausing for a deep breath, "*very* long day."

"You can say that again," Maxine agreed, before leaning in towards the desk. Her voice trembled as she said, "Kelly, I don't know how to thank you."

Kelly's smile for Maxine was heart-felt and glowing.

But Helen didn't hear a word of what Kelly said in response. She was locked on that smile.

Staring at Kelly.

As dishevelled as Kelly was, she looked amazing. Striking, sexy, strong. Helen's heart did the wildest flip flop.

She suddenly realised that both of them had stopped talking and were looking to her for an answer to … something.

Helen blinked. "Sorry, I think my brain switched off for a second there."

Kelly laughed. "That's got to be the first time you haven't responded to the word 'coffee'!" Turning to Maxine, Kelly added in a loud whisper, "Can't imagine why I bothered asking, though. It's not like we don't know the answer."

Looking over Maxine and Helen's heads, Kelly grinned towards the doorway and said, "Thanks, Chazz, that'd be lovely. Can you order two long blacks, and one flat white with three sugars please?"

Helen hadn't even heard the third woman come in. Caught off guard, she flung a quick smile of thanks over her shoulder at Chazz's retreating back.

*Bloody hell, I need to get my act together*, she thought. *That was just embarrassing.*

Taking a deep breath, Helen changed the subject.

"I overheard something about another officer who was injured. Do we know his status?"

Kelly's face turned serious. "He's going to be fine, but the wound was severe. Thankfully, Dr McGregor came out with the SES rather than waiting at the hospital, and she got him stabilised. But then we had to wait for weather conditions to clear a bit before he could be flown to the Royal Adelaide Hospital." Kelly's voice was a growl. "That bloody storm made everything take longer than it should have."

Despite knowing it wasn't really her fault, Helen couldn't help feeling responsible for the constable shot on her property. She chewed her lip nervously. "Does he have any family here to look after him?"

"Not here, no - his parents are out Murray Bridge way, and he's got a brother in Adelaide." Kelly couldn't hold back a chuckle as she added, "But don't worry about his recovery period. He's got *quite* the loyal following around here. Harry is quite the flirt. I guarantee there will be a queue of willing nurses to assist him back to full health."

"Do we know anything more about why Mr Sharpe did…" Emotion clogged Helen's throat. She didn't need to say the rest, both knew what she meant.

"Once he conferred with the lawyer, he told his interviewers everything. At least, he claimed it was everything." Kelly paused for a second, debating how to approach the conversation.

Maxine jumped in "Did he murder her? Our mother, I mean. Has he confessed, or is he still blaming me?" She stood up and paced to the window. "When we were in Sissi's house he tried to blame his wife." Her hands trembled in fists at her side. "Please, Kelly. I have to know."

"According to him, that was his wife." Kelly stated calmly.

"I knew it." Maxine sat abruptly; all energy drained from her. She shook her head. "I tried to tell the police that Mrs Sharpe already had blood on her when I found Mum. But no one would listen to me. They took her word over mine."

"But…why?" Helen's voice was small, confused. "She was Mum's friend. All those years. Community events, family barbeques." She shuddered. "And … and after, she," Helen gulped, "she looked after Dad and me. Brought us meals after the funeral." Her eyes and voice grew hard, moving from devastation to righteous fury. "And that fucking *formal dress*, Kelly! She fixed it like she was my mum or something!"

Helen didn't know whether she was going to cry or throw up.

*I'm going to burn that fucking dress,* she thought, hating that she'd hung onto it all those years.

Kelly got up, stepped around the table and pulled Helen into a hug, before reaching out a hand to squeeze Maxine's in sympathy.

"Ray Sharpe says he was in love with your mother – not that she ever did anything to make him feel that way," Kelly hastened to explain. "He was the first to say she was completely innocent of his obsession."

"He told us that when we were all in Sissi's house, but it is still difficult to believe." Helen said. Turning to her sister, she asked, "Did you ever see anything? Was I too young to notice, or was he just that good at hiding it?"

Maxine nodded slowly. "I didn't put it together at the time but looking back…yeah. He watched Mum whenever he was around. You know, *really* watched her. He was always bringing her gifts he claimed were from Lorraine. I always wondered why Mrs Sharpe didn't just bring the gifts." Her eyes filled with self-recrimination. "But I never made the connection. I was too absorbed in sport and my own dramas."

"He claimed, at Sissi's" Helen spat, "that he covered for his wife so that he wouldn't be alone." She shook her head. "If he really loved Mum, he would have wanted justice for her." She bowed her head and snarled at the table. "It was never love. It was obsession."

"He claimed he didn't want anyone to find out about his feelings for her," Kelly told them. "His wife threatened to tell everything if he didn't protect her, so he did. He claims he was protecting your mother from any gossip or rumours. He said he wanted to protect her too."

"Did he tell you that Lorraine had dementia?" Maxine asked. "He claims she said something to Dad. That Dad confronted Mr Sharpe about whatever it was and… well, you know the rest."

Helen suddenly remembered the letter. *Where's my raincoat?* She looked around, spotted it on the floor next to her chair, much worse for wear. Already old, it was covered in drying Andamooka mud, staining the original yellow with the colours of the desert.

Helen reached down and pulled the letter from her raincoat pocket. She leaned forward and thrust the wrinkled, mud splattered envelope across the desk.

"Dad sent Maxine this letter but by the time she received it, it was too late. That is evidence – proof of what Maxine is telling you."

Maxine met Helen's gaze, and Helen saw the appreciation that she had given the letter to Kelly without even opening it.

Because Helen trusted her sister. Maxine had never been a liar, much less a murderer.

Kelly read the letter and placed it on her desk. "Thank you. This will be useful in the event Ray Sharpe attempts to withdraw his confession."

"Can he do that?" Maxine wanted to know.

Helen was aware of some option along those lines, but she wasn't versed well enough in the law to respond. Surely it wasn't as simple as him changing his mind.

"He can try but it wouldn't be easy. He made his confession freely and with his lawyer present. About the only way it could be thrown out is if the lawyer were able to prove that he wasn't mentally fit to say the things he said." Kelly looked to Helen. "Based on all he said, I'm confident that after he heard from Izzy Bullock that you were coming up, he used your arrival as the opportunity to set up his wife's death, and yours. He stole Maxine's cricket bat from her room to try and implicate her."

Helen's breath hitched. "I see his motive for wanting to kill his wife. He couldn't trust her not to say the wrong thing anymore. But why would he have wanted to kill me?"

"To make it appear Maxine came back and finished off everyone involved."

"I can't believe the man I knew for all those years was so evil." Helen shook her head.

"I can," Maxine admitted, looking into the distance. "I saw it all in prison. You never know a person until you've shared time with them up close and personal."

"Mrs Sharpe understood her problem as well," Kelly went on to explain. "She went to your house that day before you arrived. She took your mother's opals and the lipstick she wore all the time as well as one of her dresses. Rather than wait for her husband to decide she was too much of a liability, she chose to go the suicide route. I suppose as a jab to him, she dressed herself up like your mother before taking an entire bottle of the Valium she'd been prescribed. Then she waited for him to come home."

"So, wait... he didn't kill her?" Helen felt confused.

"He finished her off," Kelly clarified. "She expected to be dead by the time he arrived, but two things ruined her plan. The first was Sharpe deliberately left the motel early to provide himself an alibi; he was home much earlier than she'd expected. And she'd misjudged the dose - the Valium was old and didn't kill her as quickly as she'd hoped."

Kelly drummed her fingers on the desktop. "She was still breathing when he found her and might possibly have survived if he'd called an ambulance. Instead, Sharpe flew into a rage that she'd 'ruined his plans' and was so incensed that he forgot about the bat and used a knife."

Kelly grimaced, raising her hand gingerly to the back of her skull before dropping it to her side. "I have the concussion to prove he remembered the bat later."

"They checked you over at the hospital while you were waiting for Sharpe to come out of surgery?" Helen had hoped Kelly wouldn't ignore her own injury.

"Dr Rose did." Kelly looked from Helen to Maxine and back.

"According to Sharpe, he believed that if he killed everyone related to your mother's death, the past would never be resurrected. When it became obvious that the truth would come out, he tried to kill himself rather than live with the damage to his *reputation*." Kelly's tone soured on the last word.

Helen and Maxine sat lost in their thoughts for a moment, before Helen frowned and asked, "Did he steal Mum's opals? Was it some kind of twisted memento?"

Kelly made an ambivalent wave of her hand. "Not initially, but it turned out that way. He tore them from his wife's neck, but then chose to keep them.

Then he arranged the crime scene to look as if Maxine had murdered Lorraine."

Kelly looked at Helen. "He actually hid the opals in your Dad's shed." Her voice was heavy as she added, "He planned to sneak them out again under the guise of helping clear the property after you were dead." She shook her head.

"What about the stuff in Sissi's loft? The water bottles and the empty chip packets and the sleeping bag?" Maxine asked. "Who was staying there? It damned sure wasn't me."

"We're still waiting on the forensics for that. All we have so far, excluding Helen, is that it is female DNA on the water bottle. Nothing on our data base."

Kelly looked directly at Helen. "It *was* Ray Sharpe who removed the ladder when you were in Sissi's loft, though, Helen. He'd seen you climbing up the hill and saw a way to tie up loose ends in a way that definitely couldn't be tied back to him. He was going to leave you to die of exposure to heat and dehydration."

Without turning her head, Maxine reached out to Helen's hand. Both of them thinking the same thought: *Just like he killed Dad.*

Helen released a deep breath. She'd been terrified when she'd believed that she was trapped in Sissi's loft. Yet she'd escaped.

"Sounds like nearly all the loose ends are tied up." Helen was greatly relieved. "We just need to make sure the local media – and national media, come to that – know about Maxine's innocence."

Maxine nodded heavily. "It's so hard finding work and a place in the community after gaol. I think..." she closed her eyes briefly "I think it'd be nice to be judged for *me* again. Not for Lorraine."

Kelly clapped a hand on Maxine's shoulder and squeezed gently. "I'm so sorry it took so long, Maxime. But we will make sure you're exonerated now."

Maxine nodded with slumped shoulders, before standing abruptly. "I need a shower and food," she said. "And then I need to work out how the hell I'm going to explain this to my parole officer." Her eyes were wary. "I'm surprised they haven't instructed you to take me in."

Kelly held up a hand to wave away the suggestion. "Detective Brevet Sergeant Deer has started clearing that up. It'll take quite a bit of paperwork to formally address it in the system, but your parole officer has been alerted and understands the situation."

Kelly looked back and forth between the sisters, before adding "That's the least of it though. The State of South Australia will be talking to you about compensation, Maxine. That will start with the Chief Inspector for the Far North Local Service Area. He arrived on the plane this morning." Her jaw tightened. "What happened to you was wrong. We have to make amends, at least as much as possible, given that the time you spent in prison can never really be compensated for."

Helen couldn't help herself. She shot to her feet, grabbed her sister and hugged her hard. The unshed tears glittering in Maxine's eyes spilled over in her sister's embrace, the two of them sobbing in exhausted relief.

Kelly waited until the tears started to slow, before turning to Maxine.

"Senior Constable Chadowski – Gerry - will take

you to a bed and breakfast place on the edge of town, Maxine. We'll still need you for more interviews. You'll be able to grab a shower and some quiet space in the meantime though. Gerry will stay there and provide transport, and he's organised food as well." Her voice was gentle as she added, "Try and relax. See if you can get some sleep."

Maxine rubbed her eyes blearily. "Don't have to tell me twice," she said. Turning to Helen, she gave her a last quick hug and a wide smile before vanishing down the hallway.

Waving her sister off, Helen gathered her thoughts. Maxine had been right about more than who killed their mother. It was time.

Time that she and Kelly figured out this thing between them.

Kelly's face relaxed, finally letting her true exhaustion to show now that the two of them were alone. Rubbing her hand over her head, she said distractedly, "The storm's heading down towards the Bight. We can finally start cleaning up here."

Helen sat herself on the edge of Kelly's desk. "I guess we can get on with the rest of our lives now."

Kelly winced, before admitting, "I hate to do this to you, Hels, but your place will be a crime scene for a few days. You can't go back there yet."

"Right." Helen hadn't thought about it until now. *I really should have predicted that.*

She reached down for her mucky raincoat. "That's okay. I'll be around the area for a couple more weeks." She shrugged. "Maybe I'll stay with Maxine."

Kelly stepped away from her desk.

"Actually, I was hoping you'd stay with me for a while. You have that book to finish, and the roads will be a mess for days. No need to rush." Kelly's eyes were earnest. "Maxine can do the packing up. She needs some time to adjust without a lot of outside interference. Spending time at the house alone will be good for her. It will be a while before all the clearances for her come through. Gerry can look after her."

Helen peered into those dark eyes she knew so well seeing, as if for the first time, the longing behind the façade. "Hmm, you make a good points. But," she added with a grin, "I hope you realise that bringing some strange woman under your roof is going to be gossip fodder for the entire town. It could seriously damage your single status."

Kelly chuckled in response, but her eyes held volumes – now that Helen was finally ready to read them. "Being single isn't all it's cracked up to be," Kelly murmured.

Helen weighed her options. She could leave now, and things would go back to normal.

And then what? Maybe Kelly would hook up with the sparklingly attractive Chazz at the front desk, or that capable Dr Rose.

Someone, Helen knew, would finally get the girl.

Deep inside Helen, an ache pierced her; a tight knot of fear, longing and possessiveness. No.

Helen's heart was pounding. She could hardly manage a breath.

*Now or never.*

"I see." Helen nodded. "You want me to relieve you of that problem?"

Hope, sudden and achingly raw, bloomed over

Kelly's face as though lit from within. Hands shaking, she cupped Helen's face. Taking a deep breath, she forced herself to say the words she'd held in for so long.

"If I could have married you at sixteen, I would have. I have never wanted to spend my life with anyone else."

Kelly's voice trembled, the words tumbling from her. "I should have told you this years ago, but I was afraid you didn't feel the same way. Maybe you don't now, but it feels like you do."

She took a shaky breath. "If I'm misreading the signs, tell me and we'll leave it at that. I promise you, Helen, I never want to lose you as a friend. Ever."

Helen gave a tremulous smile through happy tears. "Apparently we've been in the same boat all these years," Helen said. "We just didn't know it. But we know it now."

Finding courage in Kelly's disbelieving joy, Helen promised, "I really want to give us a try, Kelly. We can work out the logistics later."

Kelly tilted Helen's face up to meet hers and kissed her. Softly at first, then with all the desire she felt shimmering inside her.

Ex-Tropical Cyclone Kelvin had passed. This was just the beginning of a new kind of storm.

One of loving emotions and endless possibilities.

# EPILOGUE

# ABC WEATHER NEWS, KIMBERLEY REGION

BROOME, WESTERN AUSTRALIA

**8:00 pm, Monday, 19 February 2018**

"… Back to you in the studio, Gabrielle."

Ryleigh signed off with her brightest, most engaging smile, taking a moment to charm the camera operator after her segment ended. Two young men waited off to the side of the broadcast, moving in politely after the segment had wrapped to ask her for autographs. Eyes and smile glowing, she happily obliged, sending them off with some kind words, before calling an Uber.

Ten minutes later, and she was headed back to the hotel that was home for the night. And every night, until she found somewhere else to stay, far away from her sister.

Stepping through the door and carefully locking it behind her, she consciously loosened her limbs as she stripped out of her work clothes – hanging them tidily in the wardrobe – and changed into more comfortable attire.

A cartoon rabbit's buck-toothed grin stared back at her from her nightie as she brushed out her hair in the mirror. She couldn't resist grinning in return as she considered how the outfit would disillusion her viewers if they ever saw behind the curtain.

In the kitchenette, she heard the kettle turn itself off and padded out to make a cup of tea, idly grabbing her phone from her bag while the drink brewed.

*Missed call from Kelly. About time!*

Hitting playback on the message with a mixture of anxiety and righteous irritation, her face went though the entire spectrum of emotions as she listened…

*"Hi. It's Kelly. I'm sorry I missed you. Call me back when you have a moment?*

*"I am so sorry. I hate what happened, and I've been too ashamed to ever tell you. I guess you know now. But I need to say I'm sorry, properly.*

*"And Ry, you are about to get the Exclusive of your life.*

*"Trust me on this."*

Pulling up an app on her phone, Ryleigh began looking at BME to PER to ADE to OLP flights – Broome to Perth to Adelaide to Roxby Downs.

# ACKNOWLEDGEMENTS

*We acknowledge Aboriginal people as the First Peoples and Nations of the lands and waters we live and work on and we pay our respects to their Elders past and present. We acknowledge and respect the deep spiritual connection and the relationship that Aboriginal and Torres Strait Islander people have to Country.*

*To our big-hearted friends for joining us on this outback adventure by sharing early chapters around the campfire and asking for more; generously providing information about the justice system; checking technical aspects; proofreading; visiting in Andamooka and helping to dispose of the detritus of a deceased estate. Mostly, though, for leading inspirational lives.*

To Chantelle Griffin for her passion for sharing writing and publishing.

To Daria Lockwood for always knowing the people with the answers.

Digital Version published by Centred in Choice

PO Box 448 Alice Springs Northern Territory 0871 Australia https://centredinchoice.com/

# AUTHOR'S NOTE

A note to readers

*Thank you.*

Thank you for reading *Desert Deluge*. Please leave an online review where you purchased the book. Reviews are often helpful to other readers. Reviews are also helpful to authors and publishers. It is a highly competitive market, and we appreciate your support.

Connecting readers to authors is an essential match-making endeavour. Please recommend the book and share with your friends via social media.

Writing this book helped me through months of living in isolation during 2020. Thank you to the 'campfire' team, and several other individuals for feedback; for keeping me connected via technology, for the encouragement along with choosing cars, proof reading, and valuable help with justice questions. Any errors are because I didn't ask the right questions.

Thank you to Chantelle Griffin for the cover artwork and generously sharing her publishing knowledge.

Thank you for encouraging a first-time adult fiction writer. We know typos are tedious. Despite the best efforts of proofreaders, typos can still slip through. We would appreciate knowing where the typos are via email to Centred In Choice

Thank you for supporting a small Australian business.

Heather Anne Gordon and Centred In Choice

*"Sharing Australian voices, stories, strategies and skills with the world."*

What's next?

*Heather has commenced writing her second novel. She's imagining Maxine Hamilton relaxing on the River Murray in a houseboat, with her dog, Cassie. There might be recipes and inspirational quotes as well as coffee and cake and gentle water views. Some sex. A mystery or two to solve. Maybe a murder.*

*It's not clear yet. Research on the river is in progress. Mostly by dining at the pubs and bakeries along the way on the pretext of inspecting the navigation locks upstream from Waikerie, South Australia.*

*You're invited to join Maxine and Cassie on the river for sweet treats and unsavoury characters.*

*Anticipated publication date? 2023.*